John Bowen was
Oxford. His novels have been published and his stage plays performed in the United States and Europe as well as Britain. He has written award-winning television drama as well as film scripts and radio plays, critical articles and reviews, directed plays for the stage, taught in a drama school and worked as a drama producer for television.

David Cook was born in Preston, Lancashire and trained as an actor at the R.A.D.A. He has appeared on T.V. and in films as well as on stage in the West End. He began writing novels in 1969 and many of his novels have won prizes. He wrote the script for the film of his own novel, *Walter* with Sir Ian McKellen which was shown on the First Night of Channel Four and later won the Special Jury Prize at Monte Carlo. Recently his film of a later novel *Second Best* with William Hurt won the same prize at San Sebastian.

After the success of the first series of *Hetty Wainthropp Investigates*, John Bowen and David Cook have completed a second.

Also by John Bowen

The Truth Will Not Help Us
After the Rain
The Centre of the Green
Storyboard
The Birdcage
A World Elsewhere
Squeak
The MacGuffin
The Girls
Fighting Back
The Precious Gift
No Retreat

Also by David Cook

Albert's Memorial
Happy Endings
Walter
Winter Doves
Sunrising
Crying Out Loud
Second Best
Missing Persons

HETTY WAINTHROPP INVESTIGATES

Adapted from
the television series

---

by John Bowen and David Cook

HEADLINE

First published in 1996
by HEADLINE BOOK PUBLISHING

10 9 8 7 6 5 4 3 2 1

ISBN 0 7472 5347 1

Typeset at The Spartan Press Ltd,
Lymington, Hants

Printed and bound in Great Britain by
Cox & Wyman Ltd, Reading, Berks

HEADLINE BOOK PUBLISHING
A division of Hodder Headline PLC
338 Euston Road
LONDON NW1 3BH

For Patricia Routledge
But for whom . . .

Contents

Welcome to the Club 1

The Bearded Lady 4

Eyewitness 64

Fingers 107

Widdershins 140

A High Profile 177

Safe As Houses 211

Welcome to the Club

Hetty Wainthropp was sixty years old. It was too much to endure. Nobody should have to be sixty.

Robert brought her breakfast in bed. Well, that was suitable on her birthday. Orange juice, a pot of tea, hot toast in a china rack, butter and marmalade, milk and the sugar bowl, with a 3-ply paper napkin in apricot to go with her bed jacket, all arranged on a linen cloth on the breakfast tray with extensible legs which was only used for breakfast in bed on special occasions. And there were cards. Birthday cards. Some people had no tact.

'You can get musical cards nowadays,' Hetty said. 'They'll go to any lengths to induce you to buy.' She opened another envelope. The card inside was not musical, but had a picture of violets and a poodle on the front with the words *Welcome to the Club*.

'What am I meant to be joining – Crufts?' There was a message inside: 'Happy Birthday wishes from one seasoned Senior Citizen to a new arrival. Esther Chadwick.' Hetty hurled the card across the room. 'I'll kill her.'

Robert said, 'You've still one left to open.'

Of course she had. It was addressed in the instantly recognisable block capitals Robert always used when he wished to disguise his writing, and had been posted in the village. She opened it. As she took the card out of the envelope it began to play a tune. *I'll Be Loving You Always*. And there was the same old '60' on the front, the two figures looking as if they had been inflated with a bicycle pump, with the words *To My Dear Wife*.

'Read it to me.'

Robert opened the card and read the message aloud.

> '"*We've been together, my dear wife,*
> *Through all the pains and strains of life,*
> *And still together we will ride*
> *Serene into the eventide.*"
> – *With love from Robert.*'

Tears were pouring down Hetty's cheeks.

'Hey up!' said Robert. 'I knew it were soppy but I didn't expect the full waterworks.'

Hetty said, 'I hate it.' She pushed away the breakfast tray, burst out of bed and headed for the door. 'I'm not sixty and I never will be. I'm not a Senior Citizen and I'm not joining any club.'

Immediate agreement seemed to be the wisest course. 'No,' Robert said. 'No, you're not. You're right. Never.'

'If I'm an Old Age Pensioner, where's my pension?'

'Married women don't get one. I get one for us both when I'm sixty-five.'

'I worked. I paid National Insurance stamps. Eight years. Clayton's Haberdashery, Porrits' Pet Shop, Full Moon Confectioners and the Cardoma. I was a person in my own right – independent – a young woman about town: I paid my whack, and held my head high.'

'It doesn't count. Eight years isn't enough. You've to do ten for a pension of your own.'

'Then why didn't you tell me at the time, and I'd have kept you waiting for another two?'

It seemed best not to answer. There are times in any marriage when the wisest action is just to keep one's head down. A birthday – even a sixtieth birthday – ought not to be one of those times, but with Hetty a man never knew.

'Right,' she said. 'It doesn't count. All those years. But I tell you something – from this day forth it *is* going to count. I, Hetty Wainthropp, am going to count. I may start by getting a job.'

And she was gone. Breakfast over, birthday cards spread about the bed, out through the bedroom door to begin a new day and a new life. Robert didn't know what had hit him. He followed her out on to the landing, bleating pitiably.

'You can't get a job. You've still got me to look after.'

The Bearded Lady

Thursday. Market Day. The parked cars which usually filled the space had been replaced by market stalls. No passers-by lingered today outside the Bradford & Bingley Building Society, the Midland Bank or the various charity shops: it was all colour and bustle. Fruit and veg were piled high to be sold cheap. Boiled sweets and coconut ice from long trays were shovelled into paper bags with steel scoops trying to look like silver. There were cheap dresses on racks of metal hangers and cellophane packets of lambswool Highland sweaters made in Hong Kong, a stall selling second-hand paperbacks and discarded copies of Readers' Digest condensed books, the Women's Institute stall with home-made lemon curd and marmalade and Victoria sponge, and the fish stall, at which there was always a queue.

Behind the fish stall was the front of what had once been the Mechanics Institute, a building which the Town Council would have liked to sell for re-development, but was unable to because it was an historic, listed building – and anyway, there *was* no development these days within the town, only a couple of Superstores, a Do-It-Yourself Magnaplex and a Multi-Leisure Cinema Complex a couple of miles outside.

On the steps of the Mechanics Institute sat an old bag

lady. She was wearing what seemed to be at least two skirts, several jumpers, an old headscarf and a shawl of sacking against the weather. Three bulging carrier-bags lay on the ground beside her. The market people knew her. She had been coming to the same spot on Market Day for several weeks; she'd sit there for most of the day and watch the people. Sometimes shoppers would drop small coins into her lap – she never acknowledged them – and sometimes a market trader would bring her coffee in a cardboard carton or a hotdog in a bun, and for these gifts she would say thank you.

She gathered up her carrier-bags: she usually left the market in mid-afternoon, not long before it closed. She moved out of the doorway, round the front of the fish stall, past the 'You Can't Buy Fresher' stall, which had slashed the price of some dicey Dutch tomatoes, past the Bargain Antiques & Collectables, and out into the hinterland with a multi-storey car park in one direction, the bus station in another, and a waste of cheap terraced houses straight ahead of her leading to the main road.

Someone was following the bag lady, but at a distance and on the other side of the street with no intention of getting any closer, not yet, at least. The someone stopped when she stopped, loitered when she loitered, and stooped to retie a shoelace when she turned round. The someone wore gloves of soft black leather and sturdy shoes with rubber soles made for walking.

On the outskirts of town was an abandoned mill set in waste ground. Eventually no doubt it would become, as so many of the cotton mills of the North-West have done, a slipper factory or a block of yuppie apartments, maybe even a Heritage Museum with Craft Centre attached, but for the time being it was still a shell, black against the sky, the glass in all the windows shattered, holes in the roof, a broken lock on the battered door. The old lady stumped towards it with her carrier-bags, pushed open the door, and went inside. Behind her, the distant watcher began to run.

Each floor of the mill was one long shed with a skeleton of iron pillars, which had once supported the looms, connected to iron girders high under the ceiling. At one end was what had once been a supervisor's office, separated from the work area by wooden walls. Each office had two doors, one opening to the weaving-shed, the other to the stone stairway which ran from the entrance to the top floor.

The bag lady was old and burdened. She did not move quickly up the stone stairs: it was easy for the watcher to catch up. She mounted from the first floor to the second, the second to the third. The watcher was already inside the door and moving fast. At the fourth floor she heard the steps behind her and turned.

'Who are you?'

The watcher stopped, then began to move – much more slowly now – up the stairs towards her again.

'I asked who you are.'

She had a surprisingly educated voice for such a dirty old lady.

It is easy for a lady of sixty to say that she intends to get a job, but jobs these days do not hang thick on the vine, even for someone who, a mere thirty-five years ago, was an independent wage-earner in her own right and the Belle of the Cardoma. Time passed and Robert hoped the whole idea had been forgotten.

But Hetty did not forget. As the weeks passed, she kept her eyes open and her wits active. Something would turn up, not in the village where anyway she would not have wanted to work – it would be too close to home – but in the town. She said to Robert, 'We should support the small trader. How shall we survive as a great nation if we sell our souls for a supermarket's Special Offer? It's a mess of pottage, is that.' She began to go into town to shop three days a week and sure enough, making her way back towards the bus station by the scenic route via Omdurman Terrace with a nice piece of cod in her shopping basket, she saw on the door of a small corner shop, sub-Post Office with cigarettes and confectionery and a concession for the National Lottery, a sign reading:

HELP WANTED
URGENT

And pushed open the door. And went inside.

There had been a great gleaming motorbike outside – a Kamikaze or some such – and inside was the teenage biker, shouting at a young and heavily pregnant Asian lady at the confectionery counter, while her middle-aged husband remonstrated with him from behind the grille of the Post Office section of the little shop.

'Ignorant bloody Pakkis.'

'Please! Please! Politeness costs nothing. You are putting the frighteners on my wife.'

The biker hit the confectionery counter repeatedly with one gloved hand. He held the other out towards the Asian lady, showing her the packet of ten Embassy cigarettes she had given him.

'Think you can get away with it? I gave you bloody money for twenty; you gave me a bloody packet of ten. Understand? Savvy? Spikka da bloody English?'

'Please speak slowly. She is in an interesting condition.'

The pregnant Asian lady was weeping, the two men overlapping each other; there was too much noise in the shop. It seemed necessary to Hetty that she should do something about it. So she shouted.

'Quiet! All of you!'

Dead silence. The Asian lady was shocked out of her tears, her husband stood stock still behind the grille with his mouth open, and the biker had turned apprehensively to face this person who sounded so much like his mother. Hetty took the packet of ten cigarettes out of the biker's hand, put it back in the shelf behind the counter and took out a packet of twenty. Then she looked at the coins on the counter.

'They don't take pesetas in this shop.'

Still in silence the biker replaced the Spanish coins with the legal currency of the United Kingdom. Hetty gave him the packet of twenty Embassy.

'Now out!'

The biker's attempt at a swagger as he left would not have convinced even another biker. The pregnant Asian lady's expression was of admiration almost akin to love. Her husband came from behind the grille. Hetty said, 'You need help.'

'There's a notice on the door.'

'Right,' Hetty said, 'I'll do three afternoons a week to start with, and then we'll see.'

The baby was born a week later. Hetty had soon settled into the routine of the shop. Most of the time she spent behind the grille of the Post Office section, since the happiness felt by Mr Mumtaz, the owner, at the birth of his son made him, Hetty considered, too light-hearted (and consequently light-headed) to deal responsibly with the complicated traffic of Her Majesty's Mails. So he remained at the confectionery, where the occasional misplacement of a Mars Bar hardly mattered.

The Case of the Bearded Lady began early one Tuesday afternoon, before Hetty ever knew it was a Case or that she would some day have to deal with Cases. There were only three customers in the shop. Two were a couple, Wayne and Sandy, who had come in to collect a neighbour's pension, the third a young lad at the confectionery counter.

Hetty had not come across Wayne and Sandy before. Her attitude to anyone asking for money was that they should be treated with caution until proved trustworthy. She was deeply unimpressed by the neighbourly couple in front of her. Wayne seemed to have been dressed by the Women's Voluntary Services. He wore old scuffed brogues, the trousers of a pin-striped suit too large for him and kept up by a belt, a striped shirt without a collar and a double-breasted blue blazer with the badge of the Cherwell Valley Boating Club on the breast pocket and only one brass button left at the front. His wife (if she really was his wife) wore a denim boiler-suit over a blouse, trainers and flyaway spectacles.

Trainers! In her old days at the Cardoma it had always been said that you could tell a lot from shoes. She had once refused to serve a pair of open-toed sandals and had been supported in her refusal by the manageress.

'I'm not happy with this signature,' she said.

'Well, she's ill, isn't she? An old lady, bad with her legs. She lives above us. We collect her pension and then do her shopping.'

'She should get out more. Enjoy the social round. She could lose the use of those legs.'

'She *can't* get out.'

'Don't lose your rag with me, young man. I'm only doing my job. I've been warned to look out for people like you.'

'We're in every week. We've never had no trouble before.' Wayne was forty-nine years old, no longer a young man though not old. He had been made redundant – as Hetty's own husband Robert had been made redundant four years ago – before coming to the end of his useful life. Unable to keep up the mortgage, he and Sandy had lost their home and drifted further and further down in the world ever since. Had Hetty known all this she might have been more sympathetic. Or perhaps not. Those shoes repelled sympathy.

'I'll have to ask you for some identification.'

Over at the confectionery counter the young lad nicked a bar of chocolate from the counter display. It happened so quickly that Hetty could not be sure that she had seen correctly. Certainly Mr Mumtaz had not seemed to notice, but he had the baby with him, and was making kootchy-koo noises in a language Hetty assumed to be Urdu.

Sandy said, 'You're not living in the modern world. Folk like us don't have identification.'

'Driving licence?'

Wayne and Sandy looked at each other. Wayne shrugged. 'I must have left it in the glove compartment of the Mercedes.'

'Birth certificate? You were both born, I take it?'

Mr Mumtaz was whirling round like a dancing dervish while the baby chuckled. The young lad took from the counter in front of him a plastic bunny rabbit with its tongue sticking out for coins and a label, CHILDREN IN NEED, and tucked it into his windcheater. This time Hetty saw him clearly. 'Hey, you!' she said.

The young lad said to Mr Mumtaz, 'I'll come back when you're not so busy,' and left the shop, quick but casual as a traffic warden.

There was a door behind Hetty, leading out to the back of the shop. She slammed down the shutter between herself and Wayne, almost trapping his fingers. 'Call of nature. With you in a moment,' she said, and was out through that door in time to fall upon the young lad like an avenging angel as he turned the corner of the street.

'Gotcher!' She had him by the collar, and with one smooth swift movement of her free hand, she unzipped his windcheater. The bar of chocolate and the plastic rabbit fell out into the road.

'What you doing?'

'Making a Citizen's Arrest. Look at that rabbit. Children in Need! How could you?'

'I'm a child. I'm in need. I was just speeding up the procedure. Cutting through the red tape.'

'Name and address.'

'It's long and difficult to spell. You'll have to write it down.'

'Luckily I have a pencil.' But in order to get it Hetty had to loosen her hold on his collar, and at once he wriggled out of her grasp and was away down the road.

'Come back here!'

But of course he did no such thing. At a safe distance he stopped and shouted back at her: 'Want me name? You're welcome. Mickey Mouse, Sunset Boulevard, Hollywood. Donald Duck.' He did a little dancing mime. 'Goofy! Dustin Hoffman. Marilyn Monroe.' And he was off again, impossible to catch.

Wearily Hetty stooped to gather up the chocolate bar and the plastic rabbit from the pavement to return them to the shop. There was still that odd couple to deal with. She would ask Mr Mumtaz, but she supposed that she would have to give them the money, otherwise – if they were genuine – the old lady whose pension they were collecting would have nothing to eat. Three more hours to go until the end of her shift, then a trip to the only supermarket left in the town centre and a bus back home before she could put her feet into a bowl of hot water and sip at a Dubonnet.

She did not regret having found herself a job, but there were disadvantages and they were mostly to do with the state of her feet at the end of the day.

The supermarket was in a shopping mall off the High Street. Her trolley filled with groceries, Hetty arrived at the line of check-outs like a proud ship coming into harbour, and took her place at the end of the shortest queue. The shopping of two young women in front of her seemed to consist of six-packs of own-brand lager piled up with jumbo packets of crisps and a Special Offer of household bleach: it was amazing how some people could survive on such a diet. She lowered her head and began to load her own shopping on to the conveyor belt. When she lifted it again it was to meet the horrified gaze of the young lad at the till. Recognition was instant and mutual. He was the boy who had stolen the plastic rabbit.

She held out one hand. 'Pen.'

He gave her the pen from the till.

'Paper.'

He looked about him, saw an empty till-roll, and gave her that.

Hetty tore a piece off the end of the till-roll and wrote: 'Check-out number three.' She looked at her watch. 'Five-thirty p.m., Monday. I'm on my way home at the moment: I'll talk to Mr Plod in the morning. Now put those groceries through, and I'll pay for them. Unlike some.'

Speechless, the young lad put the shopping through the pinging, buzzing, clanking machines of the check-out while Hetty filled two carrier-bags. He gave her the bill and she paid cash without looking at him. Finally he spoke. 'I need this job.'

Still without looking at him, Hetty made her way out of the supermarket. His eyes never left her face, though he did not try to speak to her again. He watched the automatic doors of the Exit open for her. He watched her sweep past the plate glass of the window, carrying her shopping. A queue had built up at his check-out. He ignored it.

She was on her way home. Where was her home? Only one way to know. Follow her. Apologise. Persuade her that his was a soul worth saving. If the old lady carried out her threat to report him to the police for robbing a Post Office, he was done for with no reprieve. 'I'm sorry,' he said to the waiting customers. 'Position closed,' and set off in pursuit.

Emerging from the shopping mall at a skidding run, the young lad saw Hetty in the distance passing the sign which pointed to the bus station. On her way home with no time to call in at the police station – she must live in one of the villages outside town. He must catch her before she caught the bus.

She was in a queue at the other side of the Concourse. The queue was moving, boarding the bus. The young lad ran towards it, waving his arms and shouting, 'Please, missus! Just a moment!' and fell over two Sealyham Terriers on a single lead. Picking himself up, he saw the door of the bus closing. It was already on its way. He could see the destination, but at how many villages would it put down passengers first? Next to him, a clergyman with a bicycle was waving to a young woman in school uniform. Needs must when the Devil drives. He said to the clergyman, 'Excuse me. I'll bring it back,' leapt on to the saddle and pedalled after the bus.

There were eight gears on that bicycle, and all were needed. Luckily the bus itself, being local, was old and did not care for hills, but even so the young lad often lost sight of it. Nevertheless he toiled on and would see, from the top of a hill, the bus coming to a stop at the bottom and people getting on and off, and he would pray for arthritis, sciatica, rheumatics of every sort to strike those people and slow them down, and then he would take off downhill at a terrifying speed with his hair streaming in the wind as the corners flashed past. And at last he arrived at a village on the very top of the longest hill so far, exhausted, on the point of collapse, unable to go on, and saw the bus already pulling away from its stop and a clear road ahead, and knew that he was defeated and had better go home.

Until he saw also that one of the passengers who had already left the bus and were walking their different ways to their different houses was an old lady with two carrier-bags. So he dismounted from the clergyman's bicycle and wheeled it, following his quarry at a discreet distance and still utterly unable to decide how best to approach her.

'There's a lad outside. Hoovering.'

'Hovering,' Hetty said.

'Is he up to no good, do you think? Should I phone the police – Neighbourhood Watch kind of thing?'

'The twitchy velour curtains across the road have probably done that already.'

'He's come by bike. Could be for charity. Sponsored hoovering.'

'Just let him hoover, Robert. People have their own reasons for what they do.'

Hetty was resting her feet. She had noticed the young lad outside almost from the moment he had taken up station there. She knew perfectly well who he was, but did not feel disposed to acknowledge his presence. Instead, she and Robert had had their tea – chops and onion gravy with some nice boiled potatoes and sprouts from the allotment. But Robert, she could see, was edgy.

'He's still there.'

'I don't know why you should take on so.'

'He's only a lad. Waif-like.'

Hetty put down the teapot and came to a decision. 'All right, if it's worrying you.' She left the kitchen by the back door so that she could come at him suddenly from the side of the house. If she felt it to be necessary, she would grasp his collar again – and this time he would not get away.

No need, she saw, for collar-grasping. Robert was right: the lad was waif-like and cold with it.

'There's a Neighbourhood Watch at number twenty-seven and she's mustard at her job, so I'd go and take root on someone else's doorstep if I were you.'

He stayed where he was, looking down and scraping the side of his shoe on the ground. His bicycle had been left leaning against the garden wall. If it *was* his bicycle: it looked rather big for him.

'Well?'

Now the lad looked up and straight at her. 'I just want to know why, for something as daft as what I did, you'll get me a police record and add me to the millions of unemployed.'

'Stealing's wrong. What would happen if everyone went around grabbing what they wanted?'

'Some don't need to, do they? Not when they're retired and on a pension.'

Then the lad did something which surprised them both because it was certainly no part of his game plan – if he had ever really had such a thing beyond hanging about and staring at the window of the front room. He burst into tears. Covering his face as best he could with one hand, he turned away and took hold of the cycle. 'I'm sorry.'

Hetty was stunned. He was about to mount, get on out of it, do exactly what she had told him to do, and must of course now be prevented. She put her own hand on the handlebars to stop him. She was no longer angry. 'I'm not on a pension,' she said.

He was certainly crying: they were genuine tears. 'You're comfortable though, aren't you?'

'Not right this minute, I'm not,' Hetty said. 'You'd better come in before we both freeze.'

'Parents?'

'Divorced. I live on me own.'

Robert said, 'YMCA sort of thing? Church Army?'

'Bedsitter and lucky to get it. Communal toilet and a dodgy electric kettle which can be adapted to heat up soup. It's not very salubrious but I don't grumble.'

He was in the front room, warming his legs at the electric fire and tucking into an enormous cheese-and-lettuce sandwich with a mug of tea. He could not be more than sixteen years old. His name was Geoff.

Hetty said, 'Your mother threw you out?'

No tears now. He looked her straight in the eyes. It was clear that he would be questioned so far and no further. 'I left. My choice. Okay?'

'Well, you'd better sleep in the spare room tonight.'

There was a startled noise from Robert: it sounded a little like a moorhen meeting a stoat for the first – and perhaps only – time. Hetty said, 'I've got something I want to talk to him about in the morning.'

Robert was not sure how to express his conviction that this invitation, made so soon after first accquaintance, was rash. He made little movements with his hands which he hoped would placate yet indicate his disquiet. 'Are we sure?' he said.

Geoff looked from one to another, finished his sandwich in two bites, his tea in one gulp, and stood up. 'I'd better get back, thank you,' he said. 'I might run off in the middle of the night else with all your savings.'

Hetty came with him into the hall. Robert could sit where he was and stew in his own discourtesy. Geoff said, 'What do you want me to do?'

'I think there's a fraud going on at our Post Office. Unemployed couple – man and wife. They cash their Social Security cheques with us, but lately they've come in with an old lady's pension book and they've been cashing that as well.'

'Who's the old lady – someone local?'

'I've never seen her.'

'Has your boss seen her?'

'He says we all look alike to him: he's not bothered. What with the new baby and help in the shop, it's all roses. But *I'm* bothered. I don't like mysteries.'

Geoff grinned. 'I think you do.'

'Cheeky monkey! They say the old lady lives above them. I want to know where that is. You followed me: you can follow them. They'll be in next Tuesday afternoon. Can you get time off?'

'What option have I got?'

'I'm not blackmailing you, Geoffrey. Do it for the interest.' He nodded. She opened the door and came out with him into the bitter cold of the front garden. 'And another thing! That cycle's to go back where it came from. There's not so many churches in town that you can't find a vicar who's mislaid his transport.'

'He'll not be pleased.'

'Makes no odds. He's bound to forgive: it's in the job description.'

So it was that next Tuesday, Geoff was loitering at the corner of the road opposite the sub-Post Office. He saw Wayne and Sandy come out, then move away down the street towards the outskirts of town. Soon afterwards, Hetty appeared at the door, waved and pointed. Keeping his distance, Geoff began to follow them, his casual manner a little overdone.

It was easy. Wayne and Sandy had no suspicion that they were being shadowed; they went straight to the abandoned mill without even looking round. Once they were in, Geoff sprinted across to the entrance after them.

Unseen by Wayne and Sandy, unseen by Geoff, a gloved hand wrote in a notebook the words,

'1500 hrs. UNKNOWN BOY.'

Sandy and Wayne occupied the office space one floor below the old bag lady. There was a padlock on the door. Wayne unlocked it and the pair went in, closing the door behind them. Almost immediately the sound of Country & Western music from a cheap portable radio could be heard from behind the door. Geoff came cautiously upstairs. There was a crack in the door at an inconvenient height. In order to look through it Geoff could not sit, he could not kneel, but must crouch and support himself with one hand. In getting into position he made a small scuffing sound. When he looked through the crack, Wayne was coming towards the door.

A backward leap, a retreat up the stairs, pressed flat against the wall. At this height the staircase was illuminated by daylight entering through the holes in the roof. Wayne opened the door, came out on to the landing without looking up, and pissed into the stairwell. Then he went back indoors.

Something was troubling Geoff. There was a stench – not the eyewatering whiff of old urine on the stairway, but something much stronger – like rotting meat. It came from further upstairs. He moved towards the upper floor, nose in the air, sniffing. The stench became stronger with every step. He fumbled for a hankie, and held it over his nose as he approached the door of the office space on the top floor.

There was a padlock on this door also, brand new with new staples and hasps. Would there be a crack? Would he be able to see through? Removing the hankie from his nose, he was assailed by a putrid gust and suddenly realised what the stench must be. He no longer had any desire to see what was behind that door, or even to stay where he was. He began to descend the staircase. His job was only to tell Hetty what he had found out. She must decide what to do next.

On Geoff's way back to the sub-Post Office, something odd happened. He was cutting through an alley between warehouses when his path was blocked by a man in a brown suit. He seemed at first to have stepped out of the wall, but in fact, Geoff saw, there was a side-alley: that whole complex was a maze of disused alleys, partly filled with rubbish. Not only was the man's suit brown; his hair and Hitler moustache were brown, his glasses were brown – why wear sun-glasses in an alley? – and his shoes were brown. Only his soft leather gloves were black. This man wanted to know what Geoff had been doing at the mill. Geoff told him that the lady at the Post Office was suspicious of a pension fraud and had asked him to follow the suspects to see if they lived where they said they did. At this the man grunted. 'I hope you're the sort of boy who tells the truth,' he said. 'Any other sort could be in trouble. I hate the other sort, and so do my friends.' Then he turned smartly on his heel and was gone.

Hetty looked at the padlock on the door. There was still some light coming from the holes in the roof, but it was supplemented by a hurricane lamp which Wayne had brought from his own squat. 'She put that on herself, did she? From the inside?' Hetty said.

Wayne gave the hurricane lamp to Geoff to hold, took a key from his pocket and unlocked the padlock.

'Open the door.'

He shook his head. Sandy said, 'We're not going any further. That stink's unhealthy. You don't know what you could catch.'

Hetty took the lamp from Geoff and opened the door. The stench came out in a wave. The sacking shawl which the bag lady wore for warmth in the market had been draped over the upper part of her body, covering her head; it was alive with maggots, and at the disturbance, a cloud of bluebottles rose up towards the light. Hetty shut the door again quickly.

'Did you kill her?'

'Don't be stupid.'

'I asked a question.'

'We did not.'

Sandy said, 'We found the old woman dead on the steps, put her inside where she lived, covered her and used her pension book. Where's the harm in that? People like us have to do what we can to make a living.'

From outside they could hear the siren of a police car approaching. It stopped outside the mill and the door was kicked open. Then there were running feet on the stairs. Wayne said, 'You didn't have to call the police.'

'I didn't.'

And she hadn't. The police seemed surprised to see her and the lad, surprised by the hurricane lamp, generally surprised at everything except the dead body of the old lady, which it was clear they had expected to find. After a great many questions they allowed Hetty and Geoff to go and took Wayne and Sandy to the police station to assist them with their enquiries. Hetty and Geoff picked their way across the waste ground which was hazardous in the dark. The police had not offered them a lift.

Geoff said, 'That man must have told them – the one who stopped me in the alley.'

'But you didn't say anything about the smell, did you, or what you suspected? Just the pension fraud.'

'Right.'

'He must have come and looked for himself,' Hetty said. 'I find that interesting, Geoffrey, don't you?'

'I do if you do, Mrs Wainthropp.'

They walked on for a while in silence, then Hetty said, 'Police! They've no feelings. Why did they keep calling her "the old woman"? She had a name; it was on her pension book. She wasn't much older than me.'

Surprised at her tone, Geoff looked up at Hetty. He could see in the moonlight that there were tears wet on her cheeks. She put an arm out towards him. He took her hand and they walked on together.

The *Lancashire Evening Record* covered the story in detail. The headlines read:

PENSIONER FOUND DEAD
BEHIND LOCKED DOORS
Post Office Part-Timer
Uncovers Pension Fraud

and there was a photograph of Hetty, head-and-shoulders in her Sunday Best, emerging from the Coroner's Court, with the caption:

Mrs Hetty Wainthropp

Hetty picked the paper up from the pile in the supermarket, and held it at arm's length, squinting at it through half-closed eyes.

'I'm disappointed at the photo. It's not my best angle. You'd think they'd take more trouble.'

Robert was pushing the trolley. They had found Geoff at the fruit and veg, refilling shelves, and he had brought over his own trolley, which contained boxes of satsumas, mangoes and kiwi fruit, to admire the photograph with them. There was rather a run on kiwi fruit, which had been featured on television as a partner to gammon: it was just walking out of the shop.

'It's made a very favourable impression in the village,' Hetty said.

'A man came from Glossop to shake her hand. He brought his own video-camera.'

Geoff said, 'Nobody took my photo.'

'You weren't at the inquest. You should have asked for time off.' She put the newspaper in Robert's trolley. 'We'll take this.'

'You've got four at home already.'

'We'll send them to Australia for Derek and the children. Let that wife of his see what metal her mother-in-law's made of.' She moved back to the fruit and veg, Robert and Geoff following. 'I'll have a couple of satsumas from one of your boxes. They're bound to be fresher than the ones on display.' Hetty picked out satsumas from the third layer down, while a supervisor glared and Geoff shrank further into his maroon shelf-stacker's uniform. 'There were aspects of that inquest I didn't care for at all,' she said.

'The Coroner cut her off a bit short.'

'There was no interest shown in how the old lady died.'

'Doctor gave evidence. Cranial something. Fell on the stairs and died of her injuries.'

'But *did* she fall – or was she pushed? Kiwi fruit! There was a recipe on TV.'

'There's a run.'

'And what about that man who stopped you in the alley? If it was him phoned the police, why wasn't he called to give evidence? There's something here that doesn't add up.'

Robert said, 'Hetty likes things to add up. I offered to buy her a calculator, but she'd rather do it herself.'

The supervisor had ceased glaring and put herself in movement towards the fruit and veg. Geoff said, 'Excuse me,' and began refilling shelves with satsumas at double speed. 'I really enoyed working with you, Mrs Wainthropp,' he said. 'If anything similar comes up again, I'd be glad to help.'

But Hetty had already moved on. She had been approached by a woman shopper with a copy of the *Record* and was autographing the front page.

'Wake up!'

Robert woke. It was still dark. Hetty was lying beside him, her sharp elbow in his ribs. This was not an accident but a nudge, an intentional nudge. He had not been woken in the dark since his redundancy. 'The alarm's not gone wrong again, has it?'

'I can't sleep. My whole life is passing before my eyes and you lie there snoring.'

'It's not six yet.'

'Listen and you may learn something.'

It was years since Hetty had lain awake. How many? Three. They had lain awake together, side by side, worrying about money and how he would manage. What was she on about now?

'I've reached the time of life when I have to admit I'm not a natural subordinate.'

'No, you're not. Shall we go back to sleep now for a bit?'

'I'm wasted at that Post Office.'

'Oh!' This was different. This was good news. 'Are you going to give it up? I am glad. You're right; you're totally wasted in such a trivial occupation. A woman's place is in the home. Would you like me to appreciate you more? Congratulate you on the cooking and such? I'll do it.'

'You said yourself I've a mind like a computer. Making things add up, never satisfied until I reach the truth. Those were your very words.'

Robert was wary. 'I'm not always right. By no means.'

'What did that Coroner know? I was the one uncovered the fraud. I have aptitudes, Robert. I'm a natural detective, meant to be, just as you said.'

'I did not. I did not.'

'Lying here . . . thinking . . . it's been going round and round in my head. You must do what you're called to do in this world. If you don't follow your star you'll never hit the jackpot.'

'You're my wife. That's your calling.'

'I'm meant for better. Hetty Wainthropp – Private Eye!' Robert put the pillow over his head and his hands over his ears. If he could blot it out, it might all go away. Hetty said, 'There's fifty per cent off the Small Ads in the *Record* this week. I could put one in while they still remember who I am. Might make a nice little news story.'

This could only be dealt with in a rational way. By

reason mere fantasy could be shown up as what it was. Robert removed the pillow from his head and sat up. 'Think it over,' he said. 'Give it time.'

'I have. It's settled. I shall rely on you for advice and encouragement. And looking after the accounts, of course: you won't have to do double entry. I shall pick my cases. I won't do divorce and I won't do buggery.'

'You what?'

'Bugs. Industrial espionage. I'll put it in the advert. "No divorce. No industrial espionage."'

'What else is there?'

'Murder. I'd better get one of them Poirot books out of the Library and see how the professionals do it. Oh, and I'll need a devoted sidekick. They all have one.'

She watched him from the top of the aisle, stacking cans in a display. He was not ideal but he would have to do: there were no other candidates.

'Geoffrey!'

He left his trolley of cans where a careless shopper could fall over it, and came to her at once. Skinny, with big eyes and a face that looked as if it had been put together lopsided, he swore he was seventeen and sometimes looked eleven. 'Hello, Mrs Wainthropp.'

'I'm going into the detection business and I need an assistant. Sexton Blake had his Tinker Bell and so shall I. You're elected.'

'Tinker Bell was a fairy.'

This was a complication Hetty had not expected. But, even if she lived in a village, she was a woman of the world. 'Nobody could call me narrow-minded,' she said. 'What you do in your own time is your business, but I won't have any of that on duty.'

'How do I get paid?'

'Same way as I'll be – out of the profits. There'll be plenty of pickings when we get our first clients: I'm having cards printed. Meanwhile we might as well get our hands in by clearing up this bag lady business. We'll begin in the market.'

They began in the market.

Hetty went to the fish stall: she would need fish anyway for the evening meal, so she might as well get a bit of mileage out of buying it. There was a large bony fish with a nose like a serrated sword at the front of the stall – it was a pike brought in by an optimistic angler who did not know what else to do with it but had not wished to waste the most imposing catch he had ever made.

'Of course I knew her,' the fishmonger said. 'We all knew her.'

'How long had she been coming here?'

'Six weeks or so. Longer, maybe. She'd bring her little bits and pieces, sit in that doorway and watch the people.' He pointed to the doorway of the Mechanics' Institute, now occupied by a starveling teenager wearing jeans and two sweaters. The holes in the jeans might have been fashion, but the holes in both sweaters were clearly down to wear. In front of him there was a tin with very few coins in it, and a sign reading HOMELESS: PLEASE HELP. 'The kids used to mock her,' the fishmonger said. 'Shout after her, like.'

'Why?'

'She were a bit hairy, but no more than some I've seen.'

'You didn't know her name?'

'Nobody knew her name.'

'I did. It was in her pension book. Mary Nuttall. Does that mean anything to you?'

'Nothing.'

The pike's sword lifted the cowboy hat off a small boy whose mother was buying smoked haddock. Hetty said, 'That fish is a danger to the public.'

'I could let you have it cheap.'

'How cheap?'

'Make me an offer.'

'You might as well pay me for taking it away and saving you a summons. These bits and pieces – what were they?'

'Carrier-bags. All her worldly goods. Like a snail she carried them with her.'

'You can't imagine why anyone should want to kill her?'

'From what I've heard, she fell.'

When Hetty rejoined her assistant at the clothing stall, her two carrier-bags were full of more produce than she and Robert would be able to consume that night or many nights to come. The head of the pike protruded from the top of one of them. 'I couldn't resist this piece of fish,' she said. 'Such sad eyes.'

'You're going to eat it?'

'We'll find a use. It's give and get in this world, Geoffrey. If you want information you must be prepared to oblige. What have you found out?'

'Not a lot. They all remember her but they know nowt about her.'

'Same with me. Interesting!'

'I'm glad you think so. Was it worth the price of the fish?'

'To know that other people do not know is already to know more than they know. Remember that: it's called wisdom.'

She was struck by an idea. The consequence was that the pike suddenly became far more of a public danger than it had ever been on the fish stall. Geoffrey grabbed the two bags while Hetty took off across the market like one possessed, arriving at the doorway of the Mechanics' Institute with sparks coming off the backs of her shoes. Plopping a tenpenny piece into the teenager's tin, she said, 'Where do you lot sleep at night?'

The lobby of Lloyds Bank and the waiting room at the bus station were not popular with the homeless because the police moved them on. Hetty and Geoff found Wayne and Sandy in the octagonal bandstand in the Henry Arnaway Foundation Park: it was more exposed to the weather, specially when the wind was in the south-west, but at least you might get a complete night's sleep.

Sandy blinked in the light from Hetty's bicycle lamp. 'Haven't you done enough?' They had been turned out of their squat in the mill and, since they no longer had an address, could not claim Social Security, let alone the old lady's pension. In a remarkably short time – and as a direct consequence of Hetty's interference – they had fallen even further down the social ladder and arrived at the bottom.

'You knew you'd be found out.'

'Why? Nobody ever came there. There was no one to be inconvenienced by the smell of the dead body except us. It would've stopped in time. Or we might have moved on. You live from day to day when you're unemployed. That old lady's pension made the world of difference. We'd never have robbed her, but we couldn't let it go to waste.'

'What was in her carrier-bags?'

'Nothing. Anything. Just stuff she'd collected. There's people like that. Crazy people. They get attached to things. Worthless. Bits of newspaper. Broken toys. Orange peel.'

But the old woman had not been crazy. All the market people had agreed about that.

'We hardly spoke,' Sandy said. 'She was toffee-nosed. Superior. She had one of them la-di-da voices. Wayne saw her at the Reference Library. She wasn't there just to get out of the cold like the rest of us, not Mrs High and Mighty. She was actually reading.'

'What else did you find in the bags?'

Wayne and Sandy looked at each other, the beam of Hetty's cycle lamp moving from one face to the other. 'Nothing valuable.'

Hetty said, 'I don't believe you. There'd be letters. Photos. Mementos.'

Silence.

'I can wait for ever if I have to,' Hetty said. 'Or I could go to the police.'

Wayne said, 'There was a photo of a young lad in a silver frame. We threw the photo away and sold the frame.'

Hetty's plan worked. The conjunction of the Wainthropp Detective Agency's advertisement with her own recent success in unmasking the pension fraud persuaded the *Evening Record* to send a reporter and a photographer, and, to the delight of the village, Hetty's photograph appeared in the local paper for the second time in a month. This time it showed her best profile – Hetty had insisted. Since she was wearing her most attractive outfit, the lilac with the pink bows, it seemed to everyone a great pity that the *Record* had not moved to colour.

She spoke at length about the mystery of the old lady's death and the slipshod conduct of the Coroner's inquest. 'Who was she? Where did she come from? She may have had children,' Hetty said. 'Grandchildren. They'd want to know what happened to her. I've a public duty.' She did not make the front page, but the photograph and article were featured prominently in the Arts & Leisure section with the heading:

SUPERGRAN SLEUTH
Hetty Follows in Poirot's Footsteps
OAP in Career Move

The *Record* has a wide circulation on the North-West. A copy of the paper lay open on the red leather top of an executive desk and a well-manicured finger tapped at the headline. 'Can't have this.'

The man in the brown suit who had stopped Geoff in the alley stood before the desk. 'What exactly do you want me to do, sir?'

'Use your initiative. Play it by ear.'

It was a morning full of incident.

Hetty went to talk to the police while Geoff asked about the old lady at the Reference Library. A motorcycle courier in leathers and visor arrived at the Wainthropp house and presented Robert with a packet of 500 printed cards for which he was expected to pay.

In the Library, the plump person at the Information Desk remembered the old lady well. She had been interested in molluscs, read everything she could find on them. She had soon gone through the stock of the Reference Library and had been helped to order specialised volumes through the Public Library downstairs; when they arrived, she always brought them upstairs to read, since she had too much respect for books to take them back to the dump where she lived.

'What are molluscs exactly?'

'Oh . . . whelks . . . snails,' said the plump person. 'There's all sorts of gastropods once you start looking. Piddocks, for instance. Divine Creation, when it comes to molluscs, goes further than most of us can imagine.'

Meanwhile Hetty was having trouble at the police station. She sat on the other side of a bare desk in a bare Interview Room and got nowhere.

'All I'm asking for is information.'

'You were at the inquest, Mrs Wainthropp. She slipped on stone stairs and hit her head.'

'Who was she?'

The Sergeant consulted his notebook. 'Mary Nuttall. Of—'

'I've been to the address they gave in court. It's a mucky magazine shop, not a home.'

'Of course it is. If she'd had a home, she'd have been living in it. It's called an accommodation address.'

'Homeless people can't usually afford to pay for accommodation addresses.'

The Sergeant's patience was wearing thin. 'She was a homeless person in receipt of pension, Mrs Wainthropp, to draw which she required an address. A shop like that would've charged a pound a week – well worth the expense for the old lady to draw sixty odd pound in pension. Have you no idea how our society works?'

'I'd like to see the officer in charge of the case.'

'There is no case, Mrs Wainthropp, because no crime has been committed. Except the crime of pension fraud which is being dealt with through the usual channels.' He stood up. 'And now if you have no further questions, I'll see you out.'

The cards read:

WAINTHROPP DETECTIVE AGENCY
MISSING PERSONS FOUND, ETC.
DISCRETION GUARANTEED
PHONE 01254 812160
NO CALLERS AT THE HOUSE

The opened parcel was on the kitchen table with a few cards spilling out of the packet.

'It was cheaper if you had a lot done at once.' The intrepid private detective was wearing an old brown cardigan and bedroom slippers.

'And who's to pay for them?'

'You did, didn't you?'

'Only because he'd still be here if I hadn't. A great big chap in leather trousers with hands that could strangle an ox. I gave him a cheque but there'll be eyebrows raised at the bank. And then there's Geoffrey.'

'No problem. He's deferring his wages until we're in profit.'

'And they'll defer the rent on his room at Baden Powell Mansions, will they? They'll defer payment where he buys his groceries? Or have you sent him out thieving again?'

'Let the dead past bury its dead, Robert.'

'How much have you been giving him?'

There was a silence. This was unlike Hetty, who was more given to counter-attack than to evasion. Then, 'A little. Nowt to speak of. Expenses.'

'And where did you get it?' She could not meet his gaze and looked away. 'My God, you've been dipping into the Building Society money!'

'It is a joint account, Robert.'

'Only so's you wouldn't be stranded if I dropped down dead in the street.' He discovered that he had begun to shout. Shouting was as unusual for Robert as silence was for Hetty. 'We'll be paupers!' Somewhere inside of him a small voice whispered that shouting was fun and he should do it more often. 'We'll be on Social Security and everyone will know.'

'Don't raise your voice to me.'

It was his redundancy money, put away safely into the Building Society. They had sworn they would not touch it; they'd live on the interest until the Old Age Pension was due. Time had gone by and the monthly interest grown less and less. They had taken no holidays beyond continuing to pay a small sum every month into Sunset Years Cultural Tours, a scheme they had started before the redundancy came and they had not wanted to waste the non-returnable contributions. They had sold the Robin Reliant for less than it was worth. They had managed. And now . . .

Hetty spoke quietly. 'I stood there in the supermarket and watched him doing shelf-stacking, and I thought, "You're better than this". And since we've begun investigating, asking questions – asking other people, asking each other – it's like a flower opening: he takes your meaning so quick. I've watched you with him. Like a couple of lads.'

'What are you saying?'

'There's the spare room, never used. If he moved in here with us, he'd save on his rent and his food.'

'We know nowt about him.' Robert was desperate. She had to be made to realise the enormity of what she was suggesting without being pushed into obstinacy. Once Hetty became obstinate there was no shifting her. 'You don't take strangers into your house these days, and certainly not teenagers. He could be on drugs.'

The phone rang. Hetty could see that Robert was in no condition to answer it sensibly so she went herself. He shouted after her, 'I live here too, you know.' She would have to work on him. It would take time.

'Yes, this is the Wainthropp Agency. Please describe the nature of your problem in your own words. Take your time and speak slowly.'

She was all of a flutter inside but her voice was calm. There was a ballpoint pen by the phone and a reporter's notebook with spiral wire binding. She took notes. A part of her watched herself doing so. Then she returned to her husband, still seething in the kitchen.

'Our first client. I knew that piece in the paper would attract attention.'

Robert was gratifyingly amazed. 'Someone going to pay you? For detection?'

'A Mr Harkness. I'm to meet him tomorrow morning at Clitheroe Castle: he'll wear a white carnation. Delicate and personal, he said. I told him we didn't do divorce – ' Robert had heard her say so and had wondered whether to shout at her to reconsider, since they needed the money so badly ' – but he says it's nothing of that nature. Oh Robert, I'm on my way.'

Robert refused to be impressed. 'Not in that cardigan you're not.' If she was to be paid, that made a difference but it would do no good to say so, with the battle over young Geoff still unresolved.

It was a fine spring day. Hetty wore her lilac with the bows and a floral hat. Mr Harkness was wearing a brown suit with a white carnation in the lapel, brown boots and gloves of soft black leather. He appeared to be in a state of high agitation.

'Are you sure you weren't followed?'

'Who'd be following?'

'Nobody, I hope. I've taken every precaution.'

Clitheroe Castle is easy to find, since it dominates the town, but there is not a great deal to do when one gets there except to walk round the outside and admire the view. So they were walking round. The man in the brown suit did not seem to admire the view very much. He kept glancing nervously from side to side, and when he looked directly at Hetty it was as if he was afraid she would steal his wallet.

'I'm sorry,' he said. 'I'm extremely upset. They threatened to kill her if I go to the police.'

'Threatened to kill who?'

'Tracey. My daughter, Tracey.'

'And who are they?'

'I don't know. They could be anyone. We'd better keep on the move to avoid notice.'

They moved. A little way behind them, a large man with large hands, who looked as if he might once have been a policeman, moved also, following them. This man did not appear to be of high intelligence, but rather to be anxious to get things right which in the past had often gone wrong. His large hands swung loosely by his side like bunches of bananas.

'They won't talk on the phone, you see,' said the man in the brown suit. 'They expect phone taps. Instead they insist on a meeting.'

'You want me to go with you?'

'Instead of me. I can't go myself: I've a heart condition. Find out what they want, and then come back and tell me.'

'What about your wife?'

'She doesn't know: they phoned me at the office. I was at my wits' end. I looked at your photo in the paper and thought, "She's the one".'

'Where does your wife think Tracey is?'

'Staying with friends. She was at this party – a rave: that's where they grabbed her. You've got to explain to them, Mrs Wainthropp. They've made a mistake. I'm not a rich man. They must have got me confused with someone else.' The large man was closer now and the man in the brown suit saw him. His head jerked; his arms made broken circles in the air. 'I think we're being watched. Pretend to admire the view.'

So Hetty stepped forward to admire the view which was, as it had been for some time, of trees and the tarmac road up to the Castle, and a car park some way below. The drop to the car park was particularly steep. The man in the brown suit did not step forward with her; he stepped back and away and the man with large hands moved up behind, flexing those hands. And at that moment a boy on a skateboard (strictly forbidden at Clitheroe Castle) came from the upper level, whizzed between Hetty and the large man and on past a party of schoolchildren coming from below. The large man moved on quickly, avoiding Hetty to whom he had come dangerously close, and Hetty stepped back from the edge.

'Are you sure it's a real kidnap, Mr Harkness?' she said. She had heard of raves. 'Couldn't it just be Tracey and her friends making the whole thing up to get money out of you?'

'That's a despicable suggestion.' Hetty would not allow even a prospective client to insult her, and was about to leave but the man in the brown suit mopped his brow, smiled his sickly ingratiating smile and apologised. 'Sorry, sorry. No offence intended, and none taken, I hope. Of course I'm not sure.' He rooted about in an inner pocket and produced a brown manila envelope. 'That's one of the things I want you to find out. There's a hundred and fifty pounds here in notes, and directions on how to get to the meeting place. There'll be another hundred and fifty when you come back.'

'How do I get in touch with you?'

'You don't. I'll phone you from a public box. Now remember, they'll be expecting you and there'll be nobody else about. You'll be in no danger if you don't start anything.'

Hetty promised that she would not start anything.

'How are you going to get there? It's a long way out.'

'Please don't concern yourself, Mr Harkness. I have my own transport.'

She had. They had used her cycle and Robert's to get to the Henry Arnaway Foundation Park, but this – their first paid job – was an occasion for lashing out. Geoff had borrowed a scooter from a friend. He was licensed to drive it, having driven one before during one of his many dead-end jobs, delivering pizzas for a Chain. The Chain had broken, leaving a warehouse full of rotting mozerella, and Geoff had lost the use of the scooter, but not the skill.

Hetty did not intend to give up on the Mary Nuttall case, but it could be left on the backburner for a while. If the negotiations with the kidnappers were to drag on, as she had heard such negotiations always did, Tracey Harkness could turn into a nice little earner. She borrowed a boiler-suit from Robert. A crash-helmet came with the scooter. She was equipped for adventure. Robert suggested coming with her as added protection, but there would not have been room for two of them on the pillion, and if she arrived with too large an escort the kidnappers would panic. Even Geoffrey, in black polo-neck sweater, jeans and trainers, had been instructed to keep hidden.

It is not easy to read directions by torchlight while on the back of a scooter in motion along bumpy country roads, but Hetty managed, and eventually they came to a sign which read *Dead End* and then to a gate on which was painted FARM COTTAGE ONLY and to a track across a field with, in the distance at what they supposed was the end of it, a cottage, black against the moonlit sky. There was a tiny flickering light at the window of what must have been the front room.

'I'm expected – I'll go on in. You hide the scooter and follow me. I want you to keep me under constant observation,' Hetty said.

'What happens if they kidnap you as well?'

'Start a diversion.' She walked towards the light.

If there had been a garden it was overgrown. Hetty negotiated nettles (powerless to sting through the boiler-suit), docks, a matt of what seemed to be mainly damp chickweed, tin cans and bottles, a broken willow-pattern plate glinting in the moonlight. Light or no light, it was clear that nobody lived in the cottage or had done for years. She pushed open the front door, which was already ajar. It opened straight into the room with the light, which she could now see was a single candle fixed on top of an old paint can lid set in the middle of a kitchen table. This table and a rickety wooden chair were the only furniture in the room. If the kidnappers were thinking of a sit-down negotiation they had left themselves ill-equipped.

'Anybody home?'

No reply. Hetty came fully into the room and looked about her. 'It's Mrs Wainthropp. I've come on behalf of my client, Mr Harkness.'

She moved the chair and a leg fell off. 'I shan't sit down, if you don't mind.' Still no response. She supposed that they did not want their faces to be seen, and would talk to her from the next room or a darkened doorway. 'Well, I'm here,' she said. 'Start talking.'

They did not start talking. They were holding her in suspense in order to frighten her. 'You might as well get on with it,' she said. 'I haven't got all night.' No reaction. But there was something. Faintly at first, then louder, Hetty could hear a whimpering sound coming from above. It could be – it was, she was sure it was – a teenager in distress. She lifted her head to listen. Her night vision was coming to her. She could make out more of the interior of the cottage. There were stairs from this room leading to an upper floor. She went to the foot of the stairs. 'Is anyone up there? Tracey? Are you all right, love?'

She switched on her torch and began to climb the stairs. The whimpering sound seemed to get louder as she climbed. 'Is that you, Tracey? Don't be worried. I'm a friend, come from your dad.' There was a landing at the top of the stairs, and moonlight from a broken window. The whimpering seemed to be coming from behind a closed door. She pushed at it, but it resisted her. Was it locked? Would she have to run at it, as they did on the television, and bruise her shoulder? Well, she would if she had to, for three hundred pounds. She pushed again, harder; the door gave way suddenly and sent her careering into the room out of control.

The floor immediately collapsed beneath her. As she fell, the beam of her torch illuminated a battery-powered cassette-player balanced on a box on the other side of the room, and the sound of the whimpering was much louder.

A trap. There was a hole in the floor, covered by straw, only joists and plaster remaining and these had not been able to hold her. Plaster fell in a cloud into the room below and put out the candle. She hung, supported by her elbows, her legs dangling, and shouted for Geoff. The whimpering continued but now sounded to Hetty more like mocking laughter.

Geoff ran from outside into dark, confusion and dust. 'Mrs Wainthropp! Mrs Wainthropp, are you hurt? Have you broke any limbs? It happened so sudden. Are you asphyxiating under there?'

'I'm up here, you loon.' He looked up through the gloom and the still-swirling plaster dust and saw a pair of dangling legs. 'I'll drop the torch. Catch it.'

She still had the torch in one hand, and it was still giving light. The problem was to get her hand to the edge of the hole without moving the elbow which was holding that side of her up. She managed. More plaster fell. She dropped the torch and Geoff caught it. 'Now get me out of this. And be careful as you come upstairs. This place is booby-trapped.'

Geoff came upstairs as delicately as a cat. 'Who's that crying?'

'Tape-recorder. The bleating of the goat excites the tiger.'

'Oh, aye?' He surveyed the predicament. Her elbows were like two lions propping up a catafalque on a marble plinth, but Hetty's plinth was made of plaster and lathe and there was not much of it. 'Would it be easier if you just dropped, do you think? There's a pile of rubble underneath to break your fall.'

'If I drop, you've failed. Now get on with it.'

He failed. They both dropped. The pile of rubble broke Geoff's fall, and Geoff's body broke Hetty's: Geoff was the loser on both sides. The whimpering from upstairs continued. Hetty said, 'There'll be someone along soon. They won't leave that tape-recorder for the police to find, and anyway they've no idea whether I'm dead or alive.'

Geoff was looking out of the broken window. He could see the lights of a car approaching on the dead-end road leading to the track. It stopped at the gate and the lights were switched off. 'There's someone coming now.'

'Scarper! That garden's all cover. Just be careful of the rusty cans.'

From behind a curtain of goose grass covering a dead lilac they watched two men come up the track, one man larger than the other, with enormous dangling hands. As they drew nearer, the smaller one said, 'The candle's gone out,' and the other, 'But you can still hear the tape if you listen,' to which the first man said, 'I tell you honestly, I don't know what to expect or what to hope for. You'd better go in first. She knows my face.' And the two men went cautiously inside, while Hetty and Geoff slipped quietly away in the direction of the hidden scooter.

It would not be safe to start the engine until they were some way from the cottage. Geoff said, 'One of them two was the man who grabbed me in the alley.'

'Interesting! He was also Mr Harkness. I don't think we'll go straight home. There's a Greasy Spoon I remember on the Bury Road which does good chips. You and me had better have a bit of a talk.'

So they went to the Greasy Spoon on the Bury Road where – since only breakfasts were served whatever the time of day – Geoff had sausage, beans, bacon, egg and chips and Hetty a cup of strong tea. There, surrounded by noisy night-people, they had a little talk.

'We may be out of our depth, Geoffrey.'

'Made a hundred and fifty quid out of it so far though, didn't we?'

'I don't imagine we'll be getting the second instalment. Anyway, there's more to life than money. Like staying alive. We'll have to get out of this Bag Lady Case. Drop it and find a way to let them know. Whoever "they" are.'

He was staring at her, big-eyed, a chip speared on the end of his fork. 'We're not quitters, Mrs Wainthropp.'

'Yes, we are. I've a responsibility to your mother.'

'You've shown no sign of it up to now.'

'There'll be other cases.'

'Never close a file, you said.'

Had she said that? If so, it had been without thinking it through. 'I'm closing this one. We have to do it, Geoffrey. We've blundered into something: we don't know what, but whatever it is, they tried to kill me tonight.'

Geoff remembered the weight of her coming down on him among all that plaster. If he hadn't been there to break her fall, it was true she might have done herself an injury, but even so a sprained ankle was a lot more likely than a broken neck. Then he remembered the two men going into the cottage and the large hands dangling.

Hetty said, 'We'll talk to the police. Attempted murder – they'll have to investigate and they've more facilities. That's as far as I'm prepared to go.'

A teenager and a Senior Citizen! ('I am not,' said Hetty. 'I am not now nor ever will be a Senior Citizen, at least until *I* choose.') The lawyers would make mincemeat of them in court, not that it would ever come to court with no suspects and no proof of crime. ('We were there. It happened to us. We're witnesses,' Geoff said.) A hundred and fifty pounds in used notes and a bit of torn wrapping paper with directions written out in capital letters! ('It had to be in capitals to make it easy to read in the dark.')

Hetty rolled up her sleeves and showed the scratches on her arms where she had fallen through the floor (or ceiling if you happened to be downstairs looking up). There *was* evidence. There was the hole, the actual hole, and the fallen plaster. No cassette-recorder any more, of course, and no tape. And not a trace of any Mr Harkness or his daughter, Tracey. How could there be when these identities were bogus, invented as part of the plot?

They had been trying to kill her.

Why?

Because she was investigating the death of the old bag lady.

But the Coroner's inquest had brought that death in as an accident.

She had told the newspaper reporter that she intended to find out who the bag lady really was.

Mary Nuttall, a person of no fixed abode: that was known.

But where had she come from?

Where had any homeless person come from? That was not the problem. The problem was, what was to be done with them where they were now.

The Detective Chief Inspector was a kind man, a civilised man, a patient man. 'People think the police can investigate anything,' he said. 'But we're a public service, chronically short of cash. Broadly speaking, we investigate only two sorts of crimes – those we can't avoid and those we think we can clear up. You tell me that people are trying to kill you because you've been poking your nose into the old lady's death. It's unprovable, a waste of public money to give you more than a few soothing words.'

'You'll do nothing, then?'

'Think about it, Mrs Wainthropp. You yourself have already done something and it may well be enough. You've come to me, you've made a statement. Now suppose that you were to suffer an unfortunate and possibly fatal accident after having made that statement . . . You follow me?'

'Are you saying I've got to get meself murdered before you're prepared to take me seriously?'

'Precisely. And if anybody is really trying to kill you, they must know that. Consequently I don't think you'll be bothered any more.'

'You're telling us to go on?'

'That's your choice entirely, Mrs Wainthropp. If you did go on, and you did discover anything important, of course I'd expect to be told.'

Somewhere inside her head Hetty heard Sandy saying, *There was a photo in a silver frame. We threw the photo away and sold the frame.*

Hetty called a Breakfast Meeting. If David Frost could do it, she could too. They had found the silver frame on the Genuine Antiques & Collectables stall in the market and acquired it at a huge discount after some well-judged remarks about the danger of dealing in stolen property. Geoffrey had discovered the photograph screwed up among the contents of the old lady's carrier-bags still littering the floor of the squat in the abandoned mill. The two had been put together and they fitted. The photograph was of a young man in a mortarboard and black gown with a bit of rabbit skin round his shoulders. He had a filled champagne glass in one hand and was holding it to camera. Behind him were railings and a stone head of somebody classical in an advanced state of decomposition.

'Your brother Frank had a suit like that,' Hetty said to Robert.

She was sitting up in bed in her best bed jacket with the breakfast tray before her like some empress, with Robert and Geoff as her courtiers. Her eyes were sparkling: she was in command.

'Right – he did!' Robert said. 'Demob suit. Good cloth, is that. He wore it to funerals.'

'Demob suit?'

'Before your time, Geoffrey. I never got one. Did me National Service like, but you had to've been in the war.'

'Late forties, then,' Hetty said. 'Someone who was in his early twenties in the late forties. Drinking champagne dressed up like a schoolmaster. That old man's head behind him would tell us where if we knew which city it was, but it's probably in the South and certainly cultural. What it says to me is rich and powerful people covering up – and you remember the old lady had a la-di-da voice. Then there's the molluscs.'

'You what?'

'She went to the Reference Library and read about molluscs. Whelks and such. Cockles. What was there about whelks to make her take off and leave her home? She'd found something out and that knowledge was dangerous.'

'Some people don't care for whelks. I'm not all that keen on them meself.'

'Whatever it was, my theory is she lived where they abound.' Hetty looked again, critically, at the photograph. 'We have to know where we are before we can go where we're going. I wonder what that bit of fur means. We miss a lot by not being educated. Robert and I never had the chance and you've not taken advantage of your opportunities, Geoffrey.'

'What opportunities?'

'But it's like my Auntie Bea used to say, "If you don't know there's always others who do".'

So they all took the bus into town and dropped Robert off to make enquiries at the Grammar School about the bit of fur in the photograph, while Hetty and Geoff set off on the trail of molluscs.

Geoff went to the market and talked to the people who ran the fish stall. They did not tell him anything he did not know already – molluscs came from the wholesaler and before that from the sea – but sitting in the doorway of the Mechanics' Institute was Sandy, very much in the doldrums, and with a sign that read: HOMELESS HUNGRY. So Geoff bought her a hotdog with a double helping of mustard and took her to find Hetty who was in the supermarket examining the labels on cans of smoked oysters to see where they came from.

'Have we got to eat all those?'

'Not the ones from Taiwan.'

'Wayne's done a runner. Sandy's ready to talk.'

Robert appeared at the end of the aisle, looking almost jaunty, very much in contrast with his hangdog appearance as he went through the wrought-iron gates of the Grammar School. Initially, there had been a misunderstanding because they thought he had come about a job as a cleaner, but eventually he had found a kindred spirit in the History teacher who had been able to explain the photograph without difficulty.'

'Graduation Day – Oxford, he says. Just got his degree, like, and he'd be celebrating with his family. The bit of fur means he's a BA. It's probably just hired for the occasion; he'd have to give it back. The old gent in the background is the Emperor Trajan.'

'Never mind that now,' Hetty said. 'We have other fish to fry.'

There was an abandoned toilet on the ground floor of the derelict mill. Dirt and graffiti everywhere, no running water, but a cracked wash basin, a cracked toilet bowl, both with brown stains, and a little pile of squares of torn-up newspaper on top of the cistern.

'We'd meet in here sometimes, her and me. Well, it was somewhere to sit: Wayne used the one upstairs. She brought the bits of newspaper, all torn to size for us ladies to use and we'd collect rainwater in a bucket to flush the bowl.'

'Some of those newspapers could have been local. Where she came from.' Hetty and Geoffrey took half the pile each and went rapidly through them, while Sandy watched.

Nothing. Most were from the *Daily Telegraph* and *The Times*. 'There's more to read,' Sandy said. 'And the paper's softer. Are we done in here now?'

But Hetty was not done. 'Educated. Toffee-nosed voice. She laid down the law in the Reference Library.

She was middle-class. She had valuables. Must have.' Sandy shook her head. There had been no valuables. 'I don't mean the bit of unspent money from her pension – you'd have taken that. But the things middle-class folk can't live without. Chequebook. Credit cards. She'd have brought them with her.'

'I told you – she had nothing. Do you think Wayne and me would have wasted a credit card?'

'She'd nowhere to hide it, but she must have hid it anyway.' But Geoffrey had already sifted thoroughly through the bits and pieces in the room upstairs in his search for the photograph. Her gaze roamed over the toilet walls and corners as if the graffiti might contain a clue. 'No running water, you said. Geoffrey, look in the cistern.'

'Jackpot!'

Inside the waterless cistern of the WC was a plastic sponge-bag with a decoration of tulips, and something inside which did not feel like dentures. He handed it to Hetty, but Sandy was watching, her dejected torpor quite banished by the thought of treasure. Hetty said, 'We'll look at it later. No offence intended.'

There was a small noise. Perhaps a door had been closed at the other end of the long shed. Perhaps something had banged against the window. Perhaps something had fallen from a pigeon's nest. Where there are broken windows in abandoned buildings there are always pigeons, who are great snappers-up of unconsidered trifles and would make nests out of barbed wire if there were nothing else. Whatever it was, it startled the three of them and they turned sharply to stare up the length of the shed.

But there was nothing to see. 'Starting at shadows!' Hetty said. 'It gets to you, this job,' and she and Geoff took the sponge-bag and its contents home where they could be properly examined on the kitchen table.

There was a leather folder of plastic cards, each signed on the back, *Mary Nuttall*, and a chequebook from a bank in Windermere, and a thin packet wrapped in waterproof cloth. Hetty looked at the chequebook. 'Windermere. Nowhere near the sea. So much for molluscs.'

'What's in the packet?'

'Don't think I haven't been wondering.' She turned it over. 'It's so wrapped up I don't like to open it.'

'Let me have a feel.' Robert felt the packet. 'Well, it's not shortbread.' He passed it to Geoff. 'When in doubt, computers.'

Geoff said, 'Right! It's a disk, I'd say. Not much good to us. We haven't got a computer, and wouldn't know how to work it if we had.'

Hetty was indignant. 'Don't be daft. They've got them in primary schools, these days. Little children play with them.'

'Not where I went to school. Nobody was computer literate, or in any other way. Even the spelling of four-letter words gave us trouble.' He handed the packet back. 'Better keep this safe till we find someone as knows how to read it.'

Robert said, 'Aren't you going to give it to that Detective Chief Inspector?'

Both of them looked at him. Hetty said, 'What a funny idea! There's no crime been committed, not as far as the police are concerned, not unless we find one out.' She put the packet in her handbag with the chequebook. 'At least we know where she cashed her cheques. It's somewhere to start.'

So they started at Windermere. They went there by bus. Unfortunately, Geoff did not appear sufficiently waif-like to qualify for a half-fare, but you've got to spend money to make money in this world, and if they could solve the Bag Lady Case it would lead to better things: the bus fares were an investment. They found a phone-box and looked up Mary Nuttall. She was listed – there could only be one – with an address in a village up the valley. The bus service only ran twice a week. 'We must take as we find,' said Hetty.

So they took first a man who travelled in Teflon hardware and then a farm-vehicle – a machine with enormous wheels which negotiated the country lanes at 5 m.p.h. to the fury of traffic trapped behind it, and had recently been used for spreading muck. Hetty sat up front with the driver. Geoff stood in the back and tried to avoid touching anything.

In time they arrived at two cottages built side by side at the edge of a village, and situated about fifty yards from the nearest other building. One was Lilac Cottage – neat flowerbeds well mulched and weeded in the front garden, bulbs in flower everywhere, daffodils and crocus, tulips, anemones, Glory of the Snow and Flower of Bethlehem, still a few late snowdrops, the rose bushes pruned, the lilac itself just beginning to bloom. The other, Piddock Holme, was neglected, everything straggling and overgrown. It was easy to see which had been deserted. Except that Mary Nuttall, according to the telephone directory, had lived in Lilac Cottage.

'Something wrong here.' Hetty marched up to the front door of Lilac Cottage, Geoff following, but it was opened before she could reach it by a youngish man in cords and a crew-neck sweater.

That figured. Mary Nuttall had been toffee-nosed, according to Sandy, and this young man was wearing the uniform of Toffeenosia. Hetty recognised the type. They would come sometimes to the pub in the village of a Sunday morning and sit about, braying to each other in the Saloon Bar. 'Is Mrs Nuttall at home?' she said.

'No, she's out. Who wants her?'

'Wainthropp Detective Agency. When will she be back?'

'I'm not quite sure.'

'No, I'll bet you're not. Who am I speaking to?'

'What business is that of yours?'

A line half-remembered from something American on the telly swam into Hetty's consciousness. 'I'll ask the questions, buster.'

The young man was clearly taken aback, Geoff delighted. 'I'm her nephew, looking after her cottage while she's away,' he said. 'If you know where she is, I'd be grateful if you'd tell me.'

So Hetty told him that, unfortunately, his aunt had died under suspicious circumstances a month ago, and that she and her associate, Mr Shawcross, were investigating the case. The nephew looked at the waif-like associate with the air of a pub landlord asked to serve Grand Marnier to someone clearly under age, and Geoff grinned back at him. 'I suppose you'd better come in.' He didn't seem too griefstricken by the news.

The inside of the cottage was white walls, oak beams and tapestry cushions, with an open stair to the bedrooms above. A wall had been taken down so that the ground floor was one large room with a kitchen and WC off it. Through the window, Hetty could see the back garden, which was as well tended as the front, and the back garden of Piddock Holme, which was as unkempt as the rest. At the bottom of it was the base and twisted metal girders of a burnt-out shed.

'What happened next door?'

'To the laboratory?'

'To the garden shed.'

'It was a laboratory belonging to Professor Fisher, my aunt's neighbour. He had retired some time ago, but kept an interest. One night, quite recently, it caught fire. It was all rather upsetting, since somehow the Professor was trapped inside, and burned to death without anyone's realising what was happening.'

'Yes, it would be upsetting,' Hetty said. 'I can see that.'

Geoff gave a serious and sympathetic nod, indicating that he also could well understand how unsettling it might be to have one's next-door neighbour burn to death. 'You said, "somehow" he was trapped inside. Could somebody have locked him in?'

She was on form, no doubt of that. The complete detective. She could feel her brain ticking. The nephew said, 'I don't see why anyone should. There was an open verdict at the inquest.'

'What do the neighbours say?'

'My aunt was his only neighbour.'

'And she's dead too.'

'In suspicious circumstances, you said?'

'She fell and hit her head.'

'That's hardly suspicious.'

'It is when you don't know who pushed her. That open verdict on the Professor – means it could have been murder, suicide or an accident.'

'Hardly in that order. There's no reason why anyone should have wanted to murder Professor Fisher and none why he should take his own life.'

'You know that, do you?' Of course he did not. It seemed to Hetty that this was the same sort of cover-up as for the old lady, with everyone knowing what had happened when actually nobody knew. 'Your aunt must have had something to say at the inquest. A fire like that, she'd have heard summat, even if it was only screaming.' Her Lancashire accent grew stronger as she harried this toffee-nosed weakling to see which way he would run. 'Seen summat maybe.'

'She wasn't at the inquest. She went away: the police were rather annoyed. She was rather fond of him, you see.'

'Then why not stay and help the police find out why he died?'

'Surely that's not hard to understand. If one's

emotionally involved . . . standing up there in public, answering questions. She was a shy, sensitive woman.'

'So shy and sensitive that she preferred to run away, live rough and get herself murdered?' What a chancer! Was she going too far? Geoff rather thought she was. 'Just to avoid an inquest? It's hard to believe, is that.'

The nephew went past them to the front door. 'Mrs Wainthropp, I was totally unaware of my aunt's death until you told me just now.' He opened it. 'I'm extremely grateful to you for letting the family know, but it's hardly my business – or yours – to investigate.'

Geoff said, 'What was Mr Fisher a professor of?'

'Some sort of biologist, I think. Goodbye, Mrs Wainthropp.'

'Well, we know where to find you.' Reluctantly they went. The nephew quickly mounted the stairs to the master bedroom where the man in the brown suit was removing a head-set and switching off a tape-recorder.

'It's obvious she knows nothing,' said the man in the brown suit.

The nephew moved across to the window, from which he could watch Hetty and Geoff's progress back to the village. 'Better keep her under observation, though. You can stay here, provided you never leave the cottage: there's plenty of food.'

'What's to observe?'

'I have to get back. I'll see you're relieved if she hangs about, but my guess is she'll be gone by morning.'

'I hate these messy cases,' said the man in the brown suit.

As for Hetty and Geoff, they had not progressed far, but were looking at the front of Piddock Holme.

Geoff said, 'There's three kinds of piddock altogether. They burrow into rock.'

'Marine molluscs – what she was studying at the Reference Library! Burned to death in his own shed . . . it was never an accident, Geoffrey. And she ran off just after, and took that computer thing with her. This case is beginning to have a very fishy smell.'

'Well, he *was* a marine biologist. We'll have to ask about. There was a pub in Main Street, opposite the Spar shop.'

'There's more sources of information in a village than a lot of gossipy old men supping ale in a pub – and anyway, they'd never serve you, looking as young as you do. We'll have to spend the night here, so let's find somewhere reliable and homely.'

The landlady was baking bread. Though Hetty herself lived in a village, she was not a countrywoman. There are villages and villages, and those which cluster about Blackburn, Darwen and Bolton have little in common with the villages of the Lake District. Bread was something you bought at the Spar, often already sliced. This was a different world, but seemed a good one. What the landlady was doing did not seem difficult, though perhaps a little too time-consuming for a busy detective. Nevertheless she would watch and remember and try it out on Robert, just as she had tried out the *Boeuf catalane* which had been demonstrated on television and was now (since it gave him indigestion) cluttering up the freezer.

'Well, he was a funny man, the Professor, firm in his views,' the landlady said. 'He took against that agribusiness place they built on Mellyn Hill.'

'And what's agribusiness when it's at home?'

'It's for the farmers, isn't it? Chemicals and suchlike.' The landlady's son, Gerry, was at the kitchen table, opposite from his mother, doing his homework. He took no part in the thumping of the dough but, from time to time, would blow flour off a sociology text.

'Us old village families, we didn't care: we need the work. But the Professor got into a great state and he whipped up the newcomers, yuppies and such. Doomsday scenario, he said, pollution of the water, no telling where it would lead. There was public meetings and talk of going to law, but it all came to nothing in the end. He went a bit funny after. There's a place below Mellyn Hill where the outflow from the factory comes into the lake. He'd go out there every day, rain or shine,' – she had finished thumping, and now covered the dough with a wet cloth – 'and he'd bring back freshwater shrimps and mussels and such, like a child with tiddlers. He wanted them for his experiments, I suppose, but it looked odd. And then . . . well, he wasn't a man for pets but he got a couple of beagles – a dog and a bitch. I don't know if he intended to breed them.'

'There's a market for beagles,' Geoff said. 'I've often heard that. It's the ears.'

'And ducks. It wasn't practical – he'd no experience of poultry. And two goats to keep the grass down.'

'How did Mrs Nuttall react to all this?'

'She helped him.'

'What happened to the beagles?'

'Couple of RSPCA fellows took them away in a van after the accident. And the goats with them.'

Gerry said, 'If it *was* an accident.'

'You don't think it was?'

'The Animal Liberation Front set fire to him. Everyone knows that but they can't prove it.'

'How do you know those men were from the RSPCA? Were they in uniform?'

'They said they were.' The first batch of loaves were removed from the oven. The smell was ambrosial. Even the Cardoma on a peak day with everything fresh could not match it. 'Funny thing,' the landlady said. 'Lily Perrins down the road wanted to take the goats. She's two of her own, you see, and does sweaters with the combings. But they wouldn't allow it.'

Geoff said, 'What happened to the ducks?'

Gerry grinned. 'Better not to ask.'

Hetty said, 'We might go out and take a look at this agribusiness factory while we're here. It's a pity to come so far and see nothing. Do you think we could get hold of a couple of bicycles and a packed lunch?'

Next morning they stood at the top of Mellyn Hill looking at a locked gate of heavy steel set in a high fence of steel mesh. There was a notice on the gate:

GAIAE BIOCHEMICALS (UK) PLC
NO ENTRY TO UNAUTHORISED PERSONS
GUARD DOGS ON PATROL

Hetty said, 'It's not what you'd call welcoming.'

'We'd better go back.'

'I haven't climbed the Lake District's equivalent of the Matterhorn wheeling a bicycle to give up the moment I get to the top.'

She put two fingers to her mouth and gave a loud whistle. Almost at once a security guard appeared on the other side of the fence. He held a guard dog on a leash. The dog was wearing a muzzle and did not seem to be friendly.

Hetty said, 'Excuse me, I'm sorry to trouble you, but what goes on in here exactly?'

'If you were an authorised person, madam, you wouldn't need to ask. Now on your way, please, both of you.'

'We're doing no harm, and it's a public place out here – a natural Beauty Spot with unrestricted access, the guidebooks say.' She was making it up as she went along, but most places in the Lake District are natural Beauty Spots and it seemed a safe bet that the guidebooks would have something to say about Mellyn Hill. 'We've brought a picnic and we intend to eat it. Get out the Thermos and the sandwiches, Geoffrey.'

Geoff, who had little confidence in guidebooks or the ability of steel mesh and a muzzle to restrain a Dobermann, began apprehensively to take the packed lunch from the basket on the front of his cycle. Hetty said to the guard, 'Was Professor Fisher an authorised person?'

The security guard stared at her, blank-faced. The dog growled. Then the guard took a portable radio from his belt and spoke into it. 'Perimeter to Base!'

Geoff said, 'I think we'd best be off now, Mrs Wainthropp.' So they took their picnic down the hill and had it where the outflow from the agribusiness factory found its way into the lake.

'These feet,' Hetty said. 'They're my Achilles heel when it comes to leg-work, and that can't be denied.' She was dangling them in the water as she began to unpack the picnic basket. 'Animal Liberation Front! Some folks'll believe anything. Why should animal liberators bother about a few shrimps in a shed at the bottom of a garden?'

'You can never tell. There was a girl from our school joined them and she went about releasing bait from fishing-tackle shops.'

'There's something from that place was affecting those molluscs, and that's what the Professor was studying. That's what'll be on the computer thingummy.'

'Something in the water?'

Hetty unscrewed the top of the Thermos. 'Has to be.'

'Then should you be putting your feet in it, Mrs Wainthropp?'

The feet seemed to whip themselves out of the water. Hetty poured coffee for them both and handed Geoff one of the packets of sandwiches. He bit into haslet and salad between slices of newly baked bread and knew that he must force himself not to eat too quickly. Hetty, he saw, was brooding, her sandwich not yet broached.

'There's things you read about in the papers,' she said. 'Little kiddies born with no eyes. Leukaemia and such.'

'I don't read them bits.'

'Well, usually I don't either, but sometimes you're bound to notice. We'll have to look at what's on that disk thing. Robert can ask at the school again.'

'We can look at it here in the village.' Hetty was surprised. 'There's yuppies here,' Geoff explained. 'They've got toys – faxes and such: computers are two a penny. Gerry was telling me, there's a mate he goes over to see in the evenings sometimes, a teenage boffin with a whole room full of stuff and a police warning for hacking into Barclay's Bank. He'll read it, no problem.'

But in fact Dominic the teenage boffin could *not* read the disk; it used a software called Frogspawn which he had never heard of, and was anyway, he said, almost certainly encrypted: they couldn't get in without a password.

'Scientists! They've no consideration.' But Hetty's heart was not in mere disapproval of the scientific community. 'I was noticing, there isn't a For Sale board outside the Professor's cottage, but nobody lives there.'

Gerry said, 'Some company from London bought it.'

'I wonder how they knew.'

'About the fire? It was in all the papers.'

'If you'd read in the papers about some professor being burned to death in his garden shed, would you put in an offer for his house straight off? And it didn't look empty. There were curtains at the windows. They've not moved his things out.' All three teenage faces were turned to her, three minds moving comfortably with hers. 'Is there a way we could get in, would you suppose?'

'I think we might find one, Mrs Wainthropp.'

Both Lilac Cottage and Piddock Holme were heated by solid fuel, and behind each there was a bunker with a heavy wooden double shutter and access to the cellar. The shutter was secured with a large padlock, but the general rule for padlocks is that the larger they are, the easier to open. And the door between the bunker and the cellar of Piddock Holme was not locked; Professor Fisher had not kept it locked and nobody had given such a trivial matter any thought since his death. Many of the cottages in the village had a similar arrangement for the delivery of fuel, but it was a Neighbourhood Watch area: a break-in would be noticed. This was not the case for the two cottages at the edge, fifty yards away from any other. So Hetty and Geoff waited in the shadows of the far wall of Piddock Holme while Dominic and Gerry, both in black polo-neck sweaters, jeans and trainers and with black bobble hats, opened up a point of entry.

'It's open. Quick as you can!'

As Hetty stepped out from the wall, she glanced up and saw a gleam of light behind the heavy curtains of a room on the upper floor of Lilac Cottage. 'Interesting!' she said, and ran for the shelter of the bunker, Geoff tumbling in after her.

'It'll be that nephew.'

Gerry said, 'He's gone back down South. There's nobody in the house.'

'You could have fooled me,' Hetty said. 'Let's get searching.'

But what were they looking for? She did not know, but hoped that she would know when they found it. *If* they found it. The electricity had not been turned off, but they dared not switch on the lights. A search by torch-light could not be thorough, though they found a candle in the kitchen, lit it and set it in a saucer. First they tried what must have been the Professor's study. His computer was there, but no disks and no papers. Between them, they took every book off the shelves in the living room, opened and shook them. Five ten-pound notes, which the Professor had used to mark his place and then forgotten, dropped out, but no secret messages.

Then Geoff discovered an anomaly. All the tapes and

CDs in the shelves under the music centre were of classical music, except for one – a tape of *The Everly Brothers' Greatest Hits*. 'Let's hear it,' Hetty said. Anything odd should be investigated: her reading of Poirot and Sherlock Holmes had taught her that. She remembered the curious incident of the dog in the night.

So they listened to it, and in the middle of *Dream* the voices of the Brothers ceased abruptly and were replaced by that of someone who must be the Professor, rehearsing what must be a speech:

'You ask me what is the safety level on the presence of these hormones in the food-chain. And I must tell you that there is *no safety level, no matter what the experts may say. Because we simply do not know and we cannot know until the damage has already been done – unless we begin now to conduct the most stringent tests on a wide variety of animal species, including our own.'*

Then there was silence again, and then the voices of the Everly Brothers recommenced as if they had never been away. Geoff switched off the tape. 'He did find something then, with those experiments . . . and then someone found *him*.'

Hetty said, 'I've been thinking about that light we saw next door. Geoffrey, do you remember what I told you when they set that trap for me – the kidnapped girl in the cottage?'

'The bleating of the goat excites the tiger.'

Hetty picked up the saucer holding the candle, took it to the living-room window facing Lilac Cottage, drew back the curtains a little and set it down on the windowsill. 'And the flicker of the candleflame attracts the moth.'

'And what do we do?'

'Outside, keep stumm, and wait for moths.'

The moth was not long in coming. Behind the curtains of the lighted bedroom on the upper floor of Lilac Cottage, the man in the brown suit was writing up his Daily

Report and Expenses. An owl hooted outside, and disturbed his concentration. He went to draw the curtain fully over the window and saw a light in the deserted cottage next door.

The woman was still at it. She had only herself to blame. He had tried to frighten her off and she would not be frightened. *'Use your initiative. Play it by ear.'* He had done everything he could to avoid real violence, but if she was to be taken care of, there was nothing left but an unfortunate accident.

Gloved hands picked up a box of kitchen matches and put them into a pocket. Brown boots moved slowly down narrow stairs. The latch of the back door was lifted and the door squeaked as it was opened and then closed behind a dark figure. One black-gloved hand picked up a petrol can and the other, a crowbar from the floor of the garden shed. The can was carried along a concrete path at a jerky walk, its contents sloshing from side to side. The man carrying it reached the double wooden shutter over the bunker for solid fuel. He set down the can, bent over the shutter and prepared to force an entrance with the crowbar.

He did not need it: the padlock had already been forced. He put the crowbar down and stretched one hand out for the can of petrol. It had gone. And behind him he could hear the sound of liquid being poured into some receptacle.

He whipped around. The woman stood there in the moonlight, watching her teenage companion pour petrol from the can into a plastic bucket. There were other people behind her, two at least. He stood up fully, and the woman switched on the torch she was holding, illuminating him in its beam, and said, 'Might as well get a good look at you.' He picked up the crowbar.

'Geoffrey!'

Swoosh! The teenager threw petrol from the plastic bucket over his face and chest. It hurt his eyes and the smell of it was overpowering. The woman said, 'I've seen that done on TV.'

'You stupid bitch! It's petrol!'

'I know.' She sniffed the air. 'Nasty. If this is how it smells if you sniff solvents, I don't know why people bother. Anyway, you needn't worry. I don't carry matches and Geoffrey doesn't smoke.'

'Please! Please!' He himself was carrying matches. He must find some way to get rid of them without her noticing, then try to talk his way out of the situation.

The woman said, 'We'd better get you inside and out of those wet clothes. They use petrol for dry-cleaning. You'll be a fashion-plate when you dry out.'

The teenager said, 'There's a lighted candle inside, Mrs Wainthropp. I'd better go first and put it out.'

He sat in a comfortable armchair, wrapped in towels, and told her he was a detective like herself, so they should have a fellow-feeling. There was no malice involved – none, he said; he was only obeying orders. '"Use your initiative," he says. They never tell you what they really mean; you have to work it out for yourself. "Take care of her," he says. How? Up to me – man on the ground. That's what they pay for. They don't want to be bothered themselves, don't want to know *my* troubles.'

'And now?'

'He won't be pleased.'

'You're not working for the government, then?'

'I have worked for the Security Services. There's so much privatisation these days, you'd be surprised what I get asked to do. But not this time. Not so far as I know.'

'I'd better have a word with this boss of yours,' Hetty said.

The Rolls drew up outside the house. It was a National Heritage building, lovingly preserved by Gaiae Biochemicals. There was a long gravel drive between topiary, peacocks on the lawns and Muscovy ducks on the lake. Sandstone pineapples on plinths framed granite steps leading to an imposing front door, opened to admit Hetty and Geoff before they actually reached it by a flunkey from Central Casting who must have been pre-warned by the man at the gate.

Inside, another staircase in polished wood curved up to a landing on which stood a lady of enormous elegance in cashmere and pearls straight out of *Country Life*. This was the Private Secretary. 'Mrs Wainthropp? Mr Shawcross? How very good of you to come!' She came down to them, past portraits in oils of dead dukes and a Lord Chief Justice, and escorted them into an outer office larger than most inner offices. 'Sir Peter will see you at once, Mrs Wainthropp. I'll try to make Mr Shawcross comfortable in here.'

So she gave Geoffrey a copy of *Vogue* and settled him down in a leather armchair which almost closed over his head when he sat in it, while Hetty was ushered into the Chairman's office.

'Come in, Mrs Wainthropp. You've been putting the cat amongst the pigeons, I hear.' Sir Peter was in his sixties, silver-haired, shrewd and kindly, the very model of the acceptable face of capitalism. He got up from behind a large desk with a red leather top, and moved with Hetty to a couple of comfortable armchairs before an open fire. This was not the kind of office from which Robert had worked as a storekeeper in his days of paid employment. Except for the desk and telephone it did not look like an office at all, but was filled with flowers, books, paintings and photographs in silver frames.

A discreet knock at the door. A maid in cap and starched apron came in with coffee. Hetty sat in the armchair by the fire, Sir Peter opposite, and clutched her handbag. 'What was there in the water?'

'There was nothing in the water. Nothing to worry anyone in the water.'

'It worried the Professor.'

'He was a crank. Before any waste water leaves our plant it is treated for everything you can think of. It's always well below EEC safety levels.'

'So there wasn't a cover-up about the water?'

'There wasn't a cover-up at all.'

'Oh, there was.'

'Mrs Wainthropp, I don't know where your vivid imagination has been taking you. Did you really believe that sinister secret agents set fire to the Professor's Laboratory and then murdered an old lady who knew too much?'

'It's been known.'

'It didn't occur in this case.'

'What did happen to Mrs Nuttall?'

'She fell on the steps and hit her head. They got it right at the inquest. She was not pushed; she fell. I think you know that now.'

She did. The man in the brown suit had told her so, and she believed him. In Hetty's opinion, once she got the hang of things, she would make a better job of the private detective business than the man in the brown suit. For one thing, unlike Poirot he didn't seem to do much in the way of detecting.

'The Professor wouldn't give up,' she said. 'There *is* stuff in water, whatever the safety standards. My husband was reading in the paper how men in the Thames Valley have got this low sperm-count.' For a moment the mask of benign patience slipped and Sir Peter made a small gesture dismissing this newspaper nonsense. Hetty said, 'You'll hear me out, please: I'm not done yet. The Professor believed that nobody can say for sure what's safe till the damage has already been done. He collected shrimps and such from the outfall to your plant, ground them up and made a concentrate. He bought a couple of beagles – a dog and a bitch – and a billy and a nanny goat: goats'll eat anything. And ducks. And he took some himself.'

A silence. Hetty waited and watched Sir Peter's face, which gave nothing away. Then she said, 'And he gave some to Mary Nuttall without telling her what it was. Probably said it was vitamins.'

'Brown seems to have been remarkably indiscreet.'

'I didn't get all that from Mr Brown. I worked most of it out for myself. RSPCA! Who did you think you were kidding? Anyone from the RSPCA would have let Lily Perrins give a home to the goats.'

Sir Peter's right hand, graceful and exquisitely manicured, made the gesture by which the upper classes signify *Well done, you!* Hetty had hit her stride, carried along by indignation and the conviction of being right. 'Molluscs change sex if they're interfered with. My colleague found that out from the encyclopaedia. The market people said Mary Nuttall had facial hair.'

'Old women often do.'

'When she found out what he was doing to her, she killed him. Locked him in that shed with his shrimps and set fire to it.'

She had reached the climax. *Well done, you!* would not be an adequate response. She watched him thinking, watched the eyes: she was right and he knew it.

He said, 'She may not have known he was in there. She may have just wanted to burn the shed.'

Hetty opened her handbag and took out the photograph of the young man in the mortarboard and fur tippet which had been put back in the silver frame recovered from the Bargain Antiques & Collectables stall. She handed it across to him. 'She was frightened. She ran away, taking nothing with her except this.'

He looked at the photograph, stood up, and took from the mantelpiece a similar photograph in a similar frame, except that in this one there was a young girl beside the young man, looking up at his face with smiling pride. 'She was my sister.'

'And that was the cover-up – what your sister had done.'

'Might have done. But the press would have had a field day. It could have ruined this company and done quite a bit of harm to the country generally. Exports lost. Jobs lost.'

'Hell's bells, man! You tried to have me killed.' Mrs Wainthropp of the Wainthropp Detective Agency had finally lost her temper. 'Are you telling me that was to save jobs?'

'Brown exceeded his instructions. The inconvenience will be reflected in the size of your fee.' Sir Peter's mask had not slipped, but had simply been replaced by a different one. He went to his desk and pressed a bell. 'My secretary will give you a cheque on your way out.'

Hetty and Geoff stood at the top of the magnificent steps outside the front of the architectural gem so dear to the National Heritage Commission, looking at the Rolls which was to take them back to the Wainthropps' terraced house in an industrial village without any architectural value whatever. The cheque – the Agency's first fee if you didn't count Mr Harkness a.k.a. Brown – was for fifteen hundred pounds. They walked down the stairs between the sandstone pineapples and into the Rolls.

'Some folks!' Hetty said. 'Some folks!'

Eyewitness

Malcolm Stone lay on his stomach in a hide among scrub on the top of Hornby Head. It was a grey day and cold with scudding bursts of rain, a beast of a day. Below the cliffs the sea boiled among rocks. Malcolm was well wrapped up against the weather in gear from the Army Surplus Stores, waterproof and thornproof in camouflage colours. He could watch birds, but birds would have difficulty in watching him – not that they appeared to be interested, being preoccupied with affairs of their own, mostly to do with fish. Malcolm was happy, resting on his elbows, binoculars to his eyes, his notebook in front of him, his camera to one side. This was what he liked to do and what he did best.

Razorbill. He put down the binoculars and made a note.

About 150 yards away, a little below him and closer to the cliff-top, was a car, an ordinary saloon. He hadn't seen it arrive, so it must have been there a while; there were people in it – picnickers, he guessed, though it wasn't much of a day for a picnic. He picked up his camera with its telephoto lens, and followed the progress of a tern which swept low over the car, looking for scraps of discarded sandwiches probably, then on and up and out again, sandwichless over the open sea. Terns are common enough, but Malcolm had a fancy to catch it on camera as it swooped over the car. The shutter clicked. Either he had a photographic study of two worlds in momentary contiguity to be admired by fellow-birdwatchers and maybe even published in the *Journal* or he hadn't: he would know when the roll was developed. Mostly in these cases he hadn't.

The back door of the car was opening. A man appeared, then turned to help out a woman who seemed to have difficulty in standing, since he had to support her. Too much wine with the sandwiches, Malcolm supposed, and, since they had both been in the back, probably nooky had taken place. The man opened the front door on the driver's side and, like someone dealing with an incapable drunk, managed to heave the woman into the driving seat.

Odd. Malcolm was usually much more interested in birds than in people, but this did seem peculiar. He swapped the camera for the binoculars and continued watching.

The woman seemed to have no control over her body; it was flopping about every which way. If she was that drunk she ought not to be driving. The man attached the safety-belt to hold her upright. He stood there looking at her, then put one hand over the upper part of his face as if trying to blot her out. She remained unblotted. The man wrapped a handkerchief round one hand, took an opened wine bottle out of the back of the car, and emptied the dregs down the front of her dress before dropping the bottle at her feet. Some of the buttons at the front of her dress had been opened – yes, obviously there had been nooky – and there was a heart-shaped locket on a chain round her throat. The man opened the locket cautiously, and took out something inside, a capsule of some sort. He opened the woman's mouth, put in the capsule, closed her teeth so that she bit into it, then held up her head with one hand beneath her chin and put the fingers of the other down her throat to allow whatever had been inside the capsule to go down. He held her mouth shut for a moment, then released her, lolling in the seat, held there by the safety-belt.

The man took the woman's right hand in his and used it to turn the ignition key. The engine started. He leaned in and, handkerchief still wrapped round his hand, released the hand-brake. The car must have had automatic transmission because it immediately began to move forwards. The man jumped clear.

The car was heading for the edge of the cliff, the woman still in the driving seat. Malcolm scrambled to his feet. One foot struck the camera, knocking it into bracken, but he did not even notice. He was out of his hide, waving his arms.

The car rolled over the edge of the cliff and disappeared. He had witnessed a murder: there could be no doubt of it. The murderer turned and saw Malcolm waving.

A frozen moment. The two men staring at each other over a distance of 150 yards. Malcolm backed slowly away. The man moved as slowly towards him, maintaining the distance between them but not diminishing it. Then Malcolm turned and ran, and the man ran after him.

Stumbling through bush and bracken, Malcolm made for his car – an elderly blue Fiat Uno, which was parked on the road. Sobbing for breath, he reached it, searched his pockets frantically for the key, found it, unlocked the door on the driver's side, hurled himself into the seat and stabbed at the ignition. The murderer was much closer, but had not caught up with him yet.

The engine would not start.

Malcolm's foot pumped at the accelerator, but he only got the tired judder of a starter-motor about to give up altogether. Sweat had broken out all over his body and was running down his face. As he slumped forward, his face close to the steering wheel, trying to *will* the car to start, he felt the passenger door open. Someone got in and sat beside him.

Malcolm turned to look directly into the friendly face of the murderer, who said, 'If it's flooded, drying the plugs might encourage it a little, don't you think?'

Hetty was making a stew, not just any stew, but something called a *daube* which she had found in *Woman's Realm*. There were onions and carrots on the kitchen table, green peppers, mushrooms, stewing steak, a bottle of Passata from the supermarket, a tin of baked beans which she had decided to substitute for cannelloni, and a bottle of cheap red wine. There was a chopping block, sharp knife, a vegetable peeler and kitchen scales. Hetty had never made a *daube* before, but that was of no consequence; she often had a go at new dishes she had seen demonstrated on TV or found in a magazine; unfortunately, they seldom turned out well. On this occasion she was a little crowded at the kitchen table because Robert was sitting at the other end, with chequebook, pen, pocket calculator and lined pad, trying to do the household accounts.

'If I make three times more than we can eat, there'll be plenty left over for freezing. What's three times seven and a half ounces?'

'One pound, six and a half.'

She was piling mushrooms on the kitchen scales. There were far too many, and they spilled over.

'That can't be right for mushrooms. Oh, I see – there's a squashed fly on the recipe.' She blew it away. 'That's better.'

'How much are you giving me towards the phone bill?'

She was removing the surplus of mushrooms from the scales. Her fingers went into spasm and one of the mushrooms ceased to be a button and turned instantly into purée. 'You what?'

'You ought to give something. It's the Detective Agency makes the phone calls.'

'You phoned your brother Frank on Friday about systemic fungicide.'

'It's a legitimate business expense. You take it out of the profits.'

'You're not living in the real world, Robert.'

'Am I not?'

'There *are* no profits.'

'You got fifteen hundred pounds from that old lady's brother.'

'Five weeks ago. And what since?'

'There was that budgie lost from number seven.'

'She wouldn't pay. Her own cat ate it. Fifty-four pound seventy-three for those business cards. Small ads in the *Record*. A hundred pound for Yellow Pages. Fifty pee a week for every newsagent's board. Your wife is facing ruin and you sit there writing cheques. It's as much as Geoffrey and I can manage to keep the advertising going in even a minimal way.'

The Agency's card was placed on the board next to one reading:

STRICT SCHOOLMISTRESS
SERVES THIS AREA ONLY

Geoff said, 'They do seem to do a lot of educational work around here. Could you move it a bit closer to the lady with the quality perambulator for sale as new?'

He handed over the 50p and remounted his cycle. There were still thirty cards to distribute but he had gone his limit on newsagents' boards. Tucking what he had left into phone-boxes for free would be more cost-effective.

Meanwhile Malcolm was driving the Fiat Uno on a road new to him with the murderer as his passenger.

'This your own car?' Malcolm turned to look at him. Malcolm always looked at people who were speaking to him. He nodded. It was his own car, bought from his own money, taxed and insured. 'Watch the road!' The Fiat had swerved dangerously near the hedge. 'The road!' Malcolm watched the road. The man took a mobile phone from his pocket and punched in a number.

'Jim? . . . Steve: I'm on the mobile. Name and address, owner of blue Fiat Uno, registration number Baker Two Five Four Henry Peter Henry. Soon as you can, please.' Malcolm was looking at him again. 'Road!'

Malcolm indicated the flashing red light of the fuel gauge, which was telling them the car was nearly out of petrol.

'Don't you carry a spare can in the boot?'

Malcolm shook his head. Nobody carried cans of petrol in the boot. The mobile phone rang and was answered. 'Yes? . . . Great! . . . Just a moment.' The man tucked the phone under his chin and used his hands to get a small notebook and pencil from his pocket. Malcolm watched him do it. The Fiat swerved again, causing an approaching cyclist, who happened to be Geoff, to veer into the ditch. 'Road!'

Malcolm had seen what had happened to Geoff. It was a pity that his conduct had caused this lad inconvenience, but his own need was greater. He stared at the cyclist in the ditch, opened his eyes wide and his mouth wider, and mouthed the word 'Help!' Geoff gave him a two-finger sign, picked himself and his machine out of the hedge and continued on his journey. He only had nine cards left, but public phone-boxes were thin on the ground in this area of scenic beauty.

Inside the car, the man was writing something down. Malcolm could see what it was – *34 Kirby Gardens*. That was Malcolm's own address! He could well understand why his passenger might wish to kill or in some way silence the only witness to his crime, but had no idea why the man should want to know where he lived. Malcolm's parents had no connection with what had happened on the top of Hornby Head, and he did not wish them to suffer for what he himself had seen.

They came to a garage. The man said, 'Fill her up.' Malcolm filled the Fiat at the pump, looking about him surreptitiously for ways of escape. It would have to be here. If he got back into the car, he'd be done for. Perhaps when he paid for the petrol he would be able to alert the Asian lady at the cash desk. He put his hand in his pocket for his wallet. The man said, 'Forget it. I'm on expenses,' took Malcolm's arm in a firm but friendly way and together the two men walked side by side to pay for the petrol.

At the cash desk Malcolm gazed intently at the Asian lady as she counted out change. He wanted to ask for help, but all that came out was a sudden horrible sound, which startled her so much that she dropped the coins and bent to retrieve them, saying, 'Sorry! Very sorry!' However, this was enough to distract the man's attention for a moment and Malcolm took his chance. He wrenched his arm away and hurled himself past the racks of sweets behind them, knocking several over as he went. He reached the door marked STAFF ONLY and was through it and away. The man went after him, but stumbled over the fallen racks, and when he reached the door it was locked. He banged on it with his fist, and the Asian lady, convinced that this was some form of hold-up, stood behind the counter with her hands raised above her head in surrender.

The man turned to face her, just as the mobile phone in his pocket rang. The caller was his ten-year-old daughter.

'You're not supposed to use this number, Clare.'

Back in the kitchen of the converted farmhouse where the man lived with his family, Clare turned to her mother. 'He says he's tied up.'

The man's wife grabbed the phone. She was extremely angry. 'You're not on duty; you're on sick leave. You can't be tied up.'

It would do no good chasing Malcolm, who had escaped through the back of the garage and would be off across the fields by now. The man went out into the forecourt and sat in the driving seat of the old Fiat Uno, thinking what to do, watched by the bemused Asian lady at the cash desk.

Back at 34 Kirby Gardens, Malcolm's mother and father had become worried. He should have been back by now. Even on an ordinary day he should have been home by this time, but this was not an ordinary day. It was the day on which Malcolm had to drive to Manchester Airport to meet Penipha, the lady who was to be his wife and who would be arriving on the plane from Bangkok.

'He should be in the bath by now. Shaved – he should have shaved. I bought him cologne,' his mother said.

'What if he doesn't turn up to collect her? What if he's decided to hide somewhere until she's tired of waiting and gets back on the plane?'

'He wouldn't do that.' She replaced the navy pullover in lambswool and took out his best black. 'Oh dear! I've no experience in this kind of thing. He's never ordered a wife by mail order before.' She came to a decision. 'I'm going to the police.'

'Joan!'

'If he's not back in time, you'll have to go to the airport in his place. And if he does get back while I'm gone, make sure his shoes are clean.'

They were kind in the police station, concerned just as they should be. A young Constable took notes. 'When did you last see your son, Mrs Stone?'

'This morning, when he left to do his birdwatching.'

'Where does he normally watch them?'

'All over. The moors. Lake District. Glendale Nature Reserve.'

'Goes with a party, does he?'

'No, he's always preferred to be on his own.'

'But how does he get to these places?'

'In his car. It's a blue Fiat Uno.'

The young Constable looked at her. A certain wariness had come into his sympathetic manner. 'How old is your son, Mrs Stone?'

'Thirty-two.'

The Constable put away his notebook. 'The description would include long trousers, then, would it?'

They were beastly in the police station; they had no concern at all.

At Manchester Airport the Arrivals Board announced that the flight from Bangkok was delayed. Peter Stone went to a telephone to let his wife know.

'They wouldn't take me seriously. When I insisted, they said there's nothing they can do; he's a grown man. Unless I have a positive reason to suspect foul play, they have to treat it as domestic.'

As Peter replaced the receiver he noticed a business card by the telephone. He looked at it for want of anything better to do, because he was upset and because he wanted thinking time before returning to his seat. It was advertising the services of a Miss Whiplash and was of no interest to him. He pushed it away and saw another card beneath it. This read:

WAINTHROPP DETECTIVE AGENCY
MISSING PERSONS FOUND, ETC.
DISCRETION GUARANTEED
PHONE 01254 812160
NO CALLERS AT THE HOUSE

He phoned the number.

Hetty and Robert were in bed when the telephone rang. Awoken so brutally from sleep, Robert gave a cry. Hetty switched on the bedside light and picked up the phone. 'Wainthropp Detective Agency!'

'It's not for that Miss Whiplash again, is it?' Robert said. 'Three times this week already and always in the middle of the night. It's beyond a joke.'

'No, shut up; it's a client. Yes, I'm listening.'

At the other end of the phone Peter explained about his missing son. 'The police didn't seem interested and your card does say twenty-four-hour service.'

'I think if you look carefully you'll find that's the one offering relief correction for naughty boys. We get a lot of those. They're not the same as a good night's sleep.'

So it was arranged that Peter would do what he could to substitute for his son at the airport, and the Wainthropp Detective Agency would be along to investigate in the morning. 'There's no call-out charge as such,' Hetty said, 'but if he does turn up in the meantime, we'd like to be informed before incurring any expense.'

The Immigration Officer's expression was courteous but firm. Peter sat opposite him, still holding the piece of card on which he had written in block capitals: PENIPHA, which was the name of his son's intended bride. Penipha herself – small, frail and frightened – sat in a plastic chair against the wall with a Woman Police Officer standing beside her in case she should try to subvert the British constitution or attack the monarchy.

'But you yourself are not Mr Malcolm Stone, as I understand the situation?'

'I'm his father. I'm taking responsibility.'

'Of marrying the lady?'

'I'm already married. To Malcolm's mother.'

'Exactly. My point exactly. You are not in a position to marry the lady yourself because you are already married.

And the gentleman the lady has entered this country to marry—'

'My son,' Peter said.

'Your son, you say – is not here to vouch for her.'

'He sent me to represent him. He's tied up at the moment.'

'Tied . . . up . . .' The Immigration Officer made a careful note. 'And when will he be untied?'

'Soon. I can't say when exactly.' Peter decided to come clean. 'He's missing at the moment. He went out bird-watching and hasn't come back.'

Another note. 'Bird . . . watching. Yes, well, they do go missing sometimes: it has been known. The problem is, Mr Stone, the lady's papers.'

'You said they're in order.'

'They are – at least they *were*. She would not have been allowed to board the aircraft at Bangkok if they hadn't been. But if your son has changed his mind, that would nullify their validity.'

The language these people talked! 'He hasn't changed his mind,' Peter said. 'I'm sure he hasn't. He'll be back.'

'When?'

Peter supposed that if he were, like Eric Morecambe, to pat the Immigration Officer's cheeks and say, 'There's no answer to that, oh little man with fat hairy legs,' he would be arrested. Meanwhile the Immigration Officer continued to enjoy himself. 'Birdwatching in this weather! Bound to get cold feet. And ladies – particularly our Eastern cousins – they do tend to wander off unless watched.' He stood up. The interview was over. 'She'll be kept under supervision for one week. At your expense, Mr Stone, since you say you're responsible. After that, if your son is still away birdwatching, she'll be repatriated.'

Meanwhile, at a quarter to midnight, Malcolm walked down Allowthwaite Avenue. It had been a long journey, at first across fields, then getting what lifts he could and walking when he couldn't. He was dirty and tired, but he was nearly home.

Just by the junction of Allowthwaite Avenue with Kirby Gardens, a blue Fiat Uno was parked. It was his own car. He stopped dead. What was it doing there? He had last seen it on the forecourt of the petrol station when he had made his escape from the murderer. Something was wrong . . . He looked across the road and saw the murderer standing under a street-lamp, gazing at him and smiling.

Slowly, taking his time, the murderer crossed the road, stopped in front of him, looked him full in the face, smiled again and spoke softly. 'Who are they going to believe, Malcolm? You'd been watching her car, hadn't you, with your binoculars? Knew what she and me were up to. You like watching people doing that, don't you? Quite a hobby. And when I'd had her I pissed off. But you . . . you went and found her, Malcolm. Naughty boy! You had your wicked will of her, and then you got frightened. You thought she'd tell. So what did you do then?'

He held in front of Malcolm a police warrant card, concealing the name on it with his thumb. But his photograph was there. He was a policeman.

'Which of us are they going to believe?'

Malcolm's head dropped. He turned and walked back up the street, shoulders bowed, defeated.

Nobody would believe him. He would never be able to explain. He could not go home, could not expose his parents to the publicity. He would have to find somewhere to hide.

'He's deaf and dumb.'

'Peter!'

'Profoundly deaf and without speech.'

'Is that what they call it now?' Hetty said.

'Dumb could mean stupid.'

'There's a lot of things could mean a lot of things, but that's no reason for changing the language.'

'Yes, it is,' Joan said.

'What's blind?'

'Visually handicapped,' Peter Stone said. 'And simple's – I can't remember – educationally handicapped.'

'Not any more,' Joan said. 'It's learning difficulties now.'

Hetty said, 'You mean if a word's short, English and easy to understand, you have to say something else?'

'That's right.'

'When they shut down the mental hospitals they turned all the people with learning difficulties out in the street.'

'Into the community,' Joan said.

It seemed to Geoff that Hetty was showing herself, and therefore the Agency, up. He said, 'The word "dumb" is offensive and inaccurate. Deaf people without speech are neither more nor less intelligent than anyone else.' They were all looking at him, amazed. He cleared his throat, held his head high and continued to instruct them. 'There was a girl in our school – Lizzie – her little brother's deaf: she won't have him insulted. Why did your Malcolm want to bring a wife from Thailand anyway?'

'Because of his disability. He's always been shy. They started as pen pals and worked up. She's a school-teacher. It made a bond.'

Hetty said, 'But he does have some friends?'

The police were busy on the cliff-top. The area where the car had stood had been taped off, and mud samples were being scraped up carefully and put into plastic bags. Steel hawsers had been attached by divers to the body of the car, which had been winched at low tide on to the rocky beach; men in frogsuits were searching for the pieces which had become detached. Recovery of the driver's body had not been a problem since it was held in the driving seat by the safety-belt. The dead woman was Lynn Horrocks, a freelance photojournalist; the car was her own.

DCI Adams walked to the edge of the cliff and stared down. 'If you're going to commit suicide, why bother to strap yourself in with a seat-belt?'

'If she drove straight at the edge she'd have been wearing it already.'

'But she didn't go straight at it. She parked and thought about it for quite a while. I wonder . . .'

The car below was in a sorry mess, but the body had escaped relatively undamaged. Forensics would tell him whether she had already been dead when she hit the water. 'Parked and thought about it,' he repeated slowly. 'Maybe she needed a bit of Dutch courage. I'll want to know the stomach contents as soon as possible. Meanwhile, let the media get the impression that it was suicide. We don't want them alerting a probable murderer that we're on to him. If it *is* a him.'

The Social Club for the Deaf had once been a Methodist chapel, but the Methodists had moved to more charismatic premises and let the chapel to a worthy cause for a very low rent. There were tables and chairs set out for drinking coffee or eating vinegar-flavoured crisps or playing dominoes or all three, cardgames of various sorts in progress, Scrabble, a darts board, a bar billiards table. A TV set on the wall was showing the local news, and, although there were Teletext sub-titles, to Hetty's surprise the sound was on.

Sound! It was all sound. Hetty had imagined silence, yet it was noisy. This was because not all the forty or so people in the Club were deaf; there were friends and relations and Social Workers practising signing. These people were delighted to see each other and to communicate, and for every one who could speak there were two who could read lips. Hetty herself was adding to the racket. She had been asked to call the Bingo and was doing so, with a signer behind her to interpret.

Geoff had found Lizzie, the girl he had known at school, who was playing dominoes with forty-year-old Bennie and her brother Leonard, aged nine. 'Hey up!' he said. 'I thought I knew the back of that head. I flicked enough paper darts at it in Form Three C. You okay, Len?'

Leonard grinned a confirmation that he was indeed okay, while Hetty informed the room that she had drawn Two Fat Ladies in the Park out of the bowl of numbers.

Lizzie said, 'Last time I saw you, you were working on the check-out at the supermarket. Heard you call yourself a detective now.'

'It seemed an obvious career move.'

A news reporter was standing on the cliff-top at Hornby Head talking to camera, with some carefully staged police activity at the edge of frame and the edge of the cliff dangerously close behind him. 'Lynn, twenty-seven, from Didsbury, a former finalist in the Miss Great Britain contest, was said by friends to have been depressed for some time. She must have sat here for at least an hour, contemplating suicide.'

'Five four. Fifty-four.'

Geoff said, 'Do you know Malcolm Stone at all? I'm told he comes here regular.'

'Clickety-click. Sixty-six.'

Lizzie, Leonard and Bennie all knew Malcolm, who was well-liked among the regulars. What did Geoff want to know about him?

'Anything. Like where he's been doing his birdwatching recently.'

'It's just been on the telly – Hornby Head, where that car went over the cliff. He goes there to watch seabirds.'

'Bingo!'

The man whom Malcolm had seen pushing the car over Hornby Head was indeed a police officer, a Detective Sergeant in the CID named Steve Lennox, who had married above himself; his wife's friends referred to him amongst themselves as 'Rosemary's bit of rough'. He lived, with Rosemary and the two children, Clare and Tim, in a converted farmhouse well out of the price-range of a Detective Sergeant. This evening he sat in an expensive armchair covered with soft brown leather, Clare leaning against his side, Tim on his knee, the three of them watching the local news while Rosemary read *Country Life* at a little distance.

'. . . that she was three months pregnant,' said the cliff-top reporter. Steve used the remote control to switch the television off.

'Daddy!'

'I met her once. Said she was doing a photo-feature on the crack scene. Bloody freelances, always trying to wangle little bits of information out of the police! It's interesting, though. They wouldn't say it was suicide unless they were pretty sure it was murder.'

'Does that mean the phone's going to ring, and they'll call you back on duty before you're properly fit?'

Prompt on cue, the phone rang and Steve picked it up. 'That'll be them now,' Rosemary said. 'They've no consideration.'

Steve handed her the phone. 'Your sister.'

Janet Bleasedale of 27 Allowthwaite Avenue knocked at the door of 34 Kirby Gardens, and her knock was answered by Peter Stone.

'You know me, Mr Stone. I don't like to cause trouble; I'm neighbourly to a fault – but your Malcolm's car has been blocking our drive all day. I can't get out, and I have to take Darren to Cubs.'

Malcolm's car? Back? Peter Stone stared at Janet Bleasedale like a man demented. It was a totally over-the-top reaction to a perfectly reasonable request. Well, she had always heard that retirement could turn a man funny, and hoped it would not happen to her Jim when his time came.

Leaving her standing there in the doorway like some insurance salesman, Mr Stone turned and shouted back into the house, 'Joan! Joan!'

And when he came to move the car he was no better. 'I can't. I haven't got the keys,' he said.

Janet said, 'They're in the ignition. I've looked.'

Joan said, 'But where's Malcolm?'

Hetty and Geoff waited at the bus stop down the street from the Social Club. Hetty said, 'Hornby Head! Malcolm goes there birdwatching, that girl commits suicide, and the same day he disappears. There must be a connection.'

'Could be a coincidence. He didn't go there every day.'

'And *we* didn't go to that Social Club just to play Bingo. We went for information and we've got it. Hornby Head!'

'We should have other irons in the fire, Mrs Wainthropp. If you take my advice you'll talk to Dave the Rave.'

'And who's he when he's not in the asylum?'

'Disc jockey on local radio. I knew him at school.'

'Geoffrey, is there anyone you didn't know at school?'

'Well, it was a comprehensive school,' Geoff said. 'Dave was my English teacher.' A bus arrived and they climbed aboard. 'We really ought to have our own transport. Detectives have cars – Lagondas and such. I've mentioned it before.'

'Find us a rich client, and I'll buy a three-wheeler.'

Night and cold. Away from the lighted streets was a dark wasteland in which a small bonfire burned. Round it, in a tangle of rags, newspapers and bits of cardboard which served them for bedding, sat four winos, each with a bottle. On a comparatively clean sheet of newspaper was spread out their evening meal of bits of old rolls and pasties, biscuits, discarded sandwiches and nearly empty packets of crisps, all rescued from litter bins.

Malcolm came from the shadows, moving slowly closer to the fire. The winos saw him, ceased their incomprehensible chat amongst themselves, and watched him, four dirty bearded faces, slack-lipped and dribbling, illuminated by the wavering light from the fire. Malcolm stopped moving. One of the winos – the one called 'the Professor' because he sometimes lapsed into Latin – beckoned. Malcolm moved forward again and stretched out his hands to the fire.

The nearest wino offered a swig from his bottle. Malcolm shook his head, but pointed to the food on the newspaper.

The Professor put out a hand towards the binoculars which Malolm still wore around his neck. Slowly Malcolm took them off and handed them over. A polite pantomime which might have come out of the Royal Shakespeare Company's production of *All's Well That Ends Well* indicated that Malcolm might take as much as he wished.

Under a piece of roll spread with Salmon & Shrimp fishpaste, there was a photograph of a girl and beside it the headline:

PREGNANT BEAUTY QUEEN
IN SUICIDE PLUNGE

'*Pax vobiscum,*' said the Professor.

Hetty and Geoff examined the Fiat Uno, now parked outside the Stones' house in Kirby Gardens. 'It says thirty-two miles on the clock. That doesn't seem much.'

Peter said, 'He always put it back to nought when he got petrol. He must have had it filled yesterday. Means he's done thirty-two miles since then.'

'So he'd have been seen at some petrol station thirty-two miles away from here?'

Geoff said, 'Not necessarily. If he'd got petrol on the way, he'd have put it back to nought, gone on to where he was going, then come back here from there.'

'There may be times for negative thinking, Geoffrey, but this is not one of them.' Hetty got out of the car. 'I shall need an Ordnance Survey map and – what are those thingummies we used to have at school to do geometry?'

'We didn't have anything for geometry at our school. We didn't have geometry.'

'Compasses. I used to use mine as an offensive weapon whenever any of the boys tried anything on.'

And she was away like a terrier up the path to the front door. 'They wouldn't dare,' Geoff said, following with Peter.

By the time they caught up, Hetty already had the Ordnance Survey map spread out on the kitchen table and had sent Joan to rummage for a pair of compasses, a ruler and a yellow BB pencil. She placed the point of the compasses where she had decided Kirby Gardens would be and made a circle with a radius of thirty-two miles.

'You see?' There was Hornby Head. 'Not ten miles away.'

'Or seventy-four,' Geoff said, 'if he was going in the opposite direction.'

'Geoffrey!'

'Sorry.'

Joan said, 'I think you may have located our house in the Millfield Estate: we're the Braybrook Estate.'

'You won't mind if we use Malcolm's car to get to Hornby Head?' Hetty said. 'And we'd better have one of his friends from the Social Club to show us where he did his watching from. Someone who could drive would be best. Arrange it please, Geoffrey. We'll go this afternoon.' She looked at the kitchen clock. 'Is that really the time? You must excuse me. I've got an appointment with Dave the Rave.' The Stones were clearly not rich so she was unwilling to put them to the expense of a taxi. 'If Mr Stone can drive me to the radio station, I'll get a bus back home.'

At the radio station there were already a couple of Boy Scouts and a nun waiting in the reception area, and a teenager with freaky hair hitting the coffee dispenser which had swallowed his money and offered only hot water in a plastic cup by way of exchange. Speakers high in the wall relayed the programme in progress, and Hetty could hear Dave the Rave crooning in the microphone, 'Oh! Oh! Where I live, baby, right where I live. It's so . . . org*as*mic!' as he started a record.

She presented herself at the reception desk. 'Mrs Hetty Wainthropp!'

'Which are you, dear? Prime Minister's biography, Home for Lost Dogs, pressed flowers or the lady detective?'

'The lady detective.'

The patch of wasteground by daylight, no longer isolated by darkness, had become part of the town again, desolate, muddy and strewn with litter, used as a playground by truants and a short-cut by pedestrians. The bonfire had relapsed into dirty ashes and of the four winos, only the Professor remained, hunched beside it, his hands in front of him clasped over Malcolm's binoculars.

To him, walking delicately like a cat, came detective Sergeant Steve Lennox. 'What you got there, Professor?'

'*Libera me, domine,*' the Professor said.

'No Latin.' Without haste or brutality Steve unclasped the Professor's hands. 'Let's just have a look, shall we?'

'Libera me, domine, de morte aeterna.'

Meanwhile Malcolm, unshaven, dirty and tired after a night spent in search of sleep, had found a public phonebox. There was a litterbin close by and from it he took an empty Coca-Cola can. He carried the can into the phonebox with him, found coins in his pocket, fed 20p into the machine and punched in a number. Then he put down the can on the little shelf provided by British Telecom for the convenience of service-users who are going to have to feed in a great deal of money, held the handset over it, and began to tap out a message in Morse with a 10p piece.

'Malcolm? . . . Is that you?' She had begun to cry, could not see, did not know what to say. Blinded by tears, she held the handset out to Peter. 'He's all right. He's out there somewhere, God knows where, but at least he's telling us he's all right.'

It was something Malcolm had watched them do as a child, beating out a rhythm on the tea caddy, when they had not yet been able to accept the fact of his deafness, and had tried any sounds to see if he could make them out. He had not been able to hear, but he had watched the rhythm and replicated it and used it as a way of telling them where he was or if he needed attention.

And now – somewhere, anywhere, wherever he was – he was telling them again, using the same language.

Peter grabbed the telephone. 'I can hear you, son. We'll find you. Just hold on – please. Listen, Malcolm; it's going to be all right. We won't let you down. We're going to find out where you are. We *have* to.' He had begun to break down; he was weeping as freely as his wife, babbling and shouting into the phone. I won't let you be lost. I won't allow it.'

He had forgotten that the rhythm language only worked one way. Malcolm could not hear any of this. He looked at the handset, wishing, as he had often wished, that a miracle would happen and he would hear and understand what it was saying, but words to Malcolm were not sounds but shapes of lips, signs made with hands, characters printed or written on paper; he had no idea what words actually sounded like because he had never heard a sound. It was all a puzzle to Malcolm, but at least one he was used to, whereas the present puzzle of how to remain on the run and keep himself alive was new to him and most irksome. He looked up and the puzzle once again changed its nature. The policeman who had pushed the car over the cliff was standing outside and beckoning to him.

Obediently Malcolm left the phonebox, left the handset with the empty Coca-Cola can next to it on the shelf; and the sound of his father's voice, desperately reassuring, was dissipated into empty air until the money ran out.

'Now . . .' It was obvious that Dave the Rave could not remember her name.

'Hetty.'

'Hetty my love, these flowers you press?'

'Missing persons.'

'You press missing persons? Is that allowed? My God! What a woman!'

'I'm a detective. I look for them.'

'But there's so many.'

'I look for one at a time. I won't do more. I like to give myself completely.'

'So single-minded! I knew a young lady like that once, but I was unworthy of her devotion, Hetty my love. I was always too high . . .' he already had another record in place '. . . on the *muuuuusic*.' During the next break she must try to work in Malcolm's name and description if this interview was to do any good. It all took time, but luckily on local radio they seemed to have a lot of time, presumably because they didn't pay the people they interviewed.

She could not know that at this very moment she was in a kind of contact with the missing person she was seeking. This time Malcolm was the passenger and Steve was driving, and they were in Steve's car, not the Fiat Uno. 'I don't know what I'm going to do with you, but I'll think of something,' said Steve to Malcolm, and switched on the car radio, thus making the contact.

Hetty's voice said, 'Malcolm Stone.'

'And he's deaf and dumb?' said the DJ.

'Profoundly deaf and without speech.'

Steve switched off the radio. Contact broken. He turned slowly and stared at Malcolm, trying to take in what he had just heard. Malcolm signed at him frantically; the car was on the wrong side of the road and there was a lorry coming in the opposite direction. Hurriedly Steve returned his attention to the business of driving and the car swerved at the last minute out of the lorry's way, leaving the lorry-driver shaking.

'Well, there's a turn-up for the book,' Steve said. 'I don't know what difference it makes in the long run, but it's certainly a complication in the short.'

Lizzie, driving the Fiat Uno, parked it as close as the road went to the cliff-top, which was near where Malcolm had parked two days earlier, but today Hornby Head was not a place for birdwatchers. There was a whole line of vehicles and a sign which read NO CARS BEYOND THIS POINT; members of the public with their dogs and children were spread out on the cliff-top, some taking photographs, some peering over the edge at the vertiginous drop and the rocks and breakers below, some picnicking on rugs.

'Gawpers,' Hetty said. 'Morbid curiosity. Joe Public at his worst!'

'What else are we?'

'Professional investigators.'

Leonard ran ahead of them to the hide, which he remembered because Malcolm had once brought him along. When he reached it he threw himself down full-length and mimed putting binoculars to his eyes. Hetty positioned herself behind him. 'Well, Malcolm could certainly have seen Lynn Horrocks' car from here.'

Leonard reached over and produced a notebook which must have been left in the hide. It had been rained upon and was the worse for it. Hetty took it. She looked at Leonard, who was watching her lips. 'Malcolm's notebook?' He nodded vigorously.

She passed the notebook to Geoff.

'The writing's all run.' He squinted at the page. 'Pha . . . la . . . rope. What's that?'

Lizzie said, 'A kind of bird, I think.'

'Of course it is.' Hetty was at her briskest. 'Phalarope: anyone knows that. It'll all be birds. If he'd written anything about that poor girl's suicide he wouldn't have left the notebook here. He saw something that shocked him, and forgot the book, stands to reason. But it proves he was here.'

'You're jumping to conclusions again, Mrs Wainthropp. He could have forgot that book any day. You can't tell how long it's been here.'

Hetty took back the notebook. 'Geoffrey, there are times I despair of you. How can you hope to reach a conclusion if you don't jump?' She turned back to Leonard, who was still watching her face. 'Is there anything else in there?'

Leonard searched among the bracken to the side of the hide while they watched. He began to make little yelping sounds of excitement like a terrier; he had found the camera where Malcolm's foot had kicked it before he had turned to run. He held the object out in triumph. Hetty took it, and said to Geoff, 'He could have forgotten his camera any day too, I suppose?'

'No. If he forgot his camera, there was something – I don't know. He saw something and it frightened him.'

'Interesting to know what's on the film.'

Lizzie said, 'Are you going to give it to the police?'

The idea! 'Of course not. Why should we give it to the police? I'm the detective on the Malcolm Stone Case. He could have left this camera any day. Now – next thing. That garage where he got the petrol. It'd be back along the road about nine miles from here: there can't be many.' She held out her hand to Leonard to pull him up. 'Come on, young man. Well done so far.'

They found the petrol station without difficulty. Hetty was still in a buoyant mood. 'No need to shout,' the Asian lady said. 'I am not deaf.'

'*He* is deaf.'

'You are deaf?' said the Asian lady to Geoff. 'What an affliction! But what can I do?'

'The man who came for petrol was deaf.'

Geoff wondered whether she might remember the Fiat Uno and took her to the door to look at it. 'It would have been two days ago,' he said. 'This car.'

The Asian lady looked at the car and at Lizzie and Leonard with interest. Leonard waved at her from the front passenger seat. 'The little boy is deaf?'

'Well, as it happens, he is.'

'No time for that now,' Hetty said. 'Can you remember this car?'

'Oh, yes.'

'Two days ago? Was it here? For petrol?'

'Oh, yes. But that man was not deaf. The telephone rang in his pocket and he was able to answer clearly. He had a strange man with him – a very frightened man, I think. He did not speak, but I could readily sense his fear. However, he ran away, and that was the end of the incident.'

There was a silence. Then Hetty said, 'Thank you. You've been most helpful.'

They had left the main road and taken to smaller country roads. They drove past a farmhouse and round to the side and stopped. They got out of the car, the policeman indicating clearly at every stage which way he wanted Malcolm to go, until they came to a barn. There was a padlock on the door and the policeman unlocked it.

Malcolm was frightened. Had the murderer brought him here to kill him quietly, out of the way where nobody could see? Inside the barn there were wooden stalls in which cattle had once been kept or hay stacked, but now they contained expensive equipment for the garden. There was a lawn-mower of the kind which is used for large stretches of grass, with a seat on top. There were strimmers, scarifiers, hedge-clippers, a chainsaw, a sprinkler, anything one could want or someone with more money than sense might buy on impulse and never use. Hooks on the wall supported coils of rope and garden hose, spades, rubber rakes, a scythe. There were rolls of wire netting to keep out rabbits and rolls of green netting to keep out birds. There was petrol in a two-litre can and a fully equipped tool-bench. There was a wooden ladder leading to the upper storey of the barn.

'Up here.'

They were going upstairs. The policeman had a carrier-bag which, Malcolm knew, contained handcuffs. Once he was handcuffed he would be totally helpless. Should he resist now, struggle, try to make a run for it? But he was so tired. He would do what the man wanted and perhaps the man would not hurt him.

'I'll need rope, I suppose, to hobble you. Well, there's plenty – plenty of everything. I'll try not to make you too uncomfortable. It's only for a while until I can think what to do with you.'

At the top of the ladder was a trapdoor which pushed up. The policeman indicated that Malcolm should push it up, and Malcolm did so.

'Food. You will be fed, probably at irregular intervals: I'm on sick leave at the moment, but they may call me in. Sanitation won't be pleasant: I'll bring a bucket.' They went up through the trapdoor. 'It's not a working farm. We live in the house and rent out the land to a farmer. He doesn't come in here.'

The upper part of the barn must certainly once have been used to store hay, but now it contained empty suitcases no longer fit for use, cardboard boxes, piles of old magazines, a couple of bales of straw and some broken toys. A narrow horizontal rooflight let in daylight: there was no evidence of electricity up here, though Malcolm had noticed an overhead light in the section below. Would this barn have rats?

'My wife has the money: she married beneath her. Funny! I can say anything to you and it doesn't matter because you can't hear me. That's a liberating experience for a man who has to keep his lip buttoned most of the time.'

He took the handcuffs out of his carrier and fastened Malcolm's hands behind him. Then he pushed Malcolm down on one of the bales of straw and began to hobble his legs with rope he had brought from below. 'I do not need to work, Malcolm,' he said. 'I only continue to do so because I am a dedicated police officer.' He looked directly at Malcolm. 'Can you read lips?' Malcolm nodded. 'Right! Read . . . my . . . lips.'

But there was very little left to say, certainly nothing as personal as the conversation Steve had allowed himself to have with someone who could not hear. Steve would come back with food and a blanket when he could. Malcolm would not be hurt: this discomfort would only be for a while. After that, no more reading of lips. Steve, the gaoler, returned to his car and drove it round to the front of the farmhouse where he became once more a husband and father.

Malcolm used one elbow against the bale of straw to get himself to his feet. He contrived to reach the rooflight, but it was too high for him to see out, even standing on tiptoe. He pushed one of the suitcases under the rooflight and, after falling twice, managed to stand on it. He saw a large and beautifully kept lawn with trees and flowerbeds and a vegetable garden to one side across a dividing path, and beyond it the French windows of a drawing room, through which the man who had murdered a lady driver and was keeping the only witness hobbled and shackled in a barn as his prisoner, came strolling out on to the lawn with his wife and children.

Robert came in from the allotment though the back door as usual to find the kitchen in darkness, which was unusual at eleven in the morning. 'Hell's fire!' he said. 'I'm in the wrong house.'

'Close the door. Quickly. And don't put the light on.'

There had been a note of panic in Geoff's voice. Robert closed the door and the kitchen returned to darkness. 'Why? Has war broke out?'

'I've put a blanket up to develop that film we found in Malcolm's camera. Now I can't read the instructions.'

'I'll strike a match and you bring the book near it.'

Robert struck a match and Geoff held the book beneath it.

'Open the packet of photographic paper in the dark, being careful not to get the paper back to front. Dilute exact amounts of the chemicals with water.'

The match went out. 'Do you think we're going to get this right?' Robert said. Of course, if the instructions were carefully followed, nothing could go wrong, but neither had ever attempted to develop a film before and anyway,

Geoff's library book, being a little out of date, was describing the process of developing black and white film – and the film in Malcolm's camera had been colour.

Meanwhile Hetty, who had issued the orders, was off on another aspect of the investigation.

On the desk of the Picture Editor of the *Evening Record* was the lay-out for a centre-page spread entitled LIFE AND DEATH OF A BEAUTY QUEEN. Among the snapshots and glossy professional photographs of Lynn Horrocks, the dead model and freelance photojournalist, the Picture Editor was placing in position a blurred back-garden snap of Lynn aged eleven, her gymslip a little too short and her pose and expression a little too knowing. 'We used very little of her work,' he said.

Hetty said, 'What were her own photographs usually of – the ones she tried to sell?'

'Anything and nothing. Anything she thought she'd a chance with, and nothing worth pushing her off a cliff for.'

'Is that what you think happened?'

'I don't do thinking. I'm a Picture Editor.'

'What did she live on, if her work didn't get bought?'

'Modelling.'

'In Didsbury?'

'Utrecht. Amsterdam. Porno magazines, mainly Dutch, giving her full frontal in chains and leather.'

He fiddled with another photo, a snap of Lynn aged six in a group with other children. Hetty said, 'Where was that one taken?'

'Children's Home.'

'Where?'

'Somewhere well away from her dad, would be my guess.'

The Wainthropps' kitchen was still dark, but red Christmas-tree lights had been suspended from cup-hooks and gave just enough light for Geoff and

Robert to stare down into the tray of developing fluid. 'What happens now?' said Robert, and Geoff replied, 'We pray.'

The Picture Editor said, 'Funny to grow up winning Beauty Contests when you've had all hell knocked out of you as a nipper! He died last year, her dad. Hang-gliding. An accident.'

'At Hornby Head?'

'No, no. Life is neat, I agree, but not that neat. Inland somewhere. They don't do hang-gliding over the sea for obvious reasons. And do you know what? She was bloody nigh destroyed by it.'

'How do you know all this?'

He took from a drawer a snap of the same six-year-old with heavy facial bruising, and held it out to Hetty. 'She wanted me to use it the year she won Miss North-West and we did a spread on her. Wanted me to put it right next to the one with the trophy, the cleavage and the toothpaste smile.'

'Why didn't you?'

'Someone upstairs thought it would be inappropriate.'

Hetty said, 'Were you in love with her?'

'I'm a Picture Editor.'

Further confidences were prevented by the arrival, unnoticed, in the doorway of Detective Chief Inspector Adams. 'Are you poaching on my ground, Mrs Wainthropp?'

So it was arranged that she would break off her enquiries into the death of the unhappy Beauty Queen for the time being and meet DCI Adams for tea that afternoon to discuss the direction in which those enquiries were taking her.

Steve had brought some sandwiches, a flask of cold tea, a bucket of soapy water, some old trousers, rags and a towel; he had told Rosemary he was going to clean the car. Instead he had cleaned Malcolm of the unavoidable soiling – gently, respectfully – and was now feeding him. As Steve talked, Malcolm gazed at his lips.

'I'm not a murderer, Malcolm. If I was, you wouldn't be alive: I'd have to kill you after what you saw – you understand that?'

Malcolm nodded.

'My wife . . . It's not her being older than me; it's more the money thing. And her family. So amusing, marrying a policeman! PC Plod! But I got my A Levels and I could have gone to university, only I wanted to join the Force. You believe that, don't you?'

Malcolm nodded.

'Beauty Queen! I was flattered. She wanted info for a story: we'd have a picnic somewhere quiet. It was obvious, her intention, but why not? I was only getting me end away like anyone else. But she . . . "Hurt me," she said, "Punish me. Put your hands round my throat." It was an accident. I've never been into that. I'm not a sadist, Malcolm. What she wanted . . . I went too far: I thought she'd tell me when to stop. But who's going to believe that?'

Malcolm nodded. He believed, but could well see that it would be difficult to convince anyone else.

'And I'd be ruined anyway.'

Hetty sat in the living room, waiting to be shown the prints of the exposed film.

Geoff and Robert came from the kitchen like two conspirators in Shakespeare who know that something has gone terribly wrong and they have murdered the rightful duke instead of the usurper.

Geoff placed the prints in front of Hetty. 'They've not come out as well as we hoped'.

Hetty spread them out. They were all black. 'They've not come out at all.'

Robert said, 'The detail's not as good as it might be.'

'They're blank. It's just as well I decided you'd better have a trial run. These were Hilda Outhwaite's holiday snaps from Lanzarote; she asked me to hand them in to be developed. You'll have to tell her. She won't mind. All she ever gets is the backs of knees, usually out of focus.'

'What about that waiter in Corfu? He came out *very* focused.'

'And look at the trouble it led to. She should thank you for saving her the costs of the prints. I'd tell her myself, but I've an appointment to take tea at the police station.'

As for the real film, she took it into SupaSnaps on her way. The prints would be ready in an hour. It was a pity that the SupaSnaps people would be privy to the secret of what Malcolm had snapped, up there in his hide, but unlikely that they would understand what they were looking at.

There was tea in a pot of Buxton Early Slipware which had belonged to DCI Adams' grandmother and a cake which had come as a Christmas present from Texas: it had been waiting, said the DCI, for somebody worthy of it. He pressed a button on his desk, told the person at the other end to send in Detective Sergeant Lennox, and asked Hetty if she would be mother.

DS Lennox cut cake and passed the cups Hetty filled. He had been on sick leave, recovering at home from a stab-wound sustained in the course of duty, but had come in part-time to assist Hetty.

She said, 'Assist?'

'Liaison. Facilitate your enquiries. Now, shall we share information?'

'You first.'

'When a car falls from a height on to rocks and then into the sea, it is considerably damaged and so is any body which happens to be inside it. Lynn Horrocks was wearing a seat-belt so that her body was less damaged than it might have been, but of course the internal organs were a mess.'

'They said on TV that she was three months pregnant.'

'That was a media misunderstanding. We've let it go in the hope of flushing out any ex-boyfriends.'

'Sugar, sir?'

The DCI waved away sugar. 'Why the seat-belt? If she'd driven off the road straight over the cliff, all in one desperate plunge, you'd expect it, but the car was parked for at least an hour. During that hour she ate a meal – picnic stuff – paté and salad, French bread and wine: it was all there in her stomach, the digestive process hardly started. Why a meal if she intended to kill herself?'

'The condemned woman ate a hearty picnic. People do it for comfort.'

'Which would explain the wine. However, she was already dead when she hit the water: there was none in her lungs. So what killed her? The impact? Plain fear? And – another puzzle – there was the residue of a capsule of amyl nitrate stuck in her throat.'

The Detective Sergeant explained to Hetty: 'A popper. Gives you a kick. Heightens perception. Used in sex mainly at the moment of orgasm.'

'What people get up to! In my day most of us didn't even have orgasms.'

'You missed a lot,' the DCI said. 'Lynn Horrocks must have bitten through the capsule as the car went over the cliff.'

Lennox said, 'Supports the suicide theory, sir. And poppers stimulate the heart. I've known people overdose.'

'One capsule. Hardly an overdose.'

'I've known it, sir. People unused to poppers, trying one for kicks. Usually older punters, I agree.' This Detective Sergeant seemed to Hetty to be extremely knowledgeable about drugs, more so than his boss.

'It hadn't entered the bloodstream, Lennox: it couldn't have given her a heart attack.'

'Sorry, sir.'

'If her death wasn't suicide, it must have been murder. But by whom? Why? How did the murderer get there, and how did he get away afterwards?'

He was looking directly at Hetty as he spoke. Did he know already about Malcolm's Fiat Uno parked on the road? She supposed she would have to tell him. Meanwhile she played the game. 'Lynn must have brought him. That explains the picnic.'

'Him?'

'Whoever.'

'Whoever – yes. She seems to have had a lot of acquaintances – mainly professional – but no friends. We have to interview them all, including the people in Holland, but it will take time. So tell me please about Malcolm Stone.'

'We're still looking for him,' Hetty said. Then she told him about the Fiat Uno and its mysterious return, and the Asian lady at the petrol station, the Morse code message by telephone to Malcolm's home, and finally, under patient and persistent questioning, about the film from Malcolm's camera which was even at that moment being developed by the one-hour service of SupaSnaps. Detective Sergeant Lennox came with her to pick it up and remained with her all the way home and was still with her when they spread out the prints on the Wainthropps' kitchen table.

Most of them were of birds, rows and rows of photographs of birds, and in the last row was Lynn Horrocks' car and through the rear window could be seen the back of a man's head. The car itself was extremely clear but the man's head, which had been caught in motion, was a little blurred. The Detective Sergeant picked up the print. 'The DCI will want this.'

'He can have the negative.'

'He'll want that too.'

'We have to have a picture.'

'I'm sorry, Mrs Wainthropp. It's material evidence.'

'That's why I need it.'

'To the Horrocks enquiry. Not your enquiry.'

'Let me be the judge of that, young man.' She took the photograph out of his hand and gave it to Robert. 'Take this down to Mr James at number ten and get a large photocopy.' Robert was already on his way. 'Mr James does wood and smokeless fuel mainly,' Hetty said to the Detective Sergeant. 'The photocopying's a sideline.'

'But—'

'Please don't make difficulties: a refusal offends. I was promised full co-operation. Tomorrow morning, if you've no objection, I'd like to see round Lynn Horrocks' flat. Shall we say eleven o'clock?'

Later that night in the upper part of the barn, Detective Sergeant Steve Lennox said to his prisoner, Malcolm Stone, 'Here's something to make you laugh. I've been called in on partial attachment, keeping an eye on an old lady detective. She's looking for you, Malcolm. We'll have to try to arrange for her to find you when it's safe, but just at the moment you're a bit tied up.'

Malcolm did not exactly laugh, but he did manage to crack a smile. What neither he nor Steve knew was that, across that well-kept lawn which separated the barn from the house, a little girl was looking out of her bedroom window on the second floor, and what she was looking at was a small patch of yellow light, made by her father's hurricane lantern, which could be seen through the rooflight on that side of the barn.

In the Wainthropps' kitchen Geoff and Hetty were slumped at the table, brooding over the photocopy made by Mr James, who specialised in smokeless fuel. 'You should have gone home hours ago,' Hetty said. Robert had carried a mug of Ovaltine and a disapproving expression up to bed.

'Hardly seems worth it now.'

'What's left of the sherry trifle is in the fridge.'

'Is it?' Geoff opened the fridge door. 'So it is.'

He spooned trifle into a bowl and tucked in happily as Hetty continued to study the photocopy. 'You can tell a lot from the backs of heads,' she said.

'You can.'

'I was in the choir when I was young: it made a change from haberdashery. The organist said himself, "You're a fine mezzo, Hetty. You should turn professional." Of course he was after my body at the time, but there was some truth in it. Sunday after Sunday I sat behind Mr Dabney, bass-baritone: he got his come-uppance in the Three Counties' *Elijah* – gave too much, fell off the rostrum and fractured a fibula. I knew the back of that man's head like the back of my hand.'

They went to Lynn Horrocks' flat next morning by way of the Picture Editor. 'I want to know why none of Lynn Horrocks' boyfriends came back for more,' Hetty said.

The Picture Editor stopped working and looked straight at her. 'I don't think she wanted them to. Just once and out, you know.' He became engrossed in his work again. 'And what they had to do, not everybody would fancy it.'

'I'm listening.'

'It was dangerous, for one thing. They could do her a damage if they didn't watch themselves, and if they did watch themselves she wasn't best pleased.'

'How do you happen to know?'

He looked sideways at her. 'Because she told me.'

'When?'

'Over the phone sometimes in the middle of the night.'

'And other times?'

'Whispered. As she clung while I rocked her, waiting for the sleeping pills to work.' Silence as Hetty took this in, and Geoff shifted his weight from one foot to the other. Then the Picture Editor said, 'If I'm to be a suspect, you'd best know she considered me a parent, best friend, nanny and nurse.'

'What did you consider yourself?'

No pretence of being busy with work any more. Tears filled the Picture Editor's eyes. 'Honoured, if you must know. More than I ever realised.'

'You've a funny idea of honour,' Hetty said. She was bristling with shock and with distaste, but politeness, as she was always telling others and now told herself, costs nothing. 'Thank you for your co-operation.' She turned to go. 'Come along, Geoffrey.'

The Picture Editor said, 'Mrs Wainthropp!'

She forced herself to turn back to him.

'She didn't reckon much to herself, you see,' the Picture Editor said. 'I did; she didn't. I was the only man she allowed to be gentle with her. Sex had to hurt her, do you understand? What her father did to her . . . being sent away into care . . . even his death – she thought it was all her fault. What she wanted from other people was punishment. She believed that was all she deserved.'

Hetty shut him out. 'We don't have that kind of thing where I live.'

'Don't you?'

Geoff said, 'Thank you. We'll be on our way now if you don't mind,' and then when they were safely out of the door: 'If we're going to be a Detective Agency, we'll have to take that kind of thing in our stride, Mrs Wainthropp.'

'Right,' said Hetty. 'Sorry! Right!'

Lynn Horrocks' flat consisted of a large studio-cum-bedroom with a kitchen and bathroom off it, and was probably a conversion of what used to be the living quarters above a shop. There were odd bits of junk – a rag doll, a wicker birdcage without a bird, a Staffordshire lion. The bed had a patchwork quilt; the dressing-table was covered with a litter of brushes and bottles, paper tissues and cosmetics. There was a cooker, fridge-freezer, and shelves of dishes and cans, a TV, a computer and a music centre, and a large wooden kitchen table which must also have been a work-table since it had folders of photographs at one end.

Hetty was restless, edgy, uncertain, Geoff watchful: mostly he watched Hetty. Detective Sergeant Lennox, by contrast, was much at his ease. Hetty could take all morning to look about if she wished and he would not hurry her.

There was a plaster statuette of a virgin and child on the mantel. Hetty picked it up. 'Was she a Catholic?'

'I don't know what she was; I'm not really on the case. She may just have bought it on impulse like the other junk. Why do you want to know?'

'To get a feeling of what she was like from how she lived. I've not heard much good of her up to now.'

'I'm afraid there's really not much to see. They took all her personal stuff – letters, diary, address book.'

Hetty pointed to the folders. 'And those?'

'Portfolios. Photo-features she was trying to sell.' He opened the top folder. 'Not very imaginative.'

Hetty came to look. Morecambe Sands – guides, walkers, Danger signs, seascape. She pushed the folder aside and opened another – high-rise flats, standard pictures of teenage vandalism. Another – more teenagers, now mainly standing around in groups, a couple against a fence of steel mesh, one apparently giving the other money.

She moved away. It was going wrong: it didn't feel right. She looked back at the Detective Sergeant, who seemed interested in the third folder and was poring over the pictures, the back of his head towards her. Hardly knowing what she was doing or why, Hetty held up her hands in front of her face, making a frame with her thumbs and forefingers, and looked through it at the back of the head presented to her.

Geoff watched. He knew perfectly well what she was doing and why.

Hetty lowered her hands. 'How did you get your stab-wound?'

'Drugs squad.' He looked round with a cheerful smile. 'We get a lot of aggro. It's all part of the game.'

Case Conference in the Wainthropps' kitchen. The photostat was again flat on the centre of the table and the full staff of the Detective Agency sat around it. 'All this thinking gives me a headache,' Robert said.

'There's aspirin on the dresser. We'll go step by step. Geoffrey?'

'Malcolm took a photo of the car on the cliff. Then he saw something happen – suicide or whatever, we don't know. Whoever he saw, saw him. And caught him.'

'A man. He saw a man. Evidence of the lady at the petrol station.'

'He escaped. The man still had his car, but Malcolm had money; he could have got home somehow. Only he didn't go home. Instead the man took Malcolm's car home and parked it just round the corner.'

'So – question: how did the man know where Malcolm's home was? There was nothing in the car to say where he lived. Go on.'

'Malcolm tapped out a message on the phone to let his parents know he was okay. But for some reason he still couldn't go home, and he's not been seen or heard of since.'

'Right! Or some lynx-eyed listener would have told Dave the Rave. So?'

Robert said, 'Kidnappers do that, don't they? Make you phone home to tell your relations you're safe.'

'Nobody's asked for money, and nobody else knew about the code with a bit of metal. It wasn't a kidnap. The man found Malcolm again. Maybe he's keeping him somewhere.'

'If he's still alive.'

'I think I'll have that aspirin now.'

'What kind of person has the contacts to find Malcolm if he's drifting . . . trying to hide . . . living rough? What kind of person would be able to frighten him out of going back home or to the police? The sort of person who could persuade him he wouldn't be believed.'

The aspirin was only half-dissolved but Robert drank it at a gulp. 'How could anyone persuade him of anything when he can't hear what they say?'

Geoff said, 'He can read lips.'

Hetty said, 'You remember that folder in Lynn Horrocks' studio?'

'Teenage vandalism, the Sergeant said. But there was one picture of two kids meeting in front of a wire fence and one of them handing something over. Money. Money for drugs. The Sergeant's in the Drugs Squad.' He pointed to the photocopy. 'And then there's the back of the head. I watched you putting him in the frame.'

'You're jumping to conclusions, Geoffrey.'

'I've had a good coach, Mrs Wainthropp. Olympic standard.'

'Is Detective Sergeant Lennox at home? It's Mrs Wainthropp.'

'He's in the barn, I think.'

The little girl, Clare, ran to get him.

Steve was stacking logs, helped by young Tim, his son.

'Daddy, Mrs Wainthropp's come to see you.'

He stopped work. 'Who?'

'Mrs Wainthropp.'

He wiped his hands on his trousers, trying to think what this visit might mean. 'Where is she?'

'With Mummy.'

He could not take the children with him. They would want to know why. 'Okay. Give Tim a hand. I'll be back.'

If Malcolm had wanted to attract attention by banging on the floor he would already have done so. But he and Malcolm were buddies. Malcolm trusted him and would not give him away. Better to take the chance and get rid of the old woman.

When Steve had gone, Clare and Tim continued to stack the wood. There was a small noise from above. Malcolm was not trying to attract attention, just change position, but the two children looked up. Clare said, 'There was a light up there last night.'

She went to the bottom of the steps and looked up towards the trapdoor. Tim said, 'We're not supposed to go up there.'

'I'm not going up. I'm just going to look.' She began to mount the open stairs behind which were more bales of straw. She reached the top, slid back the bolt of the trapdoor and opened it.

'It's dark. Get the matches.'

They were not supposed to play with matches, but it was not playing if she needed the light to see inside a dark place. Tim fetched the box and climbed up behind to give it to her. They were that large kind called Cook's Matches. Clare opened the box and struck a match, holding it up in front of her to see what was in the dark space and lifting up the trapdoor with the other.

Staring down at her was a terrifying face, wild, dirty, hairy with staring eyes. She screamed. The trapdoor slammed shut, and she fell backwards off the ladder, taking Tim with her so that he was underneath when they landed, and dropped the lighted match which fell into one of the bales of straw.

Still screaming, Clare ran out of the barn, leaving Tim lying where he had fallen. He tried to get up, but had hurt his foot. Just beside him the straw was already taking fire.

Hetty and Steve heard Clare screaming and saw her running towards them from the barn.

'Tim! Where's Tim?' Steve left Hetty holding the frightened little girl and ran back to find his son.

In the barn the fire had spread from one bale to its neighbour but had not yet really taken hold. Tim was trying to crawl away from it, grunting and sobbing with the effort, when his father appeared, picked him up bodily and ran with him back through the open door. There was a crackling sound. Flames were leaping among the bales of straw behind the stair, and smoke was spreading through the lower part of the barn and filtering into the upper part through the cracks in the boards.

Outside the barn Steve released Tim, saying to Hetty, 'Here! Hold him!' Tim and Clare clung to Hetty while Steve ran back into the barn. Rosemary appeared from across the lawn, clucking like a Rhode Island Red, and although anyone could see that the barn was on fire, did not seem to know what to do about it beyond clucking, so Hetty said, 'Dial 999,' and Rosemary scurried off to do so.

Then Steve appeared again through the smoke, this time carrying Malcolm. He lowered him gently to the ground and said, 'Journey's end. Will you take him as he is or do you want him gift-wrapped?'

'Is he all right?'

Steve knelt by Malcolm's side, looking directly at him, mouthing the words, 'The lady wants to know: are you all right?'

Malcolm nodded.

A bare room. Bare and bleak. Whitewashed brick walls. A wooden table with a couple of straight chairs on each side. Steve was in collarless shirt and trousers. A uniformed Constable stood by the door.

DCI Adams said, 'Malcolm Stone refuses to testify.'

'And can't be made to.'

'We can prove you were there in the car with her.'

'I've admitted I was there. She threw me out after sex – as was her wont – and I was lucky to find a lift home. I have to tell you, sir: you have no case.'

'You'll resign, of course.'

'Of course.'

Rosemary, when he told her, was delighted. 'Now you can get a proper job at last.'

'What as? Security Guard? Night Watchman? Store Detective?' He found himself shouting at her. 'I'm a dedicated police officer.'

And at the Detention Centre close to the airport, Hetty stood at one end of a long corridor with Malcolm, Joan and Peter waiting for Penipha to be released into their charge.

Round a corner at the other end came a slight, trim, self-contained, very slightly school-mistressy figure under the charge of a Woman Immigration Officer. They stopped. The two little groups faced each other with the length of the corridor in between.

Then Malcolm ran towards his fiancée.

She stopped him with a sign. He waited. She signed again. He gave a half-laugh, half-sob, finished his run towards her and clasped her in his arms, and the two of them stood there, close, holding each other.

Hetty said to Joan, 'What was she signing?'

'"You took your time".'

Hetty discovered, to her own surprise, that she was in tears.

Fingers

When you'd seen one Leaning Tower, you'd seen 'em all. Hetty had seen the leaning spire at Chesterfield: the Tower of Pisa was nothing so special. She was in a picky mood and had been since the start of their trip. Long ago, before his redundancy, she and Robert had been persuaded by Hilda Outhwaite down the road to contribute five pounds a month to a company running something called 'the Sunset Years Off-Peak Cultural Tours'. They would never notice the money, Hilda said, and it would add up to an unforgettable life-enriching experience in the end – this was the Hilda Outhwaite who had already enriched her life with the waiter at Corfu. Well, after the redundancy they *had* noticed the money, but ninety pounds had already been subscribed and would be wasted if they did not continue, so here they were at last in a made-over charabanc with time-expired tyres, touring Tuscany with the Outhwaites and twenty-six other Senior Citizens from the Blackburn/Darwen/Bolton area, all of whom seemed already to be confused by the persistent rain in sunny Italy and five of whom were suffering from diarrhoea and requiring Comfort Stops more often than there were stops available.

And what was happening to the Wainthropp Detective Agency with its founder gallivanting abroad? Could

Geoffrey be trusted to keep it ticking over? Hetty fretted.

They were headed along a narrow valley road beyond Lucca with wooded mountains to either side of them and a series of cement lorries, all driven by madmen, coming the other way at five-minute intervals. A road sign indicated Bagni di Lucca ahead and a minor road forking left. What road could be more minor than the one they were on already? They forked left without losing speed. Robert closed his eyes. He had never been car-sick or coach-sick in his life, but was about to be chara-sick if this kept up. A wooden notice at the side of the road informed them that the Albergo Monte Fulvo (where they were to spend the night) was a mere 11 kilometres upwards and onwards. Robert concentrated on trying to work out how much 11 kilometres was in miles in the hope that the mental arithmetic would settle his stomach.

Fifteen couples, the guide and the driver filled the Albergo; off-season cultural tours could be a boon to some. It was, they were told, a typically Tuscan albergo, and looked comfortable enough, all cane chairs and stripped pine like the windows of a Habitat shop. They gathered round the tour guide while the lady at the reception desk checked over their passports. They would be here two nights beore proceeding to Siena with its internationally famous mediaeval artefacts and suchlike, including horse-racing in the streets.

'Horse-racing?' Robert said, beginning to perk up.

'In summer. We've missed it.'

Hetty became conscious that the woman at the reception desk was looking across at her in a rather personal way, and seemed to be comparing the photograph in the passport with its subject.

'Tomorrow morning, the Devil's Leap: we'll take it very slowly. And tonight a typical Tuscan menu with optional wine of the locality. You won't find Prawn Cocktail and Gammon and Pineapple here.'

'If we don't find Prawn Cocktail,' said Hilda Outhwaite, 'I'm going home.'

The woman (who was the proprietor's wife, Elena) took Hetty's passport through a bead curtain, across the terrace where the Tuscan rain beat down steadily like dried peas on the canopy covering it, and on into the kitchen, where she gave it to her husband. In the space for *Occupation* the word *Housewife* had been crossed out and the words *Private Detective* inserted. They looked at each other. Then the husband spoke quickly in Italian to a teenage kitchen helper, who nodded, ran out of the kitchen and was soon speeding on his Lambretta down the mountain road towards Bagni di Lucca.

Robert looked miserably at a plate of fried squid. Hetty was squeezing lemon over hers. When in Rome . . . 'If you can eat tripe, you can eat octopus,' she said. 'It's two sides of the same coin.'

'I hate tripe.' He tried to cut a piece. 'I'm not that keen on india-rubber in any form.'

On to the terrace there came a vision in black leather, her skid-lid tucked under her arm so that her hair flowed free. Elena, standing at the kitchen door, pointed to Hetty and Robert, and the vision strode to their table, sat without being invited, leaned towards Hetty and spoke in English with a strong American accent. 'You are the Signora Wainthropp?'

'Si,' said Hetty, 'I am.'

'I am Gianetta. You are private dick? Down mean streets you bravely walk?'

'Up to a point. What's the problem?'

'Confidential. My mama and papa speak English only for the tourists, no good for delicate matter. They send for me; I have diploma. We must talk private, you understand?'

'Is it professional?' Robert said. 'We're on holiday.'

'Detectives don't have holidays, Robert. Half the cases come when you're on a steamboat up the Nile.'

Gianetta stood up. 'We tell these people you are my pen pal from England.' She addressed the other diners, who had stopped struggling with squid to stare at Hetty and her visitor, 'She is my corresponding for many years. We will talk Girl Talk together within these walls. Ciao, Hetty! We share our secrets soon.'

And she strode back to the kitchen, watched by everybody on the terrace. 'What a stunner!' Mr Outhwaite said while Mrs Outhwaite tightened her lips.

As for Hetty, she did not intend to be discomfited in front of a load of Senior Citizens. She lifted her chin and said to Robert, 'We'll follow in five minutes. You don't want ice cream.'

'There's veal first.' So they followed in twenty minutes, by which time Guido, the proprietor, had finished cooking the main course and the rest could be left to underlings. He and Elena took them into a private room behind the kitchen where Gianetta was waiting.

The problem was Gianni, Gianetta's brother, their son, who had been sent to a Language School in Manchester to learn English. Two days earlier a small parcel had arrived at the Albergo Fulvo from England. It contained a photograph of Gianni, dressed only in his underpants, standing in front of a wall covered with very decorative spray-painting. There was also a small box containing a flask wrapped in red tissue paper and inside the flask a finger, the little finger of a right hand. On the back of the photograph was a communication in irregularly placed Letraset:

SILENZIO
ASPETTARE LE
ISTRUZIONE

'Silence. Wait for instructions.'

'Have you had any instructions?'

They had not.

'I know that wall,' Hetty said. 'One like it, any road. It's the decorations they put on. Rude mostly, but you get the occasional touch of romance.'

Robert took the photograph and examined it closely. 'You're right. Haslingden, would you say? Bacup Market? Somewhere.'

'Then you can find him?'

'I'd think he's moved by now.'

Hetty said: 'Why send him to learn English in Manchester anyway? Why not do it here?'

'My brother will inherit the albergo, so he must speak English for the tourists, more better than me – Cambridge First Certificate. Every morning he study. At night he work in a veggieburger restaurant – not Italian, Papa insist. It must be English for the idiom. When he have English good, he will come back here, find a nice girl with a diploma in Business Studies, marry and begin family. Only it goes wrong. Gianni don't like to study.'

'Don't like to work,' said Guido. 'Don't like to marry,' said Elena.

'We had the same trouble with our Derek. They grow out of it. When did you last hear from him?'

'Gianni also don't like to write letters.'

'Have you told the police?'

Guido shook his head violently. They feared a Mafia kidnap. Useless to tell the police.

'I meant the Manchester police.'

But even that was dangerous. The Mafia had eyes and ears everywhere, and would be bound to know. Gianni was their only son; they dared not risk his life by talking to any police at all of whatever nationality.

'So I'm not the police?'

'You are a woman. They would not suspect you.'

Robert was uneasy. 'Are you sure?'

'Maybe you find nothing. Maybe the ransom will not be so much and we can pay. Maybe they will kill him anyway.' Elena gave a long, shuddering sigh. 'We don't know what to do, so we must do something. We pay you seven hundred thousand lire for one week.'

It seemed a fortune to Robert. 'Seven hundred thousand!'

'Three hundred pounds. You find out what you can. Then we see.'

Hetty nodded slowly.

Geoff was waiting behind the barrier at Manchester Airport to meet them. Hetty, who had left Robert to bring the luggage on a trolley, spotted him at once and made her way briskly to him through the more encumbered passengers of their flight.

Very little had turned up in the way of work during her absence, she learned – only two lost dogs and a stolen budgie. The latter's pedigree was said to go back to Ancient Egypt.

'How much are they offering?'

'Thirty pounds for safe return.'

'We can do better. We've to trace a young language student kidnapped by the Mafia. They've been sending bodily parts to his mum and dad.' Robert appeared, sweating and pushing a trolley with bottles and a ribboned box balanced on top of the suitcases. 'Be careful with that duty-free Dubonnet. It's got to last the winter.'

She strode off across the Concourse to get a good place on the bus. 'She was talking about the Mafia,' said Geoff to Robert.

'It'll come to no good.'

'I may ask for danger money.'

'She's over-excited with the travelling.'

'What's in that box?'

'Nougat.'

Geoff concealed his perturbation until they were safely home. Lost dogs and a budgie were one thing, old ladies with facial hair, environmental polluters, even a kidnapped birdwatcher, they could all be coped with, but organised crime was in a different league. 'How can they be sure it's the Mafia?' he said.

'Who else could it be? As far as anyone in Manchester is concerned, he's an Italian waiter doing language classes. Takes the Mafia to know his mum and dad are sitting on a little gold mine in Tuscany.'

'They'd have to have informants.'

'They do. Everywhere. They've half the Manchester police in their pockets, I shouldn't wonder.' She was still on a high.

Geoff said: 'Then don't you think . . . if we're to make enquiries, like . . .'

'We are. We will. I took the job.'

'. . . that they might have informants at the Language School? At the veggieburger restaurant even?'

'Oh, that's going too far,' said Robert.

'What I mean is, these informants could inform on *us* if they heard about us asking questions. We'd need to go a roundabout way, like. Softly-softly, you might say.'

Thoughts could be seen chasing themselves across Hetty's face. Then she came to a decision. 'All right, softly-softly. By the way, that box of nougat is for you, Geoffrey. Robert and I can't eat nougat. It's death to teeth.'

So she went to the Oxfam shop and bought a disguise. She had decided that a job in Public Relations would inspire confidence and deceive any Mafia informants who might be hanging around the Language School. Black, she had read somewhere, was the fashionable colour: you couldn't go wrong with it. So she wore a black coat and skirt with a diamanté spray brooch, a black hat with a half-veil, black drop earrings, and flyaway spectacles with black rims; she carried a black patent-leather handbag.

Hetty sat across the table from the Principal, took a wrapped stick of nougat from her handbag and presented it as a gift. 'Don't worry, I'm not trying to sell you anything. Our aim is to get our nougat into every home. My card!'

The Principal received the nougat warily and examined the card which had in fact come in the box and been brought along by Hetty to add artistic verisimilitude. 'Torrone?'

'The name of the firm I represent.'

'It's the Italian for nougat.'

'Exactly. In nougat, I have to say, we're tops.'

'Aeroporto di Pisa – Pisa Airport.'

Clicking her tongue, Hetty took back the card. 'I've brought the wrong card. Luckily it doesn't affect the name of the game.'

'Which is?'

'Public Relations in the highest sense. My company intends to award a prize every year – the Torrone Prize, it'll be – to the language student who has done most to bring credit to Italy. Personal qualities will be considered as well as academic merit.'

'Will you be paying out in nougat?' The Principal applied herself to an examination of the Register. There were only two Italian students at the school that year, Gianni Pepinetto and Ernesto Torcello. Ernesto was a star pupil. Gianni seldom turned up for classes, even at the beginning and had since dropped out altogether.

'Dropped out? Did he tell you why?'

'He didn't tell us anything. He just stopped coming. Since fees are paid a term in advance, we weren't too bothered, to tell you the truth.'

Hetty the PR lady applied herself to creative thinking. This involved closing her eyes, placing one hand in front of the half-veil and then removing it sharply in a gesture of triumph. 'Just what I need! The Human Angle!'

'You what?'

'Women's Page. Top of the column with a photo of them both – I'm coming over all of a doodah just thinking about it. Gold Star and Black Spot! One dedicated, the other dead idle. I'll talk to them both. Have you got their addresses?'

'It's the same address – or was. I don't know whether Gianni's still there.'

'You mean they knew each other before they came to England?'

'I shouldn't think so; it's just their way. Italian students always stick together. I say to them, "Find a room in an English home. Mind the children, walk the dog; you'll learn more than we can ever teach you." But they never do. They crowd together into some squalid furnished flat, and go out at night to look for women. To the male Italian language student, Britain is not about the beauty and complexity of the English language. It is about easy sex.'

Meanwhile, Geoff had taken on a morning's work at the veggieburger restaurant, which always needed casual staff; he was grating carrots in the kitchen. The Salads Chef – there was only one and his previous experience had been in road haulage – stood before an enormous hatch. Veggieburgers prepared by the Burger Chef (ex-Merchant Navy) arrived on plates along a conveyor belt to his left. To them he added dollops of beansprouts and grated carrots from plastic trays on his right. The hands of waiters appeared through the hatch, grabbed the filled plates, and took them away.

The Salads Chef was a thinking man, who liked to take the wider view and comment on life's little oddities, putting them into context as he went through the day. 'No,' he said, 'they don't particularly enjoy the food; that's not the point. It's cheap and filling, and they think it's healthy.' A veggieburger dropped on to the floor and he picked it up, wiped it on his apron, and returned it to the plate, to be grabbed instantly by a waiter. Geoff, who had been watching this operation and taken his eye off the grater, cut his thumb. 'Here – don't get any blood on them carrots,' the Salads Chef said. 'We're only licensed for vegetarian food.'

'Why did Gianni leave?'

'He was always late, usually fell behind at Rush Hour and left me here like a Charlie with sod-all to put on the plates. And he needed more money than we could afford to pay.'

There was a telephone call from Gianetta. Instructions had been received. She was to bring the money to Manchester. They would book a single room for her at the Piccadilly Hotel and she would get further instructions there.

And they had sent another finger.

Why would the Mafia want the money paid in Manchester? It didn't add up to Hetty.

She sent Robert to get a blow-up of the photograph, took Geoff and went to visit the address she had been given for Ernesto and Gianni. They found Ernesto at home, ironing shirts. Italians, he explained, are fanatic ironers. Hetty introduced herself and her assistant, Mr Shawcross, with more caution than she had used in the Principal's office. As an Italian, Ernesto might be expected to know a little more about the manufacturers of quality confectionery in his homeland; she dropped 'Torrone' as the name of her firm and no longer claimed to be tops in nougat. She told Ernesto that she worked in Public Relations, was researching a project which would lead to the award of a special prize to an Italian language student, and that from what she had heard so far, he might be a contender.

'The Language School says you're their star pupil.'

'They are always so kind to me.'

The eyes roved over the grotty furnishings of the room, the crumbs on the lino and the table on which Ernesto clearly both ate and worked, the coin-operated gas fire and TV set, the pans and dishes on the draining board, the half-empty bottle of red wine, the dictionaries, newspapers and magazines, and the framed photographs from home. There were Elena, Guido and Gianetta, arms round each other's shoulders, grinning at her from a leatherette frame the colour of crushed strawberries.

'They seem to be less impressed by your friend, Mr Pepinetto.'

'Those are his mama and papa.'

Hetty pretended surprise. 'Oh, really?'

'Would you like to sit down? I cannot offer tea, but there is coffee. Or wine.'

'Oh, is there wine?' said Geoff.

'Sit down please, Geoffrey. You won't be having wine. You'll need a clear head for the note-taking. Will Mr Pepinetto be home soon? I'd really like to talk to you both. I had this idea, you see, for a photo-feature – sort of Cain and Abel kind of thing – Cox's Orange Pippin and the Rotten Apple.'

But Gianni would not be home soon. He had gone away; Ernesto did not know where. He had given up his job with the veggieburger restaurant because the pay was too bad, but said he would easily get another. 'He had such confidence, great . . .' The word escaped Ernesto and became no more than graceful Italian hand-gestures. 'What is the word for "on your bike"?'

'Tour de France? Saddle-sores?'

'Initiative. He had great initiative, but it was all talk, you know. He became ashamed that he could not pay the rent, and I must pay all. He went out one morning when

I was at the school – took nothing, only a few clothes in a bag. Left a message on the table.'

'Did you keep the message?'

'Why?'

Why? Hetty had forgotten for a moment that she was a PR lady, and had slipped back into being a detective. 'Handwriting. It's a clue to character.'

'Gianni's handwriting was terrible, maybe his character also. I don't know: we were together here only a few weeks. He seemed okay to me, but it is true he has not come back and I must pay all the rent anyway.'

They had gone as far as they could in one visit, found out very little, but had much to think about. Hetty stood up. 'Thank you so much. May we come again?'

'If you do I hope next time we shall talk about me, not all about Gianni.'

'Oh, I am sorry. What must you think of me? It's just that in my business, Ernesto – in good old Public Relations – it's the human interest angle we concentrate on. Heartbreak . . . courage in adversity. They add such values to the nougat. I'm sure you understand.'

Damn! It was the first time she had mentioned nougat. Never mind. Let him make of it what he could. If he talked to the Principal about her visit, nougat was bound to enter the conversation. 'I do,' Ernesto said, 'I really do.'

'I just can't help thinking of that poor lost lad out there on his bike in all weathers.'

They were through the door and facing the grimy stairs leading to the shared bathroom and WC, and then on down through the stale smells to the scruffy street. Geoff said, 'I made a note of the saddle-sores, Mrs Wainthropp. Do you want me to do any medical research?'

Ernesto watched them go. Then he closed the door of the flat, crossed the living area in four strides, and entered the bedroom where a young man in jeans and a soft leather jacket, who was certainly in possession of all his fingers was waiting, frightened.

'There is no Public Relations,' Ernesto said. 'No prize. They were lying. They knew you gave up your job at the veggieburger restaurant. How? Why?'

'Perchè . . .'

'Speak only English to me.'

'Can't be the polizia.'

'No. Can't be.'

'Maybe some newspaper . . . Maybe your uncle . . .' He was close to tears. 'How can we get into such a mess?'

'There is no "we". You got yourself into this mess, Gianni, and like a fool I try to help you.'

Walking away from the house, Hetty said to Geoff, 'I don't like it, Geoffrey. It doesn't smell right.'

'It were a bit pongy on the stairs, but he kept his own place in good order.'

'If you don't object to crumbs on the carpet. We'd best get home and get our heads straight. Manchester! The Agency's fees are being eaten up in bus fares.'

'If Gianni's mum and dad can afford to pay a ransom, they could afford to pay us for a second week.'

They were away up the street, round the corner, and caught the first of the four buses they needed to take them home. Gianni came out of the house, and a man who had been waiting across the street followed him.

Sensing that he was being shadowed, Gianni looked round, then quickened his pace. The man behind did not quicken his own pace to match him, but continued to follow.

Gianni glanced round again to see whether he had managed to put any more distance between himself and the follower, then to the front again. What he saw caused him fear. Another man had stepped round the corner to confront him. The man behind was tall and thin, the man in front brawny and thick, an obvious heavy.

There was nowhere to run. The two men closed on him. Then they began, methodically and without obvious enjoyment, to beat him up.

Robert had taken the photograph of Gianni into town to get photocopies and a blow-up of part of the spray-painted wall against which he was standing: the smokeless-fuel specialist in the village did not do colour. Just as well he had. The teenager in Prontaprint not only did a very satisfactory job of work – detailed and lifelike and better than the original – but she also recognised the artist.

Her name was Ruby Tuesday. She took her cans of spray paint all over the North-West, right up into Galloway. 'Tell her style anywhere, all curls and colours, dragons a speciality: you can almost smell the smoke.'

It had not occurred to Robert that experts could differentiate between graffiti-artists just as they did between Matisse and Picasso, but it seemed that in the North-West there were two schools – Ruby Tuesday and Jack Diamond, who was all spikes and jagged edges, and each had their followers. 'They've both had grants from North West Arts. Contributions to popular culture. And they've both had Youth Custody an' all for vandalism. Depends how you look at it.'

Back home, the three of them reviewed the evidence so far. Gianni had enrolled at the Language School, paid one term's fees in advance, set up in a rented flat with Ernesto Torcello and got a part-time job at the veggie-burger restaurant. Six weeks ago he dropped out of school, gave up his job and disappeared from the flat, and nobody had heard from him since, until his fingers began to arrive through the post at the Albergo Monte Fulvo.

'What other work could he do with his English so poor?'

'Have to be unskilled. Building trade or such,' Robert said. 'Except there's no work for builders these days.'

'Have to be non-speaking unless it was with another Italian. Write that down, Geoffrey: it's a line we might follow.'

'We don't know that he *did* get work. The Mafia might have took him six weeks ago.'

'I don't believe in this Mafia story. Anyway, he left a message.'

'They could have made him write it. Told him what to say.'

'Then why wait so long before asking for a ransom? There was too much that didn't add up. Why did Gianni need money?'

'Everyone needs money.'

He had enough for his school fees and for a down-payment on the rent of the flat, and he had a part-time job. Then suddenly he needed more. Why?

Robert said, 'Women can be expensive.'

'Not these days,' said Geoff.

They looked at him, surprised.

'It's a more equal society. They call it sexist if you pay for everything.'

'I am glad,' said Robert. And to Hetty, 'What about gambling?'

'Who'd give him credit?'

Geoff said, 'You're thinking of drugs, aren't you? Crack. There's plenty about.'

'I'm thinking of his mum and dad scratching about to raise a ransom.' Hetty's anger built. 'I'm thinking of that girl travelling from Tuscany with a suitcase full of money to the Piccadilly Hotel to wait for instructions. I'm thinking of a cruel trick played on folk who love him, just to get money to feed a drug habit.'

'Your little grey cells do make big leaps, Mrs Wainthropp. I've noticed it before.'

Robert said, 'He wouldn't cut his own fingers off. And pickle them, like.'

Hetty said, 'We'd better have another go at Ernesto. And this Ruby Tuesday – how are we going to find her?'

Geoff said, 'Well . . .'

'Don't tell me she was at school with you.'

'Not everyone in the West-Lancs area was at school with me, Mrs Wainthropp, but I do know someone who might be able to help.'

So they went to look for Ambo, who was a famous art critic, Geoff said, a member of the North-West Arts Forum and a Design Consultant for ICI when he could bother to turn up, and had taught Geoff Art off and on when Geoff's comprehensive had been able to afford his part-time services and a small budget for materials.

They found him taking a Master Class with a group of kids and a lot of cans of spray paint in front of a wall. 'Give me a moment,' said Geoff to Hetty, and went to talk to him.

'No, no, Jed, your arm's too stiff,' Ambo was saying as Geoff joined the group. He was a man in his mid-thirties, bearded and running to fat. He turned and looked Geoff up and down carefully, working out who he was, and the kids watched. Finally Ambo said, 'Geoffrey Shawcross. Class Five B. Freehand Drawing. You were bloody awful.'

'I had trouble at home. Can you come and talk to us? We need your help.'

'You're interrupting a class. You can have two minutes.'

He left his pupils to carry on as they were and came across to Hetty, who showed him the blow-up of the spray-painting on the unknown wall. He recognised the artist at once. 'But you're out of luck. She don't give interviews, she don't answer questions, and any road you can never find her.'

'Do you know where the wall is?'

'No problem. Middle Period, is that. All Ruby's Middle Period work was done around Addersleigh.' He shook his head. 'Decadent influences there! Rimbaud, Baudelaire, Beardsley. Still, she had to go through it.' He looked at his watch. 'Time's up. Bye, missus. See you, Geoff.' And he was off.

Hetty said, 'Addersleigh. You'll need to borrow the scooter from that friend of yours.'

There was a stone slab with a double wash basin of stainless steel with stainless steel draining shelves on each side, and a long shelf above, on which stood bottles of various coloured liquids; a pair of heavy-duty rubber gloves lay on the slab. The two doors each had a panel of dimpled glass which refracted light so that one couldn't see more than a blur through it. One of the doors bore the words SHOWER AND TOILET, the other RECEPTION AREA.

Three men stood in the room. One wore a white coat and rubber boots: this was Hebden, a subordinate. One wore a black coat and striped trousers, and he was Mr Gabriel, the boss. The third was Gianni, his face running with sweat and showing signs of the beating up, his shirt soaked, very much afraid but trying to hold himself together while remaining submissive and respectful to his employer.

'You have betrayed the trust I put in you.'

'Si, Signore, lo sò, Signore. Mi scusi, non la offenderò mai piú Signore.'

'Non posso dimenticare ciò che é accaduto.'

'No, Signore.'

'Pensero io a come meglio peuirti.'

'Si, Signore.'

Mr Gabriel turned to Hebden. 'He's disgusting. Shit-scared and sweating like a pig. He can't appear in public like that. Take care of him. Get him showered and changed.'

He left the room by the door to the reception area. Hebden jerked his head towards the door to the showers, and Gianni obediently went on through. Hebden picked up the pair of heavy-duty rubber gloves and began to put them on as he followed.

Waiting in the reception area were two Arabs, one young in a lounge suit, the other much older, in Arab dress and dark glasses. Mr Gabriel said, 'I'm so sorry to keep you waiting.'

'You have what we want?'

'Indeed, yes. And of the highest quality.'

Hetty sent Geoff to look at walls in the Addersleigh area and went by herself to see Ernesto. This time she told him part of the truth – that Gianni's parents had become worried at not hearing from him and had employed her to pursue enquiries. 'I'll be straight with you; I'm a private detective.' And she gave him the Agency's card.

'You certainly fooled me.'

'So I should hope. Disguise is part of the job.'

'Sherlock Holmes could not have done it better.'

'Fine words butter no parsnips, Ernesto. I'll have the card back if you don't mind. We're running a bit short. Now! Where's Gianni gone? And why did he need money?'

'Really I did not know him so well. He did not confide in me. He was a restless boy. He searched for the pot of gold at the end of the rainbow.'

'Women?'

Ernesto could not say for sure, but did not think so. For an Italian student in Britain, women were not a problem. As for money, every student of any race, colour or creed, needs more money than he has.

'Was Gianni on drugs?'

'I would have noticed.'

'Gambling?' Ernesto shrugged. 'Horses? Cards? Roulette?'

'Did his parents say he liked to gamble?' Ernesto asked. They had not. 'Did they say anything to help you find him, Mrs Wainthropp?'

'They said he wasn't keen on work.'

'I think maybe they are right, but it's not much help to you. Please, Mrs Wainthropp, believe me. I don't know much about Gianni's business, but if you will give me back your card . . .' reluctantly she did so '. . . I will let you know at once whenever I hear some news.'

She had got nowhere. She walked moodily down the street, round the corner, past a row of shops – a newsagent's, a small supermarket with a queue for the National Lottery, television rental, betting shop. The bus-stop was on the main street round the next corner: she would have wasted another bus-fare. Wait! Stop, Hetty – and *think*. Betting shop!

The television was on, as it always is, with a pre-race commentary. A few punters in whom gloom and hope were uncomfortably mixed were filling in betting slips. Hetty showed the photograph of Gianni to the counter clerk, who studied it warily.

'Do you recognise him? Did he ever come in here?'

'Well, I can't say.' She looked about for help. 'You get all sorts.'

'Do you? Looks like mainly regulars to me. A place like this, there'd be no passing trade.'

'There are some regulars, naturally.'

'Was he a regular?'

The counter clerk handed back the photograph. 'I really can't remember.'

'But you remember he came in. You've seen him before.'

'I never said so.'

'You've said nothing at all so far. I find that interesting.'

The counter clerk pressed a button below the counter. 'I'm not supposed to say anything. What happens between a man and his turf accountant is confidential. We learn that on the Training Course. It's like being a doctor or a priest.'

Help arrived a little more slowly than the United States Cavalry. The Manager took over. 'What's the problem?'

'This lady's harassing me.'

'I'm a detective.' Hetty showed him the photograph. 'Have you seen this young man before?'

He glanced cursorily at the photograph and handed it back. 'It's not the policy of this establishment to provide information about our clients.'

'So he *was* a client?' She held up the photograph again. 'Take another look.'

The Manager discovered that he was sweating, and since this was unlikely to add to the morale of his counter staff, he invited Hetty into his office. There, under the gimlet scrutiny of this disconcerting detective, he studied the picture again. 'He used to come in; I shan't deny that. He had a run of luck at the beginning and then lost steadily. He asked for credit and was refused. End of story.'

'Why refused?'

'We don't afford credit to students without any visible means of support.'

'His parents own a hotel.'

'In Italy. That hardly amounts to a guarantee of financial stability.'

'You know that, then? He told you?'

'He may have mentioned it.'

'I don't suppose you've any idea where he might have gone for credit?'

They looked at each other in silence. The Manager tried to smile, and discovered that his lips would not get into the right shape. He would have to get her out of his shop, but it was clear that she would not go without the information she wanted.

And after all, he had done nothing wrong. *He* had not financed the young man's losses.

Geoffrey in Addersleigh had found one of Ruby Tuesday's Middle-Period walls – curly, whirly dungeons and dragons, unsullied by any of Jack Diamond's spiky additions. The problem was that a workman up a ladder was busy covering it with white paint.

Geoff was horrified. 'You can't do that!'

'Council Clean-Up Campaign. Stimulates employment and attracts the tourists.'

'But it's Middle Period. Part of our cultural heritage.'

'Don't worry. She'll be back.'

A Victorian sampler behind the Loan Shark's desk read *In God We Trust*. The furniture was heavy and brown like something out of Dickens and a Dickensian bully-boy (who was in fact the brawny heavy who had beaten up Gianni) stood casually beside the door to protect the Loan Shark from any punters who might attempt to cancel their legal obligations by violence.

The Loan Shark himself was a genial man, open and smiling. 'Nobody lends without security. He might have been tempted to go back to Italy to avoid repayment, so we took his passport. Irresponsible, Mrs Wainthropp, to do otherwise.'

'I've heard of folk like you. Some poor woman with a bill she can't pay borrows fifty pound and by the end of the month it's three hundred. How could you hope to collect?'

'We have our ways. Friendly persuasion, you might say.' The heavy smiled.

'How much does he owe you now?'

'Nothing. Loan's paid off.'

But Gianetta would only now be arriving at Manchester Airport with the money. How could Gianni have paid off the loan?

'Gentleman paid it off on his behalf. A man of distinction – bit of a foreigner, I'd say. Well-dressed, well-spoken, carried himself well. He knew all about the debt. Paid in full, loan *and* interest. I gave him back the passport and off he went.'

Mr Gabriel led Ernesto down a row of closed coffins. Standing by the last of them was Hebden.

Mr Gabriel nodded. Hebden raised the lid of the coffin to show Ernesto the body lying inside. It was Gianni. The little fingers of both hands had been cut off and something had happened to his face.

Ernesto gave a cry of terror and began to whimper.

'Now dispose of it,' said Mr Gabriel to Hebden.

Hetty and Geoff sat side by side. She had her feet in a basin of warm water, a glass of Dubonnet within easy reach. Geoff's stockinged feet were on the coffee table.

'I've said it before, I'll say it again. It gets the feet, this job. I've been thinking of buying a pair of Doc Martens.'

'That scooter's murder on me thighs. "Addersleigh area"! It's hardly precise. I must have been to hundreds of walls and it's the same story with them all. Council's repainting.'

'You've got to persist, Geoffrey, thighs or no thighs. It's our only clue.'

The phone rang. Since Hetty could not be expected to answer it in wet feet, Robert did so. It was Gianetta, calling from the Piccadilly Hotel. Room 510. Better for Hetty not to ask for her in Reception in case someone was watching the desk.

So Hetty borrowed a maid's outfit from Hilda Outhwaite, who had last used it in a one-act play by Gertrude Jennings performed in competition by the village Drama Group, hijacked a trolley loaded with clean towels from outside the lift, and made her way in disguise to Room 510. She knocked on the door.

'Who is it?'

'Maid with towels.' This was said loudly to deceive a couple of passing guests. Then she put her face close to the door and spoke more privately. 'Hetty Wainthropp. Open up.'

She took her raincoat, hat and umbrella from the lower shelf of the trolley, and her handbag from beneath the layer of towels, and gave the trolley a push to send it whizzing down the corridor. Gianetta opened the door. 'You work here?'

'I'm a mistress of disguise. Let me in.'

Hetty had decided that it was best to come straight out with the truth, so she told Gianetta of her suspicions of Gianni.

'But he could not cut off his own fingers!'

'I can't explain the fingers.'

'You believe . . . you really believe he would do this himself? It is your professional opinion?'

'It is.'

Gianetta was upset. Unsettled. She walked about the hotel room trying to get her thoughts in order. 'Okay, he's young. Too young maybe. He likes to go out. Have a good time. Maybe he gets in debt like you say. Maybe gamble. We don't have such "Betting Shops" but of course you can bet on horses if you want, and you don't have to go to the bank to borrow money. All this may be.' A sudden burst of anger. 'Gianni loves his family. He would never hurt us.' The anger went as quickly as it had come. 'I brought the ransom money. I don't know what to do.'

'You've had no instructions so far?'

'Nothing. Just to wait in the room.'

She had never met Ernesto. Never talked on the phone. She would not know his voice. And there was nobody in Manchester, nobody in Britain as far as she knew who would have paid off Gianni's debt.

'It's a real puzzle,' Hetty said. 'Something's gone all arsy-darsy somewhere.'

The telephone rang. 'It's them!' Gianetta picked up the phone. 'Si?' The expression on her face changed from apprehension to amazement. 'Papa?' Hetty watched her. It was clear that Gianetta was deeply shocked by what she was being told, stunned: all emotion drained out of her. The fingers of her left hand fluttered without her being conscious of it, but otherwise she held herself absolutely still.

The conversation ended. Slowly she replaced the handset on its rest. She turned to Hetty. Her voice was calm. 'Gianni's body has been found. He has been . . . they have . . . mutilate . . .'

'The fingers?'

'Cut off. Little fingers like were sent. Both hands. And the eyes . . .' She swayed.

'What about the eyes?'

'Cut out. The Manchester polizia telephone to my papa. I must . . . identify. Then, if they will give me the body, I will take it back to Italy. Please go now, Mrs Wainthropp.'

Hetty began to gather up her belongings. She did not know what to say or what to think, and knew that, if she did not hold herself together, she would come out all over a-tremble. Her suspicions about Gianni now began to seem like a sick joke. 'How did the police know to phone your parents?'

'His passport was in his pocket. Signora Wainthropp, I have to say, do not blame yourself. I do not blame you. My papa and mama have no bad feelings for you. It is our fault, our mistake. We thought, being a woman of some age, the Mafia would not notice you. We were foolish. They notice everything. You did your best, signora, but you were . . . out of your league.'

Now at last Gianetta's calm broke, and she began to weep helplessly. Hetty went quickly to her, helped her to the bed, and sat by her, holding her as she wept.

'You have a good cry, my love. You have a good cry.'

Meanwhile, Geoffrey had had a highly successful morning.

He went first to Ambo and was directed to one of the kids in Ambo's Master Class, Jason, who lived near Addersleigh. Jason was a fan. He knew all Ruby's work. He took to the pillion of the scooter like a limpet to a dreadnought and guided Geoff to what had once been Glissold Park until the Council privatised it into a crematorium.

They walked along gravelled paths through flowerbeds and lawns with little metal plates set into the grass, some of which were in memoriam to some well-heeled box of ashes while others just read PLEASE DO NOT WALK ON THESE LAWNS. Eventually they came to a screen of dusty laurels; behind it were what had once been the Glissold Park Conveniences, the LADIES and GENTS sitting side by side in a friendly way, but now much vandalised with the windows broken and steel grilles over the doors. Here there was spray-painting but of a most inferior sort.

'Doesn't look much like Ruby's work.'

'Come round the back.'

And round the back they found the wall, far more of it than was shown in the photograph of Gianni. The whole expanse had been transformed into a proscenium arch, bare brick in the centre with a wonderful coloured, curvy scalloped dragon going up each side and a pair of dragons entwined across the top.

'Roll me over!' said the Junior Partner of the Wainthropp Detective Agency.

He made Jason stand within the proscenium against the bare brick. 'Bit to the left . . . bit more . . .' then held up his hands to make a frame, and looked through it. 'Bingo!'

On their way back along the gravelled paths to the entrance of the crematorium, Geoff made another discovery, which would have to be evaluated at a Case Conference, but looked as if it might be of even more importance. A hearse, with the mourners' cars following, was turning into the gate. It was a posh funeral – pricey vehicles and plenty of them, and the undertakers' men in black with top hats. Sitting next to the driver was Ernesto. He did not see Geoff. The hearse drove on, with Geoff staring after it, and stopped at the chapel. Four men, of whom Ernesto was one, took the coffin from the back of the hearse, and carried it in.

Geoff returned from Addersleigh in great good humour and found Robert deep in the glums. 'She's gone all broody,' Robert said. 'Just sits there in the front room, staring at nothing. I keep taking her cups of tea but they go to waste: she doesn't notice.'

'I've found the wall.'

'You'd better tell her. I don't know as it'll do any good.'

So he went to the living room to tell her, while Robert filled the kettle for another cup of tea. He found Hetty as Robert had described her, staring into space like a broody hen, an untouched cup of tea by her side.

She looked up at Geoff. 'Gianetta said she didn't blame me. Of course she blames me. I blame myself.'

Some disaster had occurred. He would not ask: she would tell him in her own time. 'I've found the wall.'

'I've promised we'll go no further. Ask no more questions. Discontinue the investigation. She paid us off out of the ransom money.'

'I've found more than the wall. I know where Gianni got the fingers from.'

There was a silence. Slowly she turned her head to look at him. 'Tell me.' Then she picked up the cup of tea at her side and sipped. 'This tea's cold.'

* * *

Case Conference.

'An undertaker's mute! I said – at this very table: you heard me – that if he got a job, it would have to be non-speaking. Is this undertaker Italian?'

'I've not found out yet. He only bought the firm a few months ago. Very posh premises just by the War Memorial. "Francis Gabriel Funeral Services, tact and courtesy guaranteed." He's said to be foreign.'

'I knew it! The fine gentleman who paid off the debt.'

Robert said, 'Shall we be having supper soon? I could get something from the freezer.'

'Later. Let's put the case together first. It's amazing how the little grey cells begin to work when you give them the nourishment of hard information.'

'Leaping about, are they?' said Geoff.

'Like fleas in a circus. Start writing.' Geoff's pencil went busily to work. 'The photo was taken against a wall in the grounds of the crematorium. He knew that wall.'

'Could you slow down a bit?'

'I can't. I'm in full flow.'

Robert said, 'I could put the oven on, at least.'

'Who took the photograph?'

'Ernesto?'

'Right. And it's my guess it was Ernesto got Gianni the job. I reckon Ernesto was already working for this Mr Gabriel.'

'Should I be writing this bit? It's speculation, isn't it, not knowledge?'

'If you don't speculate, you can't accumulate. Write it all down: I'll tell you when to stop. It's my guess there's a family connection.'

'Family as in Mafia?'

'Family as in family. The Mafia had nothing to do with it. Undertaking work! What student would think of it, without he already had an uncle in top hat and black gloves?'

Robert said, 'Why would Gianni go from a veggie-burger restaurant into corpses? It's not a natural career move.'

'There was money in corpses. He was trying on this Mafia trick to get money out of his mum and dad, but he needed fingers. Working in a funeral parlour, the uncomplaining dead were all around him. But think on. How did he get the idea in the first place?'

'Ernesto again?'

'Not good enough.' She concentrated. 'I must get it right. Gianni was in debt. Ernesto got him this job which paid more money than he'd been earning.'

Robert said, 'An undertaker's mute. That's not well paid without you do the embalming as well, and he'd no training in that.'

'The job paid well because all Mr Gabriel's staff had to be paid well to keep their mouths shut.'

'You've lost me.'

Geoff said, 'It's guesswork.'

'He got the idea about fingers because it was already going on.'

'Who'd want fingers?'

'Transplants.'

'You can't take them from corpses. It's got to be your own fingers stitched back on.'

'When the police found Gianni's body, it wasn't just his little fingers gone. It was his eyes.'

'Cornea transplants,' said Geoff. 'There was a piece in the paper. There's no rejection with eyes because there's no blood supply. You can keep them for ever if you freeze them.'

'They'd be sent abroad. That man Gabriel would be making a fortune. A Funeral Director! It's mainly cremations these days: not many are buried. Once they go through that curtain to the incinerator, who's going to know they're short of a few bodily bits and pieces?'

'Folks'd notice. You'd get some grieving widow wanting a last look.'

'It's eyes, Robert. You remember that stuffed ferret you tried to buy at auction until I put a stop to it? They take out the real eyes and put in glass ones. But fingers would be noticed. That's where Gianni made a mistake. That's why he had to be killed.'

Two faces, fascinated, following it through. One face triumphant, the thoughts all clear and right. 'Now! How do we prove it?'

Robert said, 'You don't have to prove it. The police do that.'

'I promised I wouldn't talk to the police. And anyway, as Geoffrey says, it's all guesswork.'

Geoff was uncomfortable. 'Ernesto will crack.'

'If he doesn't we've got no case. We need proof. We'll have to get into those premises somehow. It's the only way.'

Was it? What if they were discovered breaking and entering, and were handed over to the police? That would be embarrassing but bearable. But Gianni had not been turned over to the police. Gianni had ended up on lonely moorland, minus his fingers and his eyes.

'I think your grey cells may have taken you too far this time, Mrs Wainthropp.'

'I'm not asking you to go alone. I'll go with you.'

'No, you won't,' Robert said. He stood up with immense reluctance. Masterful action did not come easily to him. Hetty looked up warily. Was he going to forbid the whole enterprise? 'Provided – and only provided – we get our supper first,' he said, '*I'll* go with the lad. You've never been handy with tools, Hetty. I doubt they'll be well-protected: nobody burgles an undertaker. So turn on the oven. I am on my way to the freezer now.'

'Wait! I've got a better idea.' Robert's face expressed anxiety, not relief. Hetty's better ideas were so often more worrying than the ones they replaced. 'We'll need the Addersleigh local paper, and I'll need to talk to a taxidermist.'

Hetty wore the black she had used for the PR lady, Robert his Sunday-best with a black tie, Geoff the suit they had bought for the interview with Sir Peter. 'We've come to take our last leave of the late Mr Satterthwaite,' Hetty told the receptionist and they passed through to the Chapel of Rest which was dimly lit, with soothing Muzak of a religious nature.

The late Mr Satterthwaite lay in an open coffin. Three elderly mourners were filing past under the sympathetic supervision of Mr Gabriel in full fig. Hetty nodded graciously to the three mourners as they left the chapel. Heads decorously bowed, expressions solemn, the senior and junior partners and the accountant of the Wainthropp Detective Agency took their places before the coffin, Hetty first. As she drew level with the late Mr Satterthwaite's face, Hetty stopped and peered at it, then swayed as if overcome by grief, holding one hand out to Robert for support.

Robert took her arm and led her towards the exit. 'Just a momentary weakness,' Hetty said to Mr Gabriel.

Robert said, 'You shouldn't have come, Mother. You're too sensitive.'

'After so many years I had to pay my respects. Don't worry about me. I'll be all right now.' She spoke directly to Mr Gabriel. 'I must congratulate you. You've done a wonderful job. I've never seen him looking better.'

Under cover of this distraction, Geoff put both hands on the late Mr Satterthwaite's eyelids, and pressed down. Then he joined his two fellow-mourners in Reception.

'Well?'

'Glass.'

* * *

Two police cars turned in at the main gate of the crematorium. The first contained DCI Adams with a WPC as driver and Hetty and Geoff in the back, the second three uniformed Police Constables and a Sergeant. A hearse was drawn up outside the main building with the mourners' cars parked close by. The police cars stopped by the hearse. The DCI, WPC, Hetty, Geoff and one Constable from the second car entered the building by the main door: the rest of the Sergeant's detachment ran round to the back. One carried a small toolbag.

The cremation service was already in progress and nearing its close, conducted by a young clergyman who had done three cremations already that day and was just getting into his stride. The coffin rested on its rollers, ready to be borne behind the curtain. The widow in a large black hat sat in the front row, with family on both sides of her. Mere friends sat a couple of rows behind and acquaintances were at the back, along with a few OAPs who made a hobby of attending these services, partly for the warm and partly in the hope of a bit of excitement. This time they were in luck.

The DCI, Hetty and Geoff went up the centre aisle as reverently as they could, bearing in mind the urgency of their mission. The Police Constable remained at the door. Mr Gabriel stood by the curtain like Cerberus guarding the entrance to the next world, with Ernesto as a young pup by his side. The clergyman had reached his peroration. 'In certain expectation of eternal bliss in the life hereafter,' he said, nodding at Mr Gabriel, who pressed a button set in the wall. The coffin began to move.

There was taped music from a hidden source – *We'll Meet Again*, apparently one of the late Mr Satterthwaite's favourites. Suddenly, Ernesto saw Hetty and Geoff coming up the aisle; he whispered urgently to Mr Gabriel, who quickly pressed the button again, twice this time. The foot of the coffin had reached the curtain in its dignified progress towards the flames which would destroy any evidence it might contain, and was now suddenly jerked forward as if pulled from the other side. The music made a brief attempt to keep up, then droned to a stop.

DCI Adams had reached the front of the chapel and spoke to the congregation. 'We're very sorry to cause a disturbance, ladies and gentlemen. Please don't be upset. Everything's under control.' Ernesto sprinted to the door, but was stopped and held there by the Constable whose task it was to do just that. The DCI said quietly to Hetty, 'I think your friend Ernesto may be ready to talk.'

'You'll find he speaks excellent English.'

The DCI indicated the widow to the WPC, who went to her. She would be conducting Mrs Satterthwaite to the back of the premises, so that she could be sure that no hanky-panky was being done to her husband on his way to Eternal Rest. The DCI asked Hetty whether she and Geoff would like to come round the back, and Hetty replied, 'Try and stop us.' Mr Gabriel had already made an inconspicuous exit in that direction through a side door, leaving the young clergyman to cope on his own.

'Perhaps we should all remain where we are in silent prayer for a while,' he said, so the congregation, none of whom had the slightest intention of leaving, remained where they were, but without being particularly silent.

In the back of the main building, behind the curtain where the furnaces were, the coffin of the late Mr Satterthwaite lay on a table. The police detachment had unscrewed the lid, and a Constable now lifted it, watched dismally by Mr Gabriel and his men. The Sergeant was pulling on a pair of rubber gloves. The DCI, Hetty and Geoff came briskly from the chapel, followed more decorously by the WPC with Mrs Satterthwaite.

'Sergeant!'

The Sergeant went to the top of the coffin. His gloved hands moved downwards to the face of the corpse while

Mrs Satterthwaite's hands moved upwards in horror to her own face. The gloved hands made two convulsive movements in the sockets of the corpse's eyes. One of the Police Constables, a family man himself, went white and turned away. The Sergeant brought the eyes he had taken from the corpse to the DCI. Both were of glass. The DCI spoke to the widow. 'Did the late Mr Satterthwaite have two glass eyes, madam, are you able to say?'

Mr Gabriel said, 'You're fools – all fools. You don't understand! It's a public service we've been doing here. There's a need for spare-part surgery . . . ' and he was taken away to join Ernesto on his way to the cells.

Geoff said to Hetty, 'There's something I want to show you.'

The mourners had gone, still buzzing in talk: it had been the cremation of the century for the Old Age Pensioners. Mrs Satterthwaite had gone. The police had gone and taken the baddies with them. The DCI would send a car back for the partners of the Wainthropp Detective Agency, who were content to wait for it.

Geoff had led Hetty along the gravelled paths, past lawns and flowerbeds, past the dusty laurels to the back of the vandalised Public Convenience. They stood together, looking at Ruby's wall, Geoff proud and proprietorial, Hetty marvelling at the colours and the curvyness.

'Lovely work!' said Hetty. 'Lovely work!'

Widdershins

The village was in a valley, sleepy, placid, self-contained, isolated from its neighbours and liable to be cut off altogether in the ice and snow of winter. Sheep grazed on the hillsides above it and there were occasional pockets of woodland, some left over from the forests of long ago, some newly planted as tax breaks for wealthy Southerners.

April. Bees hopped from flower to flower. The snowdrops were over, but there were daffodils and tulips in all the village gardens. Traditional stone houses, 300 years old some of them, made up the centre of the village, with a little red-brick infill and modern council houses round the edges. Marian Horner, unpaid secretary to the Parish Council, rode her bicycle along the village street on her way to the church. There was a cat sitting in the doorway of the butcher's shop. She clicked her tongue in disapproval and cycled on. Cat hairs in the mince, she wouldn't wonder, but it was hardly her business.

Alan, the butcher's assistant, slapped a piece of stewing steak down on the marble counter. He was serving Tracey, a young mother from the council houses, who was wearing tight white shorts on this sunny day. His gaze moved upwards from her thighs, over the shorts and a patch of exposed midriff, up over breasts which reached out proudly from beneath shirt and bra, up again to her face, thoughtfully regarding the raw meat. 'Anything else?' he asked.

'Kidneys. None of your frozen. I like the juice.' Beside her blood dripped from a dead hare, watched by Tracey's little girl, Samantha, and by the cat, which moved from the door to dip its tongue into the little puddle of blood which had formed in the sawdust.

'Shooh!' Alan said. 'Scat! Get on out of it!' and the cat walked disdainfully out of the shop and up the street towards the church in the direction taken by Miss Horner.

From the assembly room of the local primary school came the voices of children singing *All Things Bright and Beautiful*. Outside in the playground, Hannah, Grace and Lilian, fifteen-year-olds too old for the primary, but bunking off from the Comprehensive, turned like dervishes in a trance, spinning widdershins and accompanying the movement by a monotonous wordless humming.

Marian left her cycle at the gate and walked through the neglected churchyard among long grass, broken crosses and monuments. A marble cherub had one wing missing and rusty stains ran like blood down the gravestones. She went on into the church and found the cat already there, ensconced on a hassock.

Hannah broke away from her friends in the playground and went on up the street. She passed the village shop, already preparing for summer trippers, with pots of cheap alpines, tomato plants and marigolds and postcards in a rack. Mr Lister, who had come north from Redditch with his wife to buy and run this failing business, brought from inside six corn dollies which he hung up on the postcard rack with a sign reading GENUINE COUNTRY CRAFTS ONLY *£2.50*. He gave Hannah a little nod and a sketch of a smile, both returned, and Hannah walked on without speaking.

The church door was opened from the outside, and Lottie entered. She was an OAP, one who took very little care of herself, perhaps because she was poor. She looked around the church – at the flowers in a milk bottle, the window which had been broken and mended with card-board, the sign on the pulpit, WARNING – PULPIT UNSAFE, and Miss Horner kneeling in a front pew.

Marian turned and saw Lottie, who dropped a curtsey. 'I just thought I'd come in.'

'Of course, my dear. That's what the church is for. Would you like a biscuit?' Lottie took the biscuit offered, and attempted not to make crumbs.

Just outside the village were two small cottages next to each other. Lottie lived in one, her neighbour, Albert, in the other. Hannah walked up the path to Albert's front door, knocked and opened it all in one moment.

In the centre of the room there was a wooden chair, which had been kicked over. Suspended above it were two football boots, stockings with shin-pads and above them Albert's bare knees, his whole body swinging gently from side to side.

Hannah screamed.

'He'd never do that.' Robert had brought Hetty her breakfast in bed as he often did. He sat on the side of the bed, reading a letter which had arrived by that morning's post. He took off his spectacles and put down the letter. 'There's been a mistake made.'

'Glasses!' Hetty held out her hand for the letter and spectacles and was given both. She began to read.

Robert said, 'He was never a quitter. Not Uncle Albert. There was no Substitution Bench in his day. He'd play on to the end. He were my childhood hero – my role model long before they thought up the term.'

'Readsby?'

'It's a village not far from Ackersley. Him and Aunt Em

retired there. Then she died and he was on his own.'

'That's only thirty miles away. It's no distance, but we've never been to see him.'

'No.'

'You've hardly ever spoke of him.'

'If you've a childhood hero, woman, you want him to go on being a childhood hero. Stands to reason, does that. You don't expect him to grow old.'

'We all grow old, Robert.' He could not meet her gaze. 'Take the tray. Sit by me.' He moved the tray and sat closer to her. She took his hand. 'You've not called me "woman" since the day they made you take your voluntary redundancy.'

Surprising both of them, he began to cry. She put her arms around him. 'Daft bugger!'

'You can't be expected to understand. About men's feelings.'

'I know. I know.'

'I looked up to him.'

'The letter says there was an inquest. They brought it in suicide.'

They must have got it wrong. He'd never do that. You call yourself a detective. You must investigate.' He was over his tears. 'I won't rest till I know the truth.'

Well, the Wainthropp Detective Agency had no other cases under investigation and no prospect of any. Hetty said, 'Did he, do you suppose, leave anything we could use for expenses?' Downstairs the front doorbell rang.

It was Geoff. He stood there on the doorstep clutching a bulky old Gladstone bag and a small, even older teddy bear. Around him was an assortment of parcels and carrier bags. 'I've been chucked out. I'm homeless.'

Robert said, 'I thought you'd been scrounging jumble.'

They took him into the kitchen, fed him on buttered toast, and questioned him.

'Have you stolen something?' It seemed unlikely, but

she was bound to remember the incident of the collecting box for Children in Need.

'Nothing.'

'Broken anything?'

'Not even wind, Mrs Wainthropp.'

Robert said, 'Never mind what he didn't do. What did you do?'

'Nothing. You were right first time. It was what I wouldn't do.'

'Which was?'

'The landlady. She was after me body.'

Both of them stared at him. There was a long silence. Finally Hetty said, 'Well, you can't go back.'

'He can't stay here.'

'Of course he can stay.'

'I thought . . . just for a bit . . .'

'He's exactly what we need.'

'No, he's not.'

'. . . till I sort meself out.'

'You and I, Robert, are going on a trip, if you remember, to investigate the death of Uncle Albert. We'll need someone to look after the house while we're away.'

This was a new thought to Robert. 'Oh! Right! You're right.'

Geoff said to Hetty, 'Wouldn't you rather me come with you? I am your assistant. I could leave me bits and pieces here under the stairs.'

'He was Robert's uncle.'

And so it was arranged.

Robert and Hetty took the bus to Ackersley and were driven out to Readsby in a Rover by the solicitor handling Uncle Albert's estate. They took with them a large suitcase and a carrier bag full of food, and were given the keys of the cottage by the solicitor. Uncle Albert's daughter in New Zealand was only too glad for them to stay. Houses like to be lived in, and can more easily be sold if they have been warmed up by occupancy.

'Apparently, Mr Wainthropp, you were the favourite nephew. She says her father often spoke of you as a gradely lad. But you lost touch, I gather.' Robert gave a moan, and turned away, leaving the solicitor in mid-air, but he continued his remarks to Hetty. 'His daughter blames herself for the old man's suicide, but she's no cause. She asked him to come and live with them when his wife died, but he wouldn't leave the village.'

'He was happy here?'

'He was used to it. But you and I, Mrs Wainthropp, we know how it is. The old resist change. Then they get lonely and it's easy to despair.'

'No, it's not. I don't hold with despair in young or old. I've no time for it at all. Anyway, he wasn't old. Seventy-six, that's no age at all.'

Robert was keening softly and moving in a swaying motion towards the cottage. The solicitor looked after him, worried at this odd behaviour, then coming to the conclusion that there was nothing he could or should do about it, he got back into the Rover and drove away. Hetty decided that she had better get a grip on her husband. Grief was grief and all very well in its place, but they had not come to Readsby to give way to it in public. There were still the suitcase and the bag of food set down beside her on the path. She picked them up and followed Robert to the door. 'Did you forget something heavy?'

The key to the front door was large, the cottage itself on the small side. It consisted of two up, two down: the two up were bedroom and bathroom, the two down a kitchen and living room with an extra WC added at the back in case Uncle Albert were taken short.

'Now remember,' Hetty said. 'We're relations come to mind the house. Nobody must know I'm a detective.'

'I'll take the suitcase up.'

He began to go upstairs with the case, but was stopped by a noise from the kitchen. Somebody had opened the back door. 'Hah!' Hetty went swiftly to the kitchen door and opened it.

A very old lady, not too clean, was disclosed. She was wearing an overcoat over her nightie, with her feet jammed into Wellington boots. 'Are you taking possession?'

Hetty said, 'Have I had the pleasure?'

'I have to know. Name. Number of persons. Relationship to the deceased.'

Hetty said, 'You go on upstairs, Robert. This lady must be from the Census Office. I'll talk to her in the kitchen.' She picked up the bag of food and took it in with her, putting it down on the kitchen table. The old lady watched her closely. Hetty was reminded of a hedgesparrow with a broken wing which she had adopted one winter and fed at the back door with kitchen scraps and grated cheese. 'Now,' she said. 'Who are you?'

'Have you got biscuits in that bag?'

'That's for me to know and you to wait till they're offered.'

'Or a slice of bread and cheese?'

'I may lose my patience. Who are you?'

'You're not asking the right way. Ask me name and I'll tell you.'

'What's your name?'

'Lottie Battersby. Where do you live? Bell Cottage, Badger Lane, Readsby.' That was next door. 'What day is it? Wednesday. Who's the Queen of England? Elizabeth. The second. Did I get it right?'

These questions had a familiar ring to Hetty, but she could not quite place them. She took the electric kettle from the dresser to the sink and filled it. 'Yes. Every one,' she said.

'Who's the Prime Minister? Don't care, never did. When's your birthday? August. How old are you?' She stood there, struggling to remember, and failed.

'There's biscuits in the bag. Is the electricity connected, do you happen to know?' This was a question outside Lottie's range and it clearly frightened her. 'Never mind.' Hetty plugged in the kettle. 'Were you a close friend of Uncle Albert's?'

'We shared a lilac bush.'

'Why did he hang himself?'

Lottie shook her head. 'I've got the back-door key. I can come and go as I like. We should help each other in this world.'

Which was probably as far as they were going to get for the time being. So they had tea, and Lottie finished all the biscuits, a small wholemeal loaf and a large piece of Wensleydale cheese which was most of what they had brought for lunch.

On the whitewashed walls of the bedroom upstairs there were photographs of football teams from the period during which Uncle Albert had played as a professional, 1937–9 and 1946–53, including one in particular of the presentation by King George VI of the FA Cup and medals to the winning team in 1948. Robert had found a cupboard full of Uncle Albert's football memorabilia and was making piles on top of the double bed. He seemed almost uninterested in the news that the old lady from next door had eaten nearly all the food.

'Said she comes and goes when she pleases. I said she'd better come as we please from now on, but I'm not sure she took it in.' Hetty started moving the piles of memorabilia to make room. 'Wasn't there a bed under this lot when you started?'

'Don't!' He was certainly in a funny mood. She had never known Robert so up and down. 'You've got his 1949 jock-strap there.'

'Was that a good year for them? Is this one worth Air Miles or something?'

She put it down and moved some shin-pads. Robert closed his eyes and spoke through clenched teeth. 'Shin-pads! His blood, shed at Wembley, is on the underside of the one you are holding.'

'Robert, am I permitted to sit down or not? Are we going to sleep in this bed tonight?'

'You don't understand. Uncle Albert left me his football memorabilia. It's a sacred trust, a national heritage. The bed will be free by tonight.'

'If there's any blankets. All the tea towels downstairs are torn to shreds and the rugs are held together by string.'

It was odd. Once again there were things that didn't add up. Uncle Albert had gone straight from school into First-Division Football at seventeen. The war had caught him, as it caught so many, but he had survived Norway and North Africa with never a scratch, and come back to the game in 1946 with his great days all before him. Yet all around was evidence of dire poverty.

Robert's explanation seemed lame to Hetty. 'Back in them days footballers didn't make big money like they do now. Top wage was twenty pound a week, and you'd no share of the transfer fees. And he'd only seven years to make it before his knee went.'

'Are you telling me they cast him aside like a soiled glove?'

They hadn't. Uncle Albert and Aunt Em had quite enough after his Benefit Season to buy the cottage and raise a daughter, whom they later helped through university. And there were local employers only too proud to have the great Albert Bradshaw working for them. So he would have had his savings and a retirement pension, yet there was nothing to leave but his football memorabilia and the cottage itself.

They went into the living room. Robert looked at the bookcase while Hetty stared out of the window.

'Every one a classic.'

'There's a girl been hanging about outside ever since we got here.' The girl was turning slowly in a circle in the open street, her eyes closed. 'She's turning the wrong way.'

Another oddity but probably unconnected. Hetty moved away from the window to examine the room and its furniture. There should be a clue somewhere. Robert was still working his way through the shelf of football books.

'Those were the great days. Ginger Richardson, *My Story*.'

'No ornaments.' She ran a finger along the mantelpiece. 'Someone's been dusting.'

'Four goals in five minutes. West Bromwich versus West Ham, November 1931.'

'Everything's so rundown. There's scorch-marks all over this rug where coals have fell out of the fire.'

'This one's a first edition. Eddie Hapgood, *Football Ambassador*. I suppose these'll all come to me. I must try to be worthy. Tom Finney. That's funny.'

'Tom Finney? Never made *me* laugh.'

'No, there's something here among the football books.' He had picked out a paperback and was looking at it. 'Witches or summat.'

'Show me.' He handed her the paperback which had a garish cover of old women in pointed hats – *The Witches of Readsby*. As he did so, a page dropped out, and he stooped to pick it up. 'Must have been loose.' He gave the page to Hetty.

It was a piece of red cartridge paper. Covering the edges all the way round were tiny drawings of witches on broomsticks and in the centre a black Satanic mask with horns.

'That's not a page dropped out. Somebody drew this and put it in. Witches and Satan in the middle. Was your Uncle Albert artistic?'

'No, he used to take round the plate in church.'

Hetty put one hand to her forehead and closed her eyes. 'That's very interesting. I can feel the little grey cells beginning to stir.'

But there was only one question of importance preying on Robert's mind now. 'If Loopy Lizzie next door ate all the food, what have we got for supper?'

In the village shop, Mr Lister stood on a portable step-ladder and dusted empty shelves while his wife brooded behind the counter. The shop, where once long ago cheese had been cut and bacon sliced to order before being wrapped in greaseproof paper, was now a super-market with five baskets of elderly vegetables for customers to weigh by themselves, and almost everything else wrapped in clingfilm. Two villagers, who had watched Hetty enter and decided to investigate the newcomer, stood at the Cold Cabinet picking up packets of Philadelphia Cream Cheese and putting them down again, and at a rack near the door containing videos for hire, Tracey browsed like a questing beast.

There was no bread. Hetty spoke her mind to the man on the ladder.

'Nothing? No wholemeal, wheatmeal, rye or harvest grain? No cobs, baps, tea-cakes or bridge rolls, nothing starch-reduced or gluten-free, no pitta or nan? Not even white sliced with added cellulose?'

'All bread has to be ordered.' The man had a strong Brummy accent. Hetty's hackles bristled.

'You're telling me nobody in Readsby buys on a whim? You don't understand Lancashire folk. You're a for-eigner, aren't you?'

'Redditch. It's hardly Acapulco.'

'What kind of a shop has corn dollies hanging outside and none of the staff of life within?'

'Corn dollies do not go stale, madam; they do not go

off. They are made on the premises by my wife and the profit margin is enormous.'

'But you never sell any.'

'That is their only disadvantage.'

It was clear to Mr Lister that this woman was unfamiliar with the problems of micro-economics in a consumer-led society. It was clear to Hetty that, even if she won the argument, she had lost the war; they had no bread and that was that. 'How often do the buses run to town?'

One of the pretend-customers threw back her head and gave a bark of laughter. Mr Lister said, 'The next is Tuesday.'

'Ask a silly question . . .' Hetty began to leave the shop.

'There's hand-raised pork pies at the butcher.'

But Hetty had already gone. Mrs Lister said, 'I've seen that face before somewhere. Local paper, *Evening Record*, not long after we got here.'

Tracey had been muddling up the videos in the revolving rack. Mr Lister said, 'Please don't put Mary Poppins among the Horror videos, Tracey. We like to keep them separate.'

He returned Mary Poppins to her proper place, exposing to the gaze of anyone interested the video below which Tracey had covered up. On the front was an enormous picture of a Satanic mask, very like the one on the sheet of red cartridge paper which had fallen out of *The Witches of Readsby*.

Mrs Lister said, 'There was a photo. What was it about, what was the connection? It'll come to me. I never forget a face.'

The day went from bad to worse. Jacob's Cream Crackers with bacon from the butcher does not constitute a supper. Robert and Hetty went to bed early in Uncle Albert's room.

They sat side by side propped up in the double bed, Robert working his way through the newspaper cuttings pasted into one of Uncle Albert's scrapbooks, Hetty deep in thought.

'Everything's running down; you've only to look at the church. The vicar's shared between five parishes.'

'Aunt Em made these scrapbooks. Pasted in every match. His whole career.'

'There's a smell of death in the village.'

'You what?'

'The smell of death, Robert.'

'Something dead? A rat, is it, under the floorboards?'

'That's right. A rat.'

An owl hooted under a gibbous moon, and under that same moon, Mr and Mrs Lister made their way to a patch of woodland. There in a glade in the centre of the copse they found Hannah, standing very still, her back against a tree. They took no notice of her or she of them.

Mr Lister said, 'This'll do. Circle here. Flaming torches and spikes; we don't want them too close to the trees. What are we going to use for a sacrificial stone?'

'There's a stone sink in the vicarage garden. It's full of alpines but we can take them out.'

'We'll need a wheelbarrow.'

Hannah said, 'The cat ran away.'

'Well, it would.' Mrs Lister clicked her fingers. 'That woman who came into the shop! She's a private detective – some Senior Citizen set herself up to ply for hire. They did an interview. "Supergran Sleuth", they called her. I knew it'd come to me.'

Uncle Albert had no telephone. Hetty had to use the public box outside the sub-Post Office next morning to telephone Geoff.

'There's no bus till Tuesday.' There was a sound like a

colony of beavers eating their way through a Canadian forest. 'What's that noise?'

At the Wainthropp residence the smoke alarm had gone off in the kitchen. 'Noise? What noise? Isn't it your end?' Geoff said. He turned and saw black smoke billowing from the kitchen into the hall. 'I think my toast is nearly ready, Mrs Wainthropp. I'm going to have to phone you back.'

He put down the phone and went rapidly back towards the kitchen. The front doorbell rang and kept on ringing. Caught at the kitchen door, Geoff dithered. Burning toast or someone at the door, which was the most urgent? Meanwhile both the smoke alarm and the front doorbell sent out their conflicting messages.

There would be no saving the toast. He had better deal with the visitor. He opened the front door. A woman with a suitcase was standing outside; she appeared to be in tears. 'Oh! . . . Hello, Mum,' Geoff said.

The smoke from the kitchen was blacker, the smoke alarm louder. 'I'll be back,' he said, closed the front door in his mother's face and dashed off into the kitchen to deal with the toast. One disaster at a time.

Meanwhile Hetty was talking into a dead telephone. 'Geoffrey? . . . Geoffrey? You can't ring me back. I told you; it's a phone-box.'

But Geoffrey had already returned to the front door. His mother still stood there patiently with her suitcase. 'You can't stay here,' he said.

'I don't want to stay here. I want you to come home.'

'I've left home. I'm on me own now. I'm in responsible employment of public importance.'

'You're still my boy. Come home, Geoffrey.' She began to cry again. 'Since your dad left I can't live alone. It's wrong to force me.'

Geoff was looking past her. The curtains of the house opposite twitched. It seemed to him that all the way down the road curtains were twitching like a Mexican Wave. 'You'd better come in,' he said.

Hetty put down the phone and left the box. Robert was outside.

'How's he getting on?'

'Like a house on fire.' She looked at her unhappy husband. Grief for Uncle Albert seemed to come and go in varying degrees of intensity. It was bad this morning. Hetty did not understand why there should be such sorrow for an uncle he had not seen for over thirty years, but this was not a moment for bossiness. Her tone was gentle. 'There must be some kind of taxi. You could make a bolt for civilisation, get us some proper food. It's better for me to hang on here and ask questions anyway.' He shook his head. He did not want to leave her or the cottage. 'Well, we'll go together and have a word with Mr Plod before he sets off in his Panda.'

So they went to interview the village policeman and found him in shirtsleeves, cleaning his shoes at the kitchen table, the breakfast washing-up still in the sink, children's toys littering the floor, a wisp of cotton wool still staunching the blood on his chin while his wife sponged dog hairs from the jacket of his uniform.

'Aspects of this case puzzle me,' Hetty said. 'Why football gear?'

'He was going to kill himself, Mrs Wainthropp. He put on the clothes he was happiest in long ago.'

Robert was taking no part in the interview. Well, no worry in that; he was not trained to the work. But he was standing by the kitchen door, looking out over the back garden with unseeing eyes, and humming tunelessly to himself. The policeman's wife had noticed already.

'There was a post mortem, I suppose.'

'Always is.'

'Was he suffering from any terminal diseases, did they find out – cancer and such?' Perhaps she was beginning to sound too much like a detective. She remembered her cover story. 'I speak as family.'

The policeman's wife said, 'Dog hairs! I don't know where you pick them up. They're murder to get rid of.'

'No terminal diseases of any kind. For a man of his age he was in excellent health.'

Robert began to recite football scores quietly to himself. 'Accrington Stanley four, Burnley two. Crystal Palace nil, Blackpool six.'

'And he didn't leave a note?'

'There was no note found.'

'You don't think that's strange?'

'The reasons people have for killing themselves are their own business. They're not a proper subject for police enquiry.'

'Darlington two, Manchester City three. Manchester United two, Bolton one.'

'Is Mr Wainthropp all right?'

'It's called grieving, Constable. We all have our own ways of doing it.'

The policeman's wife grunted, opened the door of the washing-machine and began to pile in clothing.

Soon the machine was going full blast. It did not seem to disturb Robert, who was staring up at the ceiling, his eyes closed and tears on his cheeks.

It did worry Hetty, who was worried enough already about the emotional condition of her husband. 'Could he have been dead already, and hung up there to be found?' Her control cracked and she shouted: 'Turn that thing off!'

They were all staring at her. Even Robert had lowered his chin and opened his eyes. Constable Pearce gestured to his wife who turned the machine off. 'I'm sorry,' Hetty said. 'I'm not at my best solving murders when someone's trying to launch their biological stains into orbit.'

'The medical evidence was clear. The drop killed him.

He took his life while the balance of his mind was disturbed.'

'Hah!'

'Nobody's mind is perfectly balanced all the time. And elderly people . . .'

'Do what?' Her anger was growing. 'Become forgetful? Selfish? Easily frightened? Revert to childhood? Spill food? Don't wash? It doesn't add up to insanity. Life's too good to throw away, particularly if you've managed seventy-six years on this earth already. You've got a nice little garden out the back. You've been working on it, haven't you? So did he. He shared a lilac bush with his next-door neighbour. That's what you do with life. Use it. Enjoy it. Love it. It's spitting in the face of God to chuck in the towel before full-time.'

'Plymouth Orient . . .' Robert's voice was small and sad. 'Can't remember.'

'We won't keep you,' Hetty said to the Constable. 'I can see you want to get on duty, let alone the laundry. Come on, Robert.' He followed her obediently to the door where she turned back, like Columbo, to deliver a last clinching question. 'We found a book in Mr Bradshaw's cottage –*The Witches of Readsby* – that's this village. Have you got witches here?'

The policeman's wife said, 'She makes it sound like mice.'

'There was witches all over Lancashire in the old days,' said Constable Pearce. 'All those old women hanged at Pendle in sixteen something.'

'Exactly!' Hetty said. 'Hanged.'

'But nowadays there's just not the interest.'

'Were you born here, Constable?'

'No, I'm from Blackburn. You're never sent for duty in your own area. My wife's local, though.'

His wife was local. The Witches of Readsby. Hetty left the cottage feeling that she had learned something but was not sure what. Constable Pearce looked at his wife and shrugged: the Wainthropp woman was clearly an oddball. Mrs Pearce smiled.

There was a cycle propped against the wall of Lottie's cottage. A lady's bike. Hetty sent Robert on indoors. She had decided that she would like to know who visited Uncle Albert's next-door neighbour and why, but that she would manage better without a running commentary of football scores.

The visitor was Miss Horner, who had already made herself at home as seemed to be her custom. She made Mrs Wainthropp welcome and dispensed mugs of instant coffee all round from a jar she had brought with her, while Lottie sat bolt upright in an armchair, her arms on its arms, concentrating on being a good girl who sits up straight and listens to what is said to her.

'And you're dear old Albert's . . . niece, is it?'

'In-law. He was my husband's uncle.'

A drop of water hit Lottie's hand. Neither of the visitors noticed. Lottie looked upwards. There was a damp patch on the ceiling. Appalled, Lottie looked down at the drop of water on the back of her hand. Another drop joined it.

'Such a sad unnecessary loss. I blame myself, Mrs Wainthropp. I should have known. I come in most days to see the old dears – that's what I always call them – my old dears.'

A third drop joined the other two. Lottie put out the dripped-on hand to the table beside her, lifted her empty mug, moved it to the arm of the chair to catch the next drip and held it there.

'It's up to the village community to care for those in need. Nobody else will do it. We hardly see the Social Services.'

'Was Uncle Albert in need? He had his pension.'

The fourth drop of water hit the bottom of the mug. To Lottie it sounded like an immense crystal earring falling into a lake. With her other hand she swiftly covered the mug. But it was too late. Miss Horner and the biscuit lady were staring at her. She gave a little yelp of fear and shrank down into the chair.

Miss Horner looked at the ceiling. The damp patch was larger and the water dripping faster. 'Upstairs! Quickly!' She left the room at a run, followed by Hetty.

Upstairs the bath was full and overflowing. Both taps had been left on. Miss Horner turned them off and pulled out the plug, then grabbed a towel and began to mop the floor. Hetty found a smaller towel and helped her. 'I'd rather you didn't mention this to anyone if you don't mind,' Miss Horner said.

'Does it happen often?'

'Not really. But the old dears get so frightened, you see.'

'What of?'

'The Cottage Hospital in Ackersley. The Old Folk's Home in Horton-le-Dale. Nobody ever comes back from either, or that's what they believe. So they struggle on.'

'Frightened of folk knowing they can't cope?'

'Taps left running, flooding the floor. Coals dropping out of the fire and setting the hearth-rug alight. Locking themselves out of their own homes. Some of them are a little absent-minded – Lottie especially so – but they're not senile. One covers for them as long as one can.'

The mopping-up done, they wrung out the towels in the bath. Hetty said, 'It's not a reason for suicide.'

'Indeed no.'

'And anyway Uncle Albert could cope.'

'Yes, he could.'

'You get about a bit in the village – visiting your old dears and such?'

'Oh, yes. The Parish Council, the Flower Show, the WVS. And I collect for charity. I'm quite a busybody.'

'Uncle Albert had a book. Witchcraft. You've never come across anything like that in Readsby?'

'Good gracious, no. It's hard enough to get them to come to church.'

Hetty returned to Uncle Albert's cottage to find Robert sitting on the bed. He was all crunched up, head down, body forward, elbows on his thighs, each hand clutching the opposite upper arm. It was a position she had seen before in old Mrs Hubbard ten doors down after her Sydney died and before she was taken to the hospital to be treated for depression.

'Any better?'

'Comes in gusts.'

'This can't go on.'

'Aye. I'd better go home, love. I'm no use to you here.'

'We'll both go. Witchcraft! I'm clutching at straws. He was an old man. He was lonely. He killed himself. End of story.'

Slowly Robert brought his head up, staring at her. It made Hetty uncomfortable. 'You can't give up,' he said.

'Childhood hero! You've never shown any interest in football.'

'I followed football regular before I met you.'

Hetty was outraged. 'You're not suggesting . . .'

'Hear me out, love. Nineteen forty-six to fifty-three – Uncle Albert's great days: I worshipped him. Nineteen forty-eight – Cup Tie at Wembley: ninety-nine thousand attendance and I were there in the best seats with Auntie Em and me brother, Frank. Then in fifty-four he did his leg in: it were never right after. Crystal Palace at home. They booed him. His own fans booed him. I'd gone to the match with me mates. I booed with the others.'

'He can't have known that.'

'I knew. I kept away after. He must have thought I was ashamed of him. I were ashamed of meself.'

She looked at him. The tears had dried on his cheeks. All this time he'd been keeping the secret. It had gone rotten inside him until Uncle Albert's death had brought it to a head. 'What do you want me to do?' she said.

'Put me mind at rest.' He got up from the bed. Hetty was glad to see that just being able to tell her had restored some of his backbone. He took the photograph of King George VI presenting the cup and medals and showed it to her. 'Here he is. Uncle Albert getting his medal with the rest. Eighteen-carat gold. And he let me hold it.' A sudden burst of emotion. 'They were heroes in them days.'

'Hang on.'

'You what?'

'Where's that medal now?' He stared at her, not understanding what she was on about. 'He kept everything. All the memorabilia – boots, jock-straps, shin-pads. Where's the gold medal?'

Robert was perplexed. Three thoughts followed each other. 'He must have sold it. But he never would. Unless he had to.'

'Why would he need money that badly?' She was turning the photograph over in her hand as she puzzled it out.

Something was tucked into the frame at the back. 'Got it!'

'What?'

'Pawn ticket.' She took it out and showed it to him.

Robert stretched out a hand, took the ticket from her, looked at it, felt it between his fingers. 'You'll go on with the case, then?'

'Just because there was no note found doesn't mean he didn't leave one.'

In the back room of the village shop Mr Lister was with Hannah, Lilian and Grace. He held in both hands a Satanic half-mask, black with gilded horns. 'You made this yourself?' Hannah nodded. Slowly he lifted the mask and fitted it over his face, then turned to the fly-specked mirror on the wall. 'It's very good, Hannah. It's really very good. And the garlands?'

'Lilian did them. She found some silk flowers half-price at the Co-op.'

'But there is ivy?'

Lilian said, 'Plenty. Interwoven with the silk. It was the stinkweed I couldn't find.'

'*Diplotaxis muralis*: it can be difficult. Luckily I have a source. What else? Blood I'll do myself. Cauldron – that's well in hand. Sacrificial knife – Alan's bringing his own from the butcher's. And the sacrifice?'

'It'll be there.'

'Goat?'

'From the Organic Dairy.'

Mr Lister said, 'I would like to have had a goat from Readsby, but needs must when the Devil drives.'

And they all began to laugh.

The elderly village taxi was at the door, its driver a gap-toothed middle-aged unshaven ruffian in a check cap called Fred. It would take Robert as far as Ackersley where he would look for the pawnshop which had issued the ticket for Uncle Albert's gold medal, redeem it and find out whether it was Albert Bradshaw himself who had pawned it. Then he would take the bus home.

He was carrying some of the football memorabilia in the carrier bag in which they had brought the food. The suitcase would remain with Hetty. 'I want Geoffrey here by tomorrow morning,' she said.

'There's no bus till Tuesday.'

'Tell him to borrow the scooter from that friend of his. If not, he can cycle. It's only thirty miles. They'd think nothing of that on the Tour de France.'

They walked together to the taxi, watched by Lottie from her window. 'You'll be in our own bed by tonight.'

'I've missed it.' He sat in the passenger seat next to the driver, his carrier bag on his lap. Hetty said to Fred, 'Will this taxi get as far as Ackersley, do you think, in its condition?'

'Always has,' said Fred. He started the engine. The noise was extraordinary. He shouted above it, 'Has to be a first time, though.' The taxi moved away in a series of shudders before it picked up speed and turned the corner. Hetty watched it go. Lottie let her net curtain fall back into position.

Robert looked for and found the three brass balls in Ackersley, but the manager of the pawnshop refused to part with the medal; the time for redemption had gone by. He could not remember who had brought it in and any record made at the time was confidential. So much for the pawn ticket.

Robert walked up the street to his own home thoughtful and still a little huffy about his treatment at Ackersley. The man had said he was a football aficionado, but in Robert's opinion he had been corrupted by the 18-carat gold. Geoff saw him coming from an upstairs window and was at the door to meet him.

'You can't come in, Mr Wainthropp, without I talk to you first.' He closed the front door behind him. 'We'd better go for a little walk, I think.'

So they went for a little walk and Geoff explained that he had lied about the landlady at Baden Powell Buildings being after his body. The reason for his hurried removal was that his mother had found out where he was living; she kept coming around, wouldn't leave, nagged on at him all the time to go back home. And now she had found him again. 'And this time, not to beat around the bush, to come straight out with it, to put it to you like just as it is, not making a meal of it, to tell the exact truth man to man as I know you would expect . . .' He took a gulp. Robert was glad Geoff was not making a meal of it. If he did, at this rate they would have to walk round the houses several times, and Robert had already done a fair bit of walking in Ackersley. 'This time she's moved in entirely,' Geoff said.

'With us?'

'She goes round the kitchen singing *There's No Place Like Home*.'

'Well, there isn't if it's your own. Will she be moving out again?'

'I thought maybe you'd have a word with her. I won't go back, Mr Wainthropp. Since me dad walked out, it's too heavy.'

Robert grunted. 'Well, I tell you what. You don't have to live with her but you ought to visit sometimes. If you never visit folk while they're alive, you only feel bad when they die.'

So Robert had a bit of a confab with Geoff's mum and explained that, with him back home already and his missus due as soon as she'd cleared up a hive of criminal activity over at Readsby, whither in any case Geoffrey himself would be going next morning to assist Hetty with her enquiries, it might be better if Mrs Shawcross were to return for the nonce to her own home where, from time to time, her son would visit her.

'Promise?'

'It's not up to me to promise. He's promised. It is a proper job, missus. The pay's not much at the moment, but there's prospects.'

Thus reassured, and with some reluctance and much looking back, Geoff's mother took herself off. She had managed to get through two bottles of Dubonnet in twenty-four hours. Robert did not know how he would be able to explain it to Hetty.

Meanwhile Hetty had spent the afternoon eating one of the butcher's hand-raised pork pies and reading *The Witches of Readsby*. She finished the last page, let the book fall, and looked up, blinking. The schoolgirl who had been spinning the wrong way was at the window. Hetty went over and opened it.

'You're a detective,' the girl said.

'How do you know that?'

'Everyone in the village knows by now.'

'You'd better come in.'

The girl's name was Hannah. It was she who had found Uncle Albert. 'We were doing a project at school.'

'What sort of project? We didn't have them in my day.'

'Social Studies. Care for an old person for a month and then write a dissertation. Stupid! You can't stop after a month.'

'No, you can't, though I expect some did. We learned our tables and the Kings and Queens of England. Probably did less damage.'

'I used to come round most days. Darn his socks, do a bit of shopping, talk about the old times. He'd talk, I'd listen.'

'Miss Horner came round most days too,' she said.

'We never overlapped. He didn't like her.' She noticed the book on the floor. 'You're reading my book.'

'There was a drawing in it. Satan.'

'I did that.'

'I thought it might be his. Something he'd left. Like a message.'

'He never left a note. They asked me. I'd have seen it.'

'Why did you give him a book about witches?'

'We were talking about it. He was interested. It's the Old Religion, isn't it? Never died out. Better than ours in some ways.'

'What ways?'

'Women in control.'

That night Hetty lay alone in Uncle Albert's double bed. She closed her eyes but could not sleep. Outside an owl hooted, the same owl, she supposed, as on the night before. 'Walpurgis Night!' she said aloud.

* * *

Day Three of the investigation. Geoff arrived at midday by bicycle, exhausted, carrying round his neck a bag of food out of which a long baguette projected dangerously over the handlebars. Hetty took no notice of his exhaustion, only of the food. 'We've a lot to do, Geoffrey.'

'I've done a lot already – cycled thirty-three miles mostly uphill with that French stick knocking a dent in me chin.'

'That's nothing to a lad of your age. Why didn't you borrow your friend's scooter?'

'It was in use. Brass-rubbing in the Cotswolds.'

'There's been times these past few days I could have killed for spring onions and a loaf of crusty bread. We'll have a bite to eat and then set off. I've watched two people cross that field with an old stone sink in a wheelbarrow. That has to mean something.'

They ate cold meatloaf sent by Robert with the baguette, butter, tomatoes and lettuce, radishes, a cucumber, Lancashire cheese, apples and bananas. Geoff was hungry from his long ride, Hetty from food deprivation: it was the most satisfying Case Conference the Agency had enjoyed for several weeks.

'There's something strange about this village. You know there were witches here?'

'There were witches all over Lancashire. Daft old women getting themselves hanged because of the neighbours' tittle-tattle.'

'But some of them confessed.'

'They all confessed. Put any innocent person in a police station for half an hour and you'll get a confession. Standard practice is that.'

'They confessed to congress with Satan. They had Sabbaths where they all met and carried on. They had familiar spirits, cats mostly. It's in this book, *The Witches of Readsby*.'

'Mrs Wainthropp, it's me you send to the Reference Library. I do the books.'

'Listen and you may learn something. It's beginning to add up. Small things. Corn dollies sold at the village shop. Girls in the street spin widdershins – that's anti-clockwise, the way witches spin. A cat that's everywhere, almost as if it was human, and they all take it for granted. The church neglected. Blood dripping from dead beasts in the butcher's shop. Pictures of Satan on red paper. I don't know where it's going. There's no doubt the old man committed suicide: we can't get away from that. But tonight is Walpurgis Night – that's one of the festivals; they're all in the book. Starts at midnight.'

The back door opened. Lottie stood in the doorway. She had remembered what she'd been told, did not enter, but waited for permission.

'You want to come in?' Lottie nodded. 'You saw the food arrive?' Another nod. 'All right.' Lottie moved to the table, her attention totally on the groceries. 'This is Lottie from next door. Cut her some bread please, Geoffrey. I'll pop over in a moment, Lottie, and make sure you've not left the bath running again.'

Lottie sat demurely at the table. 'Old ladies my age don't have baths unless there's someone standing by to fish us out.'

Something about this answer puzzled Hetty. Old ladies Lottie's age . . . but she dismissed it. If it was important it would surface later. Meanwhile she had other fish to fry.

'Who's the Queen of England?' said Lottie to Geoff.

They took Lottie, burping gently, back to her cottage and set off across the field the way the wheelbarrow had gone with the stone sink. They came to woodland and the glade in the centre of the copse in which a circle had been drawn in white paint, and within the circle a white pentagram with its joints touching the edge. The stone sink had been turned upside down and set up within one point of the pentagram, and behind it, fastened to a tree, was a wooden cross, also upside down.

Hetty looked closely at the white paint of the pentagram and touched it with one finger. It was wet.

Just outside the circle, a ladder had been fastened to another tree, giving access to a branch which projected over the circle. All obstructing twigs and leaves and side-shoots had been cut away from this branch.

'Looks like a hanging tree,' Geoff said. 'Shouldn't we go to the police?'

Hetty said, 'There are three reasons why not, Geoffrey. One is that Constable Pearce won't be back until this evening. Two is that, unless they actually hang somebody, there's still religious freedom in this country, and they're not committing a criminal offence. And three, I'm not sure his wife isn't one of them.' She took his arm and led him away from the circle. 'We'll be back here at midnight. We won't take any risks. We'll black our faces and hide in the undergrowth. And then we'll see what we'll see.'

Midnight. Clouds passed over the moon, leaving it clear. There was the sound of tuneless humming and the faces of the Satanic worshippers turned upwards, marking the moment. A fire blazed in the centre of the pentagram and cresset torches on stakes were set around the circle. On the sacrificial slab which had once been a stone sink containing alpines (and would be again), two iron candlesticks had been placed and candles were burning in them, turning it into an altar. Nearby, a black billygoat was tethered to a stake.

Seven handmaidens, three of whom were Hannah, Lilian and Grace, dressed in loose robes of a cinnamon colour with patterns of snakes in face-paint on their bare arms, were spinning widdershins. Two dirty half-naked children were stretched out near the fire, luxuriating in its heat. A plump middle-aged masked man wearing an executioner's leather mask and leather trousers with a red shirt open to the waist was pouring what looked like blood into the wooden bowl held by an old crone in a black cowl and bare arms. She drank the blood, spilling some on her chin, smearing it over her face, licking her fingers and laughing.

Hetty and Geoff were hiding in the bushes in the darkest clothes the suitcase had been able to provide, their faces blackened with burnt cork. Geoff shuddered. 'Where'd they get the blood?'

'Must have brought it with them.'

There were other old crones among the Satanic congregation, some drinking blood from bowls, some spinning clumsy widdershins around their broomsticks. Hetty could make out Mrs Lister and Mrs Pearce, the policeman's wife, among them. The men were fewer, their costumes less imaginatively improvised, being mainly variations on smocks and corduroy trousers, but they all wore half-masks and face-paint to disguise their identities. All kept up the wordless humming.

The voice of Mr Lister cut through the revelry. It seemed to be coming from a loud-hailer somewhere above the action. 'Do you hear the maid who steals the bread and hides behind the door? Some say the Devil is dead and buried in Cold Harbour.'

Geoff looked sideways at Hetty. What was the man on about? Hetty shrugged.

'Satan!' the voice cried through the loud-hailer, and those below took it up, 'Satan! Satan!' and turned to face the altar.

From the darkness beyond the circle came Alan, the butcher's assistant, naked but for a leather loincloth, sandals with wings and, over his face, the half-mask of Satan which Hannah had brought to the stock-room of the shop. He carried his butcher's knife held across his chest; his body had been oiled, and glistened in the firelight. He walked proudly to the altar and took his place behind it. All fell silent as Satan appeared.

'Welcome, my children,' said Alan. 'Feast and fornicate, but first I shall require due sacrifice. Let the Chosen Virgin come forth.'

Tracey, who was certainly not a virgin, appeared from the shadow of the trees. She was all in black – black cloak, black dress, black cowl pushed back to show her white face, and her black hair hanging free. With her she brought her little girl, in white dress and white shoes and socks and wearing a coronet of white silk roses. They moved slowly towards the altar, the worshippers falling back to give them space, until they stood before it, facing Alan.

The Chosen Virgin. A child. Hetty had read about such practices in the Sunday papers. She and Geoffrey would have to do something to stop it, but she did not know what.

'Do you give this child to me unconditionally?' Alan said.

'I do.'

'Has she been soothed with the juice of poppies?'

'She has.'

'Is she unsullied and unblemished, pure in thought, word and deed?'

'She is.'

'I may have to interfere,' Hetty whispered to Geoff.

'We can't. There's too many.'

'Garlands!' the loud-hailer said. 'Let the maids bring garlands.'

Led by Hannah, Grace and Lilian, the handmaidens of Satan brought garlands of silk flowers interwoven with ivy and stinkweed, which they placed on the altar and round the neck of the little girl, who at once began to weep. This worried Satan, who said to Tracey, 'She's not supposed to cry.'

Hetty said, 'We can't have this. It must be stopped.'

'How?'

'Run back to the village. Go straight to the policeman's house. I'll hold them somehow until he gets here.'

Geoff crawled backwards out of their hiding place and set off as quietly as he could. There was not much danger of discovery. All the villagers were intent on what was happening at the altar.

Satan spoke to the little girl who was still crying. 'It'll soon be over and it doesn't hurt at all.'

'All right!' said a commanding voice from a bush at the edge of the glade. 'That's enough.' Hetty stepped out of her shelter and advanced boldly into the circle. 'You can stop this. I won't have it.' They had all turned towards her. There could be no doubt about the quality of their attention. 'Freedom of worship, that's one thing. No objection to that. But you lot are going too far.'

All but Alan, Tracey and the Chosen Virgin began to move slowly towards her. The plump man in leather and two of those in corduroys slipped round behind to cut off her escape. Alan leapt on to the altar, holding out his knife. When he brought it down, she supposed, they would make their pounce. She would have to face them down.

'My advice to you would be to make yourselves scarce, quick as you can. The police have already been alerted, and are on their way.'

Very slowly the closest of the men in corduroy removed his half-mask. It was Constable Pearce.

The plump man in leather began to laugh; it was not a pleasant sound. All the others took it up. Satan was laughing, holding his knife towards her. Tracey was laughing. The handmaidens, the crones with their broomsticks and wooden bowls, all were laughing at Hetty Wainthropp.

Hetty discovered that she was very angry, and the anger drove out fear.

'Don't laugh at me! Don't dare laugh at me! A woman

of my age has to be taken seriously. I'm a fully-qualified private detective, well known in the West Lancs area and with an advert in the Yellow Pages. I've got connections.'

Constable Pearce smiled kindly and spoke gently. 'Of course you have, Mrs Wainthropp.' The effect was chilling.

Then the voice came again from above. 'All right! Cut it there!'

Mr Lister descended with difficulty from the Hanging Tree, his loud-hailer in one hand, his camcorder slung round his neck. A crone hurried to take the loud-hailer from him.

'Set up to go again, please, from Satan's entrance. I'll talk to her.' The Satanic worshippers bustled out re-setting props, Tracey removed the garlands from the Chosen Virgin, and Mr Lister spoke to Hetty. 'I don't care which comes first, madam, explanation or apology. Both are due.'

Hetty said, 'It's not up to me to explain myself. I'm not the one engaged in Satanic practices.'

'What you've blundered into is the making of a community video, *The Witches of Readsby*, in aid of Muscular Dystrophy. There have been no Satanic practices. No human being or animal has been or would be hurt. The goat will be returned to the Organic Dairy in the morning and the blood drunk from wooden bowls by the crazed acolytes of Satan is tomato juice from my own stock – liberally laced, in the case of Mrs Erdington, with vodka from a hunting flask.'

'The little girl was crying. She was terrified.'

'She was crying because the stinkweed in the garlands brings her out in a rash. Anti-histamine cream has, however, been provided.'

'Don't try to soft-soap me. I've talked to Hannah. She told me about the Old Religion.'

'She's an intelligent girl: she'll go far. She read up the whole subject and wrote most of the script.'

Slowly Hetty took in the fact that she had made a fool of herself in front of the whole village. 'You're telling me I've made a mistake?'

'We've put six weeks of preparation into this, and if it rains we've wasted Walpurgis Night. Now, if you wish to satisfy yourself, you're welcome to watch, but please don't interrupt again.'

'Thank you. I shan't bother. No offence intended.'

'None taken.'

Hetty began to go, then had a last thought. 'Why did you choose witches for your community video?'

'This village isn't famous for anything but witches.'

'Ready when you are, Mr de Mille,' said Satan from outside the circle. Mr Lister gave Satan a thumbs-up and returned to his tree.

It was a long time since Hetty had been so angry – with Hannah, with Constable Pearce, with the Listers, the whole sniggering village community, most of all with herself. She sat in an armchair in Uncle Albert's living room at one a.m. and brooded.

Geoff brought in two mugs of strong tea from the kitchen.

'Just set it down, please.'

He put her mug within easy reach and sat to watch her, his hands warming round his own mug. 'Jumping to conclusions!' she said.

'You always have jumped, Mrs Wainthropp.'

'I was supposed to be a grieving relative, not a detective, but I blundered about, cross-examining everything in sight. None of them was deceived. Laughing at me behind their hands! "You're welcome to watch," he said. Even Loony Lottie next door must have—'

Suddenly she remembered something. She had filed it away in her mind to surface later if it was important, and it *was* important, and it *had* surfaced. She sat there with her mouth open, struck dumb as she realised the significance of what she had remembered.

'Are you all right in yourself, Mrs Wainthropp?'

'Well, walk me over the wallflowers and I'll go up to our house!'

'You what?'

'Old ladies my age don't have baths unless there's someone standing by to fish us out. And those scorch-marks on the hearthrug. But Uncle Albert could cope, she said. A fool, a fool; I've been a fool. Don't agree with me – it's not polite. I suppose it's too late to go over and talk to Lottie?'

It was too late, of course, but Lottie came to breakfast in the morning. 'She does put it away,' Geoff said.

Lottie lifted a face sticky with buttered toast and nodded enthusiastically. Hetty said, 'When I came over to see you and Miss Horner was there . . . the day the bath ran over – you remember that?' Lottie was doubtful when it came to the exact reckoning up of days, but nodded again. 'Did Miss Horner go upstairs just before I arrived?'

'What day is it? Saturday?'

'Right. Saturday today. Thursday then. Did Miss Horner go upstairs?'

Lottie was wary. 'Who's the Queen of England?'

'I'll put it another way. Is Miss Horner always with you whenever anything bad happens? Water overflows? Cooker left on? Do things like that ever happen when she's not there?'

'Most days she comes to see us. Albert Bradshaw and me. Albert first, then me.'

'Albert first? Did she come the day he hanged himself?'

'Hannah found him. Darned his socks for him and all sorts.'

'I know who found him, Lottie. But did Miss Horner come to see you that day? And go in to see Albert first the way she usually did?'

Lottie was unhappy. 'Are you taking possession?'

Hetty decided to ask the big one. 'Did you give her money, Lottie?' Lottie put her hands in front of her face and began to wail. 'I thought so. How many other of her old dears in the village does Miss Horner visit most days? I'll need the names, Lottie.'

The cat was sitting on the ledge of the broken window of the church. Marian Horner, kneeling before the altar, heard the sound of the church door opening, rose, genuflected and turned to face Hetty, striding towards her.

'Eight of them!'

They met in the space between pulpit and lectern. 'Eight old dears, desperate to stay in their own homes, terrified of dying unnoticed, out of sight and out of mind in the Old Folk's Home. But you were their friend. Visited nearly every day. Protected them, taught them what they must always know to keep out of the funny farm – what day is it? where do you live? who's the Queen of England? And when water flooded the floor, or the bottoms burned out of pans, or coals set fire to the carpet, you were there to cover up. Except that these things didn't happen when you weren't there.'

'You're jumping to conclusions, Mrs Wainthropp.'

'Always have done. Its the grey cells working overtime. I'll jump on. You took money from your old dears, Miss Horner. Easy to do; everyone knew you collected for charity. You never took much; they couldn't afford much, but it all added up. And more from Uncle Albert because he had his pension. Then you went too far. His gold medal. He daren't accuse you openly. Too dangerous, he thought; nobody'd believe him, lost his marbles, away with him. So he dressed up in his football gear to remind folk that they owed him some respect, and he wrote a note and hanged himself. But you came along as you always did, took the note before anyone else found him, and went on to Lottie.'

'I came here. I came to pray. Lottie found me here.'

'You admit it?'

'Prove it.'

A long silence. Two strong-minded women measuring each other up. Then Hetty said, 'I don't have to prove it. This is a small village. There are no secrets.'

And left the church.

Robert had hung a model aeroplane from the ceiling of the spare bedroom. 'It's a Sopwith Camel.'

The room had been transformed into that of a tidy twelve-year-old. Robert had done the transforming using his memory of what the room had been like when it was Derek's, though Derek had not been tidy.

Hetty said, 'That plane's come from the attic. What's it doing in our spare room?'

'I thought it would interest Geoffrey.'

'It does,' said Geoff.

'I put it together for our Derek when he got his Swimming Certificate.'

Hetty said to Geoff, 'You can do the breast-stroke for half a mile, I take it?'

Robert said, 'She knows damn well what I mean is you're welcome to use this room till you get back on your feet.'

'Thank you, Mr Wainthropp.'

'When business picks up, we'll decide what's a fair rent.'

Geoff was looking at a photgraph hanging on the wall. It was of His Majesty King George VI presenting the cup and medals at Wembley in 1948.

The village taxi drew up outside Miss Horner's cottage and Miss Horner emerged carrying two heavy suitcases.

Fred, the driver, made no move to help her. She carried the suitcases to the taxi herself, put them in the boot herself and closed it, opened the rear door herself and got in. There was a 'For Sale' board outside the cottage, though nobody had yet come to view.

The taxi moved away down the village street. At every cottage door, at the door of the butcher's and the village shop, outside the primary school where the little ones were taught, the villagers stood in silence to watch her go.

Lottie stood at the gate of the churchyard with the other old dears. 'We has to stand together now,' she said. 'Help each other as much as we can. Who's the Queen of England?'

A High Profile

Robert was at the kitchen table doing the Agency's accounts. He had a lined pad of yellow paper, two pens (one red, one black), a calculator and a serious expression. Invoices were spread out all over the table with an overflow on the dresser.

It was bad. If they had to pay for office space instead of using their own house, telephone instead of using their own phone and a book-keeper instead of using Robert, they'd be bankrupt several times over. As matters were, the position was dicey. Three hundred pounds from the Italians gone, a hundred and fifty from Malcolm Stone's parents gone, the fifteen hundred from Sir Peter, way back when they started, gone, and nothing from the case of Uncle Albert, not even his gold medal. Lost dogs and budgies were usually on a payment by results basis, and the results so far had been poor.

Hetty said, 'It's no good asking me to cut Geoffrey's wages; he gets no more than pocket money as it is. We could try another advert in the *Record* – just a little one, well-crafted and in a good position. They'd want cash, I dare say.'

'They would. After last time, they would.'

'I won't give up, Robert.'

'I'm not asking you to give up.'

'We need a higher profile, that's what it is.'

The Elim Chapel was round the corner at the bottom of the Wainthropps' road. It was a building of great ugliness, identified as what it was by a board with a hellfire text outside. Inside were stackable plastic chairs, an old piano and a banner reading JESUS SAVES. Nothing to suggest idolatry.

It was so cold. Hetty wore her deerstalker and cape, bought on a whim from the Oxfam shop. It was a badge of her profession, but did not arouse the same confidence in clients as her more usual beret. Old Harry Jasper, in a thick dark suit, woollen mittens, boots and muffler was dusting a sandwich board with a feather duster. The board read PREPARE TO MEET THY GOD on one side and THE DAY OF JUDGEMENT IS AT HAND on the other.

After a while Mr Jasper realised that he was being watched and turned to face the intruder. 'I heard you were bad with your chest,' Hetty said. Mr Jasper was immediately taken by a fit of coughing, indicating that once again the Supergran Sleuth had hit the nail on the head. 'Best not to go out in all weathers, then. I'll borrow your sandwich board if I may. Short-term.'

So Hetty and Geoff set out to raise the Agency's profile locally, beginning with the market. Geoff walked ahead, ringing a hand-bell and improvising a spiel, with Hetty a little way behind wearing the sandwich board which now bore the same message on both sides:

WAINTHROPP DETECTIVE AGENCY
FREE CONSULTATION
MISSING PERSONS A SPECIALITY
DISCRETION GUARANTEED

and the phone number. It had been difficult to cram

everything on and keep the writing easy to read, but Hetty hoped they had managed it.

They stopped for rest and nourishment at the Hot Dog 'n' Hamburgers stall, and Geoff fetched two plastic cups of coffee and a hamburger squishy with ketchup for himself. 'You could have got me one of those.'

'Wouldn't be suitable, Mrs Wainthropp. You lack the freedom of movement for complicated eating. You'd get ketchup all down your chin. I'd take over from you, but my shoulders aren't wide enough. The straps'd keep slipping.'

There was a knocking on the back of the sandwich board just as Hetty was about to drink so that she spilled some of the coffee and blurred the 'W' on WAINTHROPP. She turned slowly, partly because her dignity was offended and partly because it is difficult to turn quickly in a sandwich board. The knocker was a woman in her fifties.

'I'm Hilda Savage,' the woman said. 'Are you free for a consultation?'

'I am. I'd be glad to get this board off for a while, to tell you the truth.'

Hilda had been shopping, had seen the board, and acted on impulse. 'I thought, if I don't do something now I never will. So I ran after you. I need to know, you see. How Michael is. If he's managing, if he's all right. Reg won't have him in the house, not any more.'

She was the wife of a dentist, and lived above the premises. She entertained Hetty and Geoff in her kitchen, wandering about as she spoke, making instant coffee and then forgetting it. Reg was the husband, Michael the son. She showed them Michael's graduation photograph, cap and gown in full colour, holding a scroll. 'Too smart for his own good, that one, they used to say. He had a wonderful brain.'

The sandwich board rested against the wall. Hetty made notes on the back of a shopping list she had found on the kitchen table. Michael was not Reg's son. Hilda had been three months pregnant by someone else when they married. They had not been able to have any children of their own, as it turned out, but Reg had never blamed her. He had been a true father to Michael. So proud of the success at school and university. 'You drive that boy too hard,' she'd say. 'Not a bit of it,' he'd reply. 'A bright boy needs encouragement.' and then . . .

'And then?'

'It's the label, you see. We never called it "schizophrenia". "Nervous breakdown" was the expression we used. But everyone knew and it was bad for the practice. What you're asking people to pay for bridgework these days, you've got to be like Caesar's wife.'

Geoff said, 'I hate dentists.'

Hetty gave back the framed photograph. 'Do you have anything more recent? Snapshot? Something smaller.'

'There's nothing recent. Michael changed, you see, with the illness. The first time he went to hospital, we thought they'd make him better. And he was, but not the same, not like himself; he'll never be that again. There's things about him you can't explain to people. Little things. Not getting out of bed in the mornings. Washing and getting dressed – he didn't see the necessity. "I'm not going anywhere," he'd say.'

Geoff said, 'It is a point of view.'

'Yes, it is, but Reg didn't understand it. It wasn't a happy atmosphere.'

'And then you moved away? Came here, started again.'

'Not at once.'

'Michael got sick again?'

'Right. And when he came out of hospital this time, Reg wouldn't allow him home. The Social Services found him a bedsitter but he'd come over to see me and . . . If he didn't want to leave you couldn't put him out into the street.'

'But Reg did?'

'Only the once. But it brought on . . . The symptoms got worse. Talking silly. Stopping people in the street. Wandering into places. He tried to walk through glass once: it was just a mistake, I think. And the canal. It was in the local paper. And Reg said, "He's beyond our help, Hilda. Not our responsibility. We do more harm than good." So we sold up and came here.'

'What happened to Michael's real father?'

'Hit by a train. It could have been an accident, but they said not. He was a gentleman, never put himself forward. Shy, like Michael in that way. We met at evening class. I was that taken with him, I made all the running. Reg never held him against me. I owe Reg a lot. But I keep thinking . . . wondering.' Hetty had never taken her eyes off the dentist's wife as she wandered, distracted about the kitchen, mostly avoiding those eyes. Now she turned and looked Hetty straight in the face, desperate for help. 'It's not wanting Michael back. I know I can't have him back. But I have to know he's all right. Do you see?'

Hetty stood. Geoff supposed that, now they had a job, she would no longer be wearing the sandwich board, and he would have to carry it. 'I'll do what I can. It'll cost, but not too much. You'll want a monthly report, I suppose?'

'You're very good.'

'I'm a professional. Just like Reg.'

Michael had hitched to the seaside. What with the wind and rain, people had not wished to stop for him, but a few had done so. He had ridden much of the way in the cab of a lorry. He had seen the Floral Clock and found his way to Sunnysands, where it was a rule that you must not track sand over the carpet. It had been dark. He had looked through the window, and been turned away. That was all right. His mother had not been there. He had spent the night under the pier.

'Oh no, it isn't!'

'Oh yes, it is!'

He stood at the end of the Crazy Golf, looking at the place where the Marionette Theatre used to be. It would be there again. If he concentrated, he could make it happen. Making things happen through concentration was different to what happened in spite of him, and which he did not like. He sat cross-legged on the wet paving and heard the distant sound of the children and their parents waiting for the show to begin. A faraway voice shouted, 'It's starting.'

The curtains were closed, but suddenly the head of Baron Hardup popped out from between them.

'What's the time, children?' And the children shouted, 'It's Playtime!'

Baron Hardup shook his head slowly from side to side. 'Oh no, it isn't.'

'Oh yes, it is,' Michael shouted, louder than any of the other children, and an elderly woman, walking her Sealyham in the rain, gave him an odd look.

'Your wish is my command,' Baron Hardup said. 'Let battle commence.'

Breakfast was over and Hetty was dressed for a journey. Her suitcase was by the door. She would only be away two days. She would ask Michael's social workers where they had found for him to live, take a look, talk to the neighbours, make sure he was not walking into any canals, and come straight back.

'You don't have to stay overnight.'

'There'll be contacts to interview. The Wainthropp Detective Agency doesn't skimp, Robert: we've a reputation to consider. And the B & B will be on expenses.'

'What about Geoff and me?'

'There's food in the freezer and Geoffrey can cook.'

'Only hot-pot.'

'There's nourishment in hot-pot. If you were on a desert island you'd be glad of it.'

Geoff said, 'I should come with you.'

'You'll be at the Public Library. I wasn't going to display ignorance in front of a dentist's wife, but we know damn all about this schizophrenia. So find out all there is to know, and if I've a spare 10p, I'll phone in from a box. Now I must go, or I'll miss the bus.'

And she was away. Robert said, 'It's being so long without work makes her picky.'

Hetty took the bus to town, a bus to Bolton and another on to Wakefield in Yorkshire. She had been supplied with the address of the community centre where Michael's Community Psychiatric Nurse had his office. It was no great way from the bus station and her suitcase was not heavy, so she walked; there was something in Hetty which was reluctant to take taxis, even on expenses.

The CPN had a round face and Denis Taylor spectacles. He was twenty-eight years old and looked eighteen. 'Michael's gone,' he said.

'Gone where?'

'I don't know where.'

'When?'

'I don't know when.'

'You don't know much.'

'Not as much as I'd like.'

'His mother told me he had to have an injection every fortnight.'

'Right.'

'But if he's just taken off . . .'

'He's not having it.'

'Won't he get ill?'

'He will get ill. Probably.'

There was a knock at the door and a shy teenage girl entered without waiting for permission. Hetty could hear music, conversation and laughter from the canteen just down the corridor. The CPN said, 'It's okay, Doreen. I'm with this lady,' and Doreen gave Hetty a smile of singular sweetnesss and went out again, shutting the door carefully behind her.

'What was that about?'

'She thinks you're a patient.'

Hetty was affronted. 'How dare she!'

'Easy mistake to make.'

'But I don't look like a—' She stopped herself. 'A mentally ill . . .'

'You look like yourself. Most people do.'

She stared at him, hostile. Was he making fun of her? He looked back. Slowly a smile formed. But he wasn't making fun. He liked her. Maybe it was his job to like people. If so, Hetty discovered that she didn't care. She liked being liked by this young man. 'We've got off on the wrong foot,' she said.

'No wonder. Those feet are swollen: I can tell. Would you like to take your shoes off, and I'll get some coffee?'

So she took her shoes off, and when he came back with the coffee, Ian – his name was Ian – showed her some exercises which would be even more effective than putting her feet in a basin of hot water and having a glass of Dubonnet, but probably not quite as enjoyable.

'What am I going to tell his mother?'

'She knows.'

Hetty was surprised. 'No, she doesn't, or I wouldn't be here.'

'I informed the family as soon as I knew myself.'

'She never said.'

'His stepfather answered the phone. I asked him to let me know if Michael turned up.'

'Are you saying he never told her?'

'Does that surprise you?' Hetty realised that it didn't. 'Don't blame him, Mrs Wainthropp.'

'She will.'

'Probably. But it's not easy for families. Worry – yes, they expect to worry – but it's the little things. Personal neglect. Dirt. Beds never made and bits of food left on the carpet. It wasn't a good atmosphere. Stepfather disapproving, mother over-protective. If he could have managed independence . . .'

'Did he really try? His mother said he kept coming back home. They had to push him out.'

'How can our people manage to be independent when there's nowhere for them to live that won't make them ill again? Bedsitter, maybe a one-room flat in a tower block. And no work, of course. Day after day of nothing to do but walk about listening to your own thoughts.'

'They can come here.'

'Yes, that's why it's called the Drop-In Centre. Cheap meal in the canteen. Meet people. Get your medication. Talk. Occupational Therapy, Art Therapy, Group Therapy – we're great on therapies providing they're cheap.'

'Did Michael come in regular? For the therapies and such?'

'He had on and off periods. Times he'd come in, times he'd keep away. You're surprised I can't tell you when he went?'

'I am.'

'He was having one of his off periods. That's okay; he's a free man – he doesn't have to come in. He missed an injection. I wrote to him; he didn't reply. Went to see him; he wasn't in. I asked around; nobody knew. I informed the family.'

'And that's all?'

'Once he's gone out of the area, there's nothing I can do.'

'You could tell the police.'

'He hasn't committed a crime.'

'You said yourself, without his injection he'll be ill.'

'He can't be forced to take it. He has the right to refuse.'

Hetty put on her shoes. 'I'd like to see this flat you found him.'

'We'll have to go to the Town Hall first for a spare key.'

'Won't the caretaker have one?'

'Caretakers were privatised long ago. You never see one these days.'

Ian drove her to the Town Hall and then to the tower block in his elderly Renault. 'Don't mistake me, Mrs Wainthropp,' he said. 'I want you to find Michael. He's an intelligent educated man. I'm afraid he may have reached what we call the "rational suicide" stage. He knows he'll be on medication all his life and he can see the empty days stretching ahead of him – always the possibility of a relapse, not much chance of work and any he does get will be well below his capacities – a BA Hons packing boxes, making cocktail sticks or sweeping floors. He doesn't like what he sees. He may make a rational decision that he doesn't want it.'

'He may be right.' They had reached the tower block. Hetty eased herself out of the passenger seat like a sardine deciding to leave the can.

'Are you sure you'll be okay? I'd come with you, but I'm needed back at the Centre.'

'I'll manage. Always have. Thanks for the lift.'

He watched her stomping over to the vandalised entrance of what had once been the cream of community housing. 'Indomitable!' he said.

Michael's flat was tiny – a small main room with a microscopic bathroom to the right of the door and a narrow kitchen opening off the bedsitting-room. Both bathroom and kitchen had curtains across the entrance; there was no room for doors. Just inside the front door was a jumble of junk mail, free newspapers, cards from minicab companies and takeaway restaurants; the few actual letters were lost in it and it has to be admitted that Hetty, the meticulous detective ever on the *qui vive* for clues, did not look for any.

Instead she looked about her at the room. The walls were grubby, like the windows; the furniture consisted of a single bed, unmade with stained blankets, a two-seater sofa with a dirty cushion, two old wooden chairs, a whitewood bookcase, an overhead light which was just a naked bulb, a cheap lamp on a packing case by the bed, a built-in cupboard with rusty metal hangers, worn linoleum on the floor instead of carpet. There was a litter of newspapers, paperbacks, dirty mugs and plates, empty containers from takeaways. An unremarkable room really.

With three exceptions. There were two areas of tidiness within the clutter. One was a shelf of the bookcase, on which a lined manuscript pad had been set out with a couple of Pentels and some envelopes in a box. The other was a folding table, which had been set up in the middle of the room with the two hard chairs on each side of it and a chessboard laid out ready for a game. The table and the area of floor around it were clean.

Most remarkable was that one wall of the room had been painted black, and a white skeleton, man-sized, had been painted on over the black. Hetty stared at it. 'I knew I was right not to go to Weight Watchers,' she said.

She became conscious of the smell of rotting food coming from the kitchen, pulled back the curtain and took a look inside. The dirt and squalor were stomach-turning. A voice behind her said, 'Gone bad in there, has it?' She turned to see that an old man had come into the room through the open front door. 'He never washed up much at the best of times.'

'Who are you?'

'Todd from next door. I used to clean up a bit sometimes. Michael never did, never thought of it. But since he went away I've not been able to get in. You're from the Social, are you?'

'Wainthropp Detective Agency, acting for the family.

His mother's paying me to find out how Michael's getting on.'

'He's not getting on; he's not here.' He indicated the chessboard. 'We used to play chess; he taught me. He were a funny sort of chap, but I miss the company. You don't play chess yourself, I suppose? The board's all set up.'

'Did he say where he was going?'

Michael stood in the drizzling rain, gazing at the outside of the Sunnysands Private Hotel. He wore a black plastic bag over his shoulders. From the window of the front room the landlady looked out at him. No sand on the carpet. He gave her a friendly smile and a wave.

Indoors the landlady picked up the phone, dialled 999 and asked for the police. Time passed; she continued to watch from the window and after a while a young Police Constable arrived in a Panda car to speak to Michael. 'What do you think you're doing, hanging around?'

Michael's responses were slow. There was always a short pause before he answered. He liked to give every question his full attention. 'Sunnysands. Allerton Road. Don't track in sand on the carpet.'

'We've a Neighbourhood Watch here, you know.'

'Sometimes they ask you questions. It's different stories but there's always a skeleton.'

'Do you need help? Something to eat, like? A bed? I can take you to the Sally Ann.'

Michael said, 'Ann. Man. Ran.' The sounds pleased him and could be extended. 'Can. Flan. Dan. Fan. Tram. Mam.' He nodded his head at the friendly policeman and turned away to look for food in a litter bin; he soon found a soggy crisp packet with a few crisps left in it. 'Wham,' he said. 'Pram. Slam. Sam,' crammed the crisps into his mouth and moved on down the street.

The policeman watched him go, then turned back to the

front door of the Sunnysands Private Hotel, in which the landlady now stood like an avenging archangel.

'Why didn't you take him in?'

'Not committing an offence.'

'He's a loony. Standing outside my hotel for hours, staring. Who knows what was in his mind?'

'If he's not in immediate need of care and control, I can't do nothing.'

'Well, if he gets in the papers it's your responsibility.'

'What about the skeleton?' Hetty said to Todd. 'Was that part of his illness?'

'I don't think so. He took a lot of trouble doing it. He were quite proud of it, I think. It's not meant to be frightening.'

'And he went off the week before last? Monday? – ten days ago?'

Todd did little sums on his fingers, and nodded vigorously. 'Right. I knocked on the door. Special knock, same as always, then he'd answer. This time he didn't.'

'He could have been dead.'

'What odds if he had been? He'd've been found. They allus are.'

'You were his friend. Maybe his only friend.'

'I wouldn't say that. You're making assumptions there. Presuming there. He'd got no friends. Nor have I.'

'You came round every day. You tidied up.'

'We were neighbours. I like to keep tidy. We didn't talk much. We'd play chess. Sometimes I'd get him a bite to eat. We had the same problem, y'see. Getting through the day.'

There was no more to be found out in Wakefield, not for the time being, and she'd a lot to think about. Hetty took the bus from Wakefield to Bolton, Bolton to Darwen, then back to the village. Her suitcase seemed to grow heavier during the course of the journey. She put it down in the kitchen. 'You were right,' she said to Robert. 'I didn't need a suitcase.'

Robert looked at Geoff, and Geoff at Robert. 'I'll get the Dubonnet,' said Geoff.

Later that night, Robert brought Hetty cocoa in bed and a mug for himself at the same time to be companionable. '"Rational suicide"!' Hetty said. 'Community nurses, social workers, they've a language all their own.'

'They do it to fool people really,' Robert said. 'That's my belief. Conceal their meaning, like.'

'They talk about community care, but there's no money provided for it. That flat was a pig-sty. They need hostels . . . Housing Associations . . .'

'They would.'

'That poor woman! What am I going to tell her?'

'And the skeleton?'

'He never had one. Not as a toy. You wouldn't. And there was nothing like it on the wall of his room at home.'

'It wasn't part of his delusions?'

'No, that was different. It was all muddled up of course, but mostly it was to do with Reg's dental drill. When Michael was younger, he'd smelled that scorched smell you get sometimes from the drill, and now he thought it was the pain from the patients' teeth polluting the atmosphere. He had it all worked out but it made no sense, and they told us at the hospital not to discuss it with him.'

'I talked to the nurse at the Drop-In Centre.'

'Ian?'

'He said he'd phoned to let you know Michael had disappeared. He said Reg took the call.'

Hilda was staring at her. She was taking in what had been said, then trying to reject it, then realising that it must be true. 'Excuse me,' she said, walked quickly to the door and went downstairs to the surgery.

In the small and soothingly furnished reception room

with its cinnamon armchairs and copies of *Hello* and *Country Life*, the secretary told her that her husband was with a patient. She took no notice and went on into the surgery. Reg had his drill in his hand, his nurse standing by with amalgam and a patient at his mercy, lying back in the padded chair, mouth open, staring at the ceiling in an ecstasy of quiet fear.

'Ian phoned you from Wakefield. You knew Michael had gone.'

'Yes.'

'And never told me.'

'I didn't want to upset you.'

'Well, now you have.'

'Did you tell me when you hired a detective?'

'Out of my own savings.'

Reg said to the patient, 'I'm so sorry for this interruption. Please bear with me.'

'It won't take a moment,' said Hilda. 'And it'll hardly hurt at all,' and left the surgery as abruptly as she had entered.

She went back upstairs to Hetty in the kitchen. 'Please continue your investigations, Mrs Wainthropp. I'll find a way to pay you if I have to steal the gold fillings from the patients' teeth.

Case Conference.

Geoff had been to the Public Library and brought back a stack of books on psychiatric illnesses generally and schizophrenia in particular. He sat at the foot of the kitchen table with the books beside him, and a manuscript pad, on which he had made copious notes, in front of him and five sharpened pencils. 'I'll spell it out.'

If Michael's injections were still working, the only place he'd want to go would be his mother's house. But he didn't know where she'd gone, so he could be searching for her, anywhere and everywhere. Worse! He was supposed to have an injection every fortnight and he'd already been away a fortnight, and had missed the injection before that. So his symptoms would probably have come back.

Robert said, 'What symptoms?'

'Seeing things. Hearing voices. Delusions.'

'Like thinking you're Hercule Poirot?'

'Try not to be negative, Robert.'

'What I'm trying to say is, if he was still in control and trying to find his mum, we don't know where he'd try. And if the symptoms had come back and he was hearing voices, he might go where the voices told him to go, and we don't know where that would be either. So whatever's happened, we can't win.'

'Give me that character profile again. Not what his mother said; what the books say.'

Geoff read from his notes. 'Isolated, sullen or moody, sometimes hostile. No job, nowhere to go, no friends. Poor concentration, wanders off the point. Conversation becomes difficult; letters are easier. Reliant on routine, upset by change.'

Hetty said, 'Letters are easier. So who did he write to? And who wrote back? I'm sure that skeleton's in it somewhere. I've a feeling in my bones about that skeleton.'

So she and Geoff went back together for another look at the skeleton. This time they took more notice of the pile of letters inside the door. Among all the junk mail there were three handwritten envelopes postmarked Sutton & Cheam all in the same writing, and three postmarked Stoke-on-Trent on which Michael's address had been printed by something like a word processor or computer but the address on the back was clearly not that of *The Readers' Digest* or the Sun Life Assurance Company but that of a private person, Miss Geraldine Camrose of 17, Penfold Avenue.

'Two people wrote to him regular.' She handed the Stoke-on-Trent letters to Geoff. 'You take one, I'll take the other.'

The skeleton said nothing, but remained where it was on the wall, above the action.

Michael looked at the entrance to the pier where the Amusements were. It would be warm in there. There was a sign to tell him that entrance was free. That was a good sign. He decided to take its advice.

He heard his stepfather's voice from behind him: 'You've always been a time-waster.' That was another reason to go inside, to get away from Reg.

A small boy was playing a video game. Such games were dangerous; like the TV set at home they might taunt him, tell him things he didn't want to hear, give him orders he didn't want to obey. But the presence of the small boy reassured him. If he was close to a child, he would be safe.

There was a fat man in uniform looking at him in a hostile way. He moved close to the small boy. The money had run out and the game was over.

The boy said to Michael, 'You pong. You know that?'

'Pong. Wrong.'

'Right!'

'Song?'

'No way. Now piss off.'

The small boy put more money into the machine, and the fat man in uniform came over to Michael and made him leave the pier.

Miss Geraldine Camrose was seventeen years old, serious and dedicated to her hobby, which was correspondence. On the wall of her room in 17, Penfold Avenue, there was an enormous photographic blow-up of the cover of *Pen Pal Magazine*, showing Geraldine receiving the

Correspondent of the Year award at a ceremony in Ditchling. On her desk was a computer (with Pentium chip) and a laser printer, telephone, dictionaries (not just English but of various foreign langauges), reference books, an In-Tray and an Out-Tray, and behind the desk were low shelves of box-files, arranged alphabetically and labelled with the name of the correspondent and a year – YURI 1995, DARLENE 1994–6, MICHAEL 1994–5, YVES 1995 and so on. Also behind the desk, tacked to the wall, was a banner with words embroidered on it: THE MOVING FINGER WRITES.

Geraldine was in a wheelchair. She seemed to be comfortable about it, very much at ease and in command of events. Her desk had been specially adapted so that the chair would fit and everything she needed was within reach. She took Geoff's announcement that he was a private detective investigating the disappearance of one of her pen pals in her stride, and treated him as if he was someone from local radio come to interview her.

'I've got ten pen pals altogether. French. German. Darlene's American. She's a born-again Christian at the moment. It's the third time; it makes her letters monotonous. I don't think people should be born again more than once. And Yuri's Russian. He doesn't write often because he can't afford the stamps.'

'And Michael?'

Geraldine took Michael's box-file from the shelf. 'He's in a special sub-group – Mentally Challenged. I've two of them. He's been rather naughty lately about replying.'

'I hate writing letters.'

'That's the advantage of word-processing. Provided you stick to general subjects, you can send the same letter, just slightly altered, to each one.'

There was a knock at the door, and Geraldine's mother brought in a tray with two mugs and a plate of biscuits. 'Isn't she wonderful?' she said to Geoff. 'A network of positive thoughts across the world. We're all so proud of her,' and was gone again.

Geoff said to Geraldine, 'I know it's confidential, like, but if there's anything Michael's written to you lately about his state of mind . . . if he was thinking of going anywhere . . . wondering where his mum might be. Any suicidal thoughts even.' He took a sip from the mug he had been given. The contents tasted extremely strange. 'I think something may have gone wrong with this coffee. Unless it's cocoa.'

'Oatorola. Essence of organic oats fortified with every known vitamin. Just let it cool. The cactus likes it.' She opened the file.

'Any clue there might be to his intentions. We represent the family. We have to find him.'

She flicked through the letters in the file, reading odd bits, while Geoff watched anxiously. Then she closed it. 'Sorry, there's nothing. I told you, I keep my correspondence general. Religion and philosophy. Environmental issues, particularly penguins. It's the only way. If you let pen pals get too personal, you'll be sucked in.'

Hetty went to Sutton to meet Aileen, who had worked in the Public Library at Wakefield, leaving three years ago to look after her parents. She had known Michael as a lad; he had been a regular user of the Library. 'He was what I call a reading boy. Three books a day sometimes, anything as long as it had a story. We'd have great chats.'

She kept the door of the living room open. Her father was upstairs in bed. He had been bedridden for over a year ever since Aileen's mother had died. It was his way of protesting at the unfairness of old age. There was the sound of a handbell and then his voice. 'Aileen!'

She shouted up the stairs. 'I can't come now, Father. I'm with a lady.' And to Hetty, 'I was so proud when he went to university. He took a BA in English: I almost felt

I had a part in it. And I've kept in touch. He'd already had his first breakdown, you see, when I left. It seemed important to keep some kind of contact. It's not much to write a letter.'

'Aileen!'

'I'm busy, Father. He doesn't understand. I can't go every time he calls. I'd be up and down all day.'

'Has there been anything unusual in Michael's letters recently?'

'Just the poems.' She took a thick manila envelope from the writing desk. 'Keeping things is a habit with me. These are just scraps, really. But interesting.'

'They do Art Therapy at the Drop-In Centre. Would they do Poetry too?'

'Bound to. Poetry passes the time.' She took a couple of sheets of paper – lined sheets like the ones Hetty had seen on the shelf in Michael's flat – and read:

> '*Lions, when sick, look for a place to die.*
> *Birds crouch in corners.*

Then it breaks off, but there's quite a cadence, don't you think?'

'Morbid.'

'Here's a longer one:

> *Old Bones is a merry fella.*
> *Comes into every story.*
> *Sinbad, Aladdin or Cinderella,*
> *Old Bones takes all the glory.*'

The handbell again from above. 'Aileen!'

'Old Bones?' said Hetty.

'Death, I suppose. The skeleton with the scythe.' Her glance wandered in the direction of the stairs. '*He* certainly comes into every story.'

'Aileen! Aileen!'

'There was a skeleton painted on the wall of Michael's flat. I didn't notice a scythe.'

'Aileen!'

'I'll have to go this time. He may have wet himself.'

'Sinbad, Aladdin or Cinderella,
Old Bones takes all the glory.'

Hilda's face was blank. She knew very well what the verse meant, but did not intend Hetty to know she knew. 'Michael wrote that?'

Nothing gives more away than a face composed to give nothing away. Hetty knew she was on to something. But why was the woman clamming up? 'Would it have anything to do with the skeleton on his wall? Does it give you any idea where Michael might have gone?'

'No . . . No, none.'

'Comes into every story. Does that mean anything?'

'Nothing at all.'

It did. Hetty knew it did. Hilda took her chequebook from her bag and wrote out a cheque to cover a week's work and expenses – the fares alone, even taking Hetty's bus-pass into account, were considerable, and they'd had to eat. 'I'm sorry I've been wasting your time. It was silly of me to think you could find him.'

'I can, I hope. With your co-operation.'

'Anyway I can't afford to pay for a long enquiry. I'm sure you understand that.'

'It's got something to do with that poetry, hasn't it?'

Hilda tore off the cheque and held it out to Hetty. 'Thank you so much for all your trouble.'

What to do? In her short experience of detective work she had never been taken off a case while still hot on the trail. But you can't help people if they don't want to be helped. She took the cheque. 'Thank you. It's been a pleasure.'

She walked down the road from the surgery, the cheque in her handbag. There was a phone-box on the corner. She looked back. She could see the gate, and a small section of the front garden, and a patient in pain arriving. She entered the phone-box and dialled the number of her own phone. Robert answered, rather flustered because he was in his wellies on his way to the allotment. 'I'm in a phone-box on the corner of the road where the dentist's is. Tell Geoffrey to get down here with the scooter as soon as he can. I'm not giving up the case. That woman knows something.'

The box was ideal concealment. She was ejected twice by an angry person wishing to telephone, but remained outside, watching the dentist's gate. Time passed. A taxi arrived, driven by an elderly Sikh. Would Geoffrey never come? Hilda emerged from the front door, dressed in outdoor clothes and carrying a small suitcase. She gave directions to the driver and got into the taxi.

Hetty looked about her, distraught. Should she leave her post and run after the taxi? Then she heard the heaven-sent familiar *putta! putta! putt!* of the scooter and Geoffrey was with her. She took the skid-lid he offered and climbed on the back. 'Follow that cab!'

They followed it with ease to the railway station. Hilda paid the driver and scurried inside. Hetty said to Geoff, 'She knows where Michael's gone, and she's off to find him. But she's no experience; she'll make a mess of it. There must be somebody in that ticket office you were at school with.'

Geoff set off at a run and returned soon afterwards. 'Staverton Sands. There's a train in ten minutes.'

'Too soon, and anyway she'd see us. Let her have the evening to fret, and we'll be there tomorrow.'

'Mrs Wainthropp, I have to say we can't afford to work for nothing.'

True. It would lead to reproach from their accountant, and although Hetty was well able to shrug off a reproach from Robert, he would in this case be in the right. A moment's thought to allow the little grey cells to apply themselves. Then she said, 'There's more than one way to skin a rabbit,' and they went back to the surgery.

Like Hilda before her, Hetty brushed the receptionist aside and went straight in to Reg, who was with the same patient. 'Do you know your wife's gone to Staverton Sands?'

Reg put down his drill, removed the hook which sucks away moisture and a wad of wet cotton wool from his patient's mouth, and handed the patient a glass of pink water. 'Rinse!' The patient rinsed his mouth. 'Open!' Reg popped in another large wad of cotton wool. 'I'll be back.' He took Hetty into the outer office. 'Why does it always have to be me?' the patient said to the nurse, indistinctly through the plug of cotton wool.

'How much do you need?' Reg said to Hetty.

'Seven days' daily rate and reasonable expenses.'

'Very well. I shall require strict confidentiality, you understand? Nothing to come out.'

Michael stood outside the Sally Ann. The friendly policeman had spoken of it. There would be warmth and food and somewhere to sleep. Maybe Todd would be there or someone he knew.

The skeleton sat on the canopy over the front door. 'Go in?' Michael asked the skeleton. But the skeleton shook its head. 'Shut me up?' The skeleton nodded and pointed away in the direction of the harbour. 'Right!' Michael said. 'Right! Freedom. Oh, for the wings?' The skeleton nodded; it had always been on Michael's side and given good advice. A woman in the uniform of the Sally Ann appeared at the door beneath it, and again the skeleton shook its head. 'Right!' Michael trotted away through the rain towards the harbour.

Reg said, 'Useless! Worthless!' As usual he did not bother to appear in person, but sent his voice as a sign that he was always watching.

Freedom! 'You keep out of this,' Michael shouted back at Reg. The Salvation Army Captain watched him go.

Down at the harbour Michael found a boat. It was called *White Bird*: the name was painted on the side. The skeleton appeared on the roof of the wheelhouse and beckoned. But there was a fence of steel mesh between Michael and the jetty. The skeleton did not use words. It expressed its meaning either by manipulating its strings to make gestures, or else by entering Michael's mind so that he knew what to do without being told.

What to do was wait. The boat would wait.

Freedom.

He waited until it grew dark and the people of the harbour went away. All was quiet save for the lapping of the water, and distant noises from the town and the motors which passed along the harbour road, and very faintly the sound of music from a radio.

The boat was still there. There were electric lights in the harbour, but they were well spaced. Michael climbed the fence and went towards the boat. The tide was low so the level of the deck of the boat was well below the level of the harbour wall, but there were stone steps cut into the wall. Michael stood on the wall and looked down at the boat. Freedom.

Reg said, 'You get nothing for nothing in this world.'

From the deck the skeleton was beckoning.

Baron Hardup said, 'What's the time, children?' and all the children replied, 'It's Playtime!' Michael descended the steps and jumped on to the deck of the *White Bird*.

The owner of the boat, a large clumsy man, was sleeping off a skinful on a bunk in the living quarters below, and woke at the impact of Michael landing on deck. Vandals! He would have to investigate.

Michael was looking for a way to cast off. Once the boat was floating he would be free. He muttered to himself:

'Don't Care was made to care.
Don't Care was hung.
Don't Care was put in a pot
And boiled till he was done.'

He heard a voice. 'Oi! What do you think you're doing?' It was not one of his regular voices, though you could never tell. He looked round and saw a fat man coming towards him, holding a baseball bat.

Then there was a bad time.

He was running, falling, climbing the fence, falling back, climbing again. He was over the fence, the fat man gone away, there was blood on his face and arms, head hurting, arms still over face for protection. He could not see and kept falling over in the dark. Passed some people. They looked. Some made moves, shouted, laughed. He ran, fell over, ran on, knew now where he must go to be safe.

All the time Reg's voice, getting in the way, putting him down:

'Useless, useless! Hide, hide!
Rubbish, garbage! Better dead.
Don't Care was made to care.
Teach you a lesson you won't forget.
Bone idle, and always has been.
Useles, useless, out of sight!
Useless garbage, out of mind!
Find a grave and crawl inside.'

He had reached the Crazy Golf and had to slow down to negotiate its hazards. There was wood and wire and steel hoops, sand, all sorts; he did not know how the children these days found space to sit. He came across a building, a sort of kiosk which must be where Baron Hardup and the others lived. They would look after him until he felt better.

He pulled out one of the hoops, smashed a panel in a door, opened it from inside, entered Baron Hardup's castle and closed the door carefully behind him.

It was very cold in the castle, and there was nothing to cover him, but he wedged himself into a corner and folded his arms to wait for the day.

Hetty and Geoff found Hilda at the Sunnysands. Reg had given Hetty the address. Hilda and Michael had stayed there for three weeks of every summer when Michael was a small boy, when it had been a mere boarding house, not yet aspiring to the grandeur of a Private Hotel. Reg had never gone with them; crowns and bridges kept him too busy.

'Will you be taking luncheon?' said the landlady.

'We might as well: we're on expenses.'

So they took luncheon.

Hetty said to Hilda, 'Now what about this skeleton who gets into every story?' and Hilda – since Hetty and Geoff had come to help and there no longer seemed to be any point in economy with the truth – told them about the Marionette Show which had once been in a booth in the Gardens near the Paddling Pool, but had now been superseded by Crazy Golf. They had performed all the old pantomime stories, from *Aladdin* to *Babes in the Wood*, and the skeleton had come into them all, couldn't be kept out, he was so cheeky and disrespectful. He had been Michael's favourite.

After lunch they questioned the landlady.

'Come down in the world, has he? Well, it can happen to anyone. You're bound to find him. He's been seen everywhere. There've been complaints.' She did not mention that she herself had complained. 'The Pier . . . the esplanade . . . the Floral Clock . . . what you might call the scenic features of the town, he'd be there loitering.'

'And he loitered here?'

'For hours in the rain, peering in windows and upsetting the guests.'

'He'd been happy here. In the old days.' Hetty meant before it had become a Private Hotel.

'If I'd known who he was I'd have asked him in. But you can't know, can you?'

Geoff said, 'Mind you, we can't be sure its him. We've no positive identification.'

'Geoffrey, there are times when I despair of you.'

Hilda said, 'I looked all round the town this morning, but I couldn't find him. It's not as easy as you think.'

'There's three of us now. We can go three different ways.'

Staverton Sands on a winter afternoon. The ice-cream stalls, hotdog and hamburger stalls, and shops selling humbugs, home-made fudge and candy floss were all shut. So were the Fortune-Tellers, Gypsy Sarah and Gypsy Susan. So was the Open Air Aquadrome and the Fun Fair.

They went three ways. Geoff made for the Amusements on the Pier, played a couple of video games, a fruit machine and one of those machines with flippers, little steel balls and bumpers that light up producing enormous scores which never quite add up to enough for a prize. He talked to the attendant, who gave him a highly coloured account of rescuing a small boy from the loony, and he looked under the pier and under every building which jutted out over the sands on stilts.

Hetty tried the doors of the Beach Huts but they were all locked up for the winter. She walked round the drained and deserted Paddling Pool and noticed that kids seemed to have run amok in the Crazy Golf and vandalised the door of the kiosk. She looked behind shrubs in Marine Gardens and walked among the sand-dunes to the north of the town between the Esplanade and the sea, and observed that everywhere floribunda roses had seeded themselves and grew freely among the litter and dog turds.

Hilda examined every seat and shelter on the esplanade, then went to the Reference Library to stare at the old tramps sleeping among the quality periodicals, and on to Tourist Information where she was offered a potted history of the town and a list of hotels.

They looked in doorways and into those cheap cafés which were still open, and the waiting rooms of the bus and railway stations. Everywhere they looked, they asked, and there were people who had noticed the loony, seen him hanging about in the rain and eating from litter bins, but they had not seen him that day. And it grew dark.

It was growing dark in the kiosk by the Crazy Golf. Michael was still huddled in a corner, around him all the summertime paraphernalia of putters, balls, deckchairs, trays, umbrellas, some of which he had pushed against the inside of the door to keep it securely closed. He was still very cold, and hungry, and he had soiled himself, but did not dare to go out. In the opposite corner he could see the skeleton sprawled out, no longer cheeky and disrespectful but lifeless now, no help to anyone, no comfort, no advice. Anyway, too late for that. His voices had gone out of control, overlapping, all mixed up, coming from every direction. He screwed his eyes tight shut, put his hands over his ears, and gave a silent scream.

The search-party of three sat together in Hilda's room, all with glasses of Dubonnet from a bottle purchased on expenses at exorbitant cost from the Bar downstairs. Hetty had her bare feet in a plastic bowl of hot water; she had tried to remember the exercises Ian had taught her, but they had faded. 'So much of this job is legwork. You have to keep in trim.'

'Most of the time it's not the illness that makes them act strange. It's the drugs they take to control it.'

Geoff said, 'I don't know why he couldn't have gone to Blackpool. There'd be more to do in the evenings.'

'Dubonnet's a great comfort at a time like this. We'll tackle the police and such tomorrow.'

So Hetty and Hilda tackled the police, Hetty asking the questions since Hilda was scared and out of her depth.

The Sergeant said, 'We've got no jurisdiction if he's not in immediate need of care and control.'

'But he was. He was eating from litter bins.'

'It's not a crime.'

'He needed care. You won't deny that?'

'Not our care, Mrs Wainthropp.'

And not the Hospital's care since he had not reported himself sick. And not the care of the church. The church door was locked.

They were advised to try the Salvation Army and did so. Michael had been seen hovering outside by the Salvation Army Captain in charge of the Shelter.

'He may have wanted to come in.'

'We don't drag people in off the street: we've no resources and no authority. People come to us if they need help. He walked away.'

'Would the Good Lord have taken your commission away if you'd walked a few steps after him and offered him a cup of coffee?' said Hetty bitterly. And they left the Sally Ann and went to the Community Centre where the lady at the canteen said the young man had not been in but some of her regulars had seen him and commented on his appearance.

Meanwhile Geoff had gone to the Holiday Caravan Site outside the town. It was a rundown place with the site office in a Portacabin. Geoff found the Site Manager staring gloomily at a blocked drain in the Toilet Facilities.

'It's out of season. There's no occupancy to speak of, just a few regulars on Social Security.'

'That's what I mean. You'd have caravans empty.'

'Locked.'

'They could be broke into.'

'I'd notice.'

'He could be hiding. Lying low, like. Only using the toilet in the middle of the night.'

'I go round every day, trying the doors.'

'When?'

'When I feel like it.'

Geoff took a ten-pound note from the inside pocket of his jacket and rubbed it between his fingers. 'If you felt like it now, maybe I could go with you.'

The Site Manager tried the doors of all the caravans in a row while Geoff looked underneath. They went on to the next row. The Site Manager began to fall behind. Now Geoff tried the doors *and* looked underneath. Another. Geoff was well ahead. Another door. From behind him the voice of the Site Manager. 'Not that one!'

Too late. Geoff had already opened the door. A middle-aged bald man with a moustache and horn-rimmed spectacles was on a bunk, grappling with an equally middle-aged lady with dyed black hair, too much mascara and Romany earrings, both in a state of partial undress, and both were staring at Geoff in the doorway, appalled by his interruption of their afternoon's enjoyment. Seated demurely in its basket beside the bunk was a small white poodle. Geoff closed the door of the caravan.

'I did warn you.'

* * *

'Try to sleep.' Hilda sat in an armchair looking out of the uncurtained window at the Esplanade. She was ready for bed in her nightie and slippers, but Hetty suspected that she would sit up most of the night.

'I will. Goodnight, Hetty. Thank you.'

'Goodnight, Hilda. We'll have some new ideas by morning.'

Geoff was waiting outside on the landing. 'She took a pill but I doubt she'll sleep. I've promised some new ideas, but I don't know what they'll be.'

'Case Conference?'

They could hear raucous male laughter coming from the Bar downstairs. 'Yes, but not here. Get your coat.'

They went out together and sat in a deserted shelter on the Esplanade. Geoff felt strongly that the word 'shelter' was a misnomer. Both were in overcoat, scarf and gloves, and Hetty's beret was pulled down well over her face, but sea mist and the winter chill got into their bones.

'He came here out of the blue. He could have gone back into it.'

Hetty said, 'Won't do. We know why he came: he was trying to rediscover something he'd lost.'

'You can't know that, Mrs Wainthropp.'

'I do know it.' She touched her chest. 'Here.'

'You don't allow for disordered thoughts. I'm the one had to read the books. If his symptoms have come back, there's no logic.'

'It's nothing to do with logic.'

'If he decided he couldn't find what he was looking for because it isn't here any more, then he might just have given up and gone back to Wakefield.'

'They'd have told his stepfather and he'd have told us. Forget logic, Geoffrey. It's feelings in this case.'

'That's your department, Mrs Wainthropp. That and the little grey cells.'

'It is.' She closed her eyes and breathed deeply. Geoff waited. These were Hetty's indications that the little grey cells were being given a work-out. In this cold, he doubted whether it would do much good. Hetty said, 'Those bits of poems. Do you remember what they said?'

'Old Bones, was it?'

'No, the other.' He had brought a copy with him. '"Lions, when sick, look for a place to die. Birds crouch in corners".'

Hetty's gloved fingers clicked. 'In corners? Fool! Of course. We'll have to be quick.'

'Oh! Right! To do what?'

'He's in a bad state. He may not last. Lions, when sick . . . Feelings. He's come back and been rejected, so he's given up – looked for a place to curl up and die. We've been searching in public places. He's found somewhere private, somewhere nobody would come across him, somewhere . . .'

They were looking at each other, keeping step with each other's thoughts. 'Somewhere he felt safe, like? Somewhere he was happy before?'

'Come on!'

They were out of that shelter and off together down the Esplanade. The pace was almost enough to keep them warm. Hilda was still in the armchair when they erupted into her room at Sunnysands. 'The marionettes!' Hetty said. 'Where were they?' Hilda didn't understand. 'Where did they hold the Marionette Show exactly?'

Geoff had borrowed a torch from the landlady, which helped them to negotiate the Crazy Golf. They found the damaged door.

'Someone broke in.'

Hilda gave a cry and surged forward, but Hetty held her back. 'No, love. Stay. Let Geoffrey go.'

There was something inside the door, holding it shut;

Geoff supposed that the damage would have been discovered otherwise. He pushed hard and managed to get the door open wide enough for him to squeeze inside. It was dark. He shone the torch around, saw deckchairs and the clutter of Crazy Golf and someone scrunched up in the corner.

Whoever it was did not move or speak. The beam of the torch moved upwards from body to face, which was white and unshaven except for the black of dried blood and the purple of bruises. Geoff forced himself to go over to that face and touch it. It was stiff and cold and the eyes were open.

He moved the stuff which had been holding the door shut and opened it. 'He's in here.' Hetty and Hilda entered.

'Michael?'

The beam of the torch illuminated Michael's face. Hilda walked slowly to the body and knelt by it. She cradled Michael's head in her arms. There were no sobs, just total silence from all three. Then Hetty said, 'Go and get the police, Geoffrey,' and Geoff gave her the torch and left the kiosk.

Hetty moved over to the body, knelt on the other side of it, reached over and took Hilda's hand in hers.

People came and took the body away. There was no sleep that night. Hetty sat up in the armchair next to Hilda's bed, and went to the police station in the morning.

'Somebody beat him up. It's murder, and you know it.'

'The beating didn't kill him, Mrs Wainthropp. He died of cold and lack of nourishment.'

'If he hadn't been beaten, would he have gone there to die?'

The Desk Sergeant looked at her. This woman was trouble. However . . . 'There's some evidence – signs of a struggle down by the jetty. We've had problems there before. Some boat-owners . . . There's been vandalism: you can't blame them.'

'Someone's got a club, iron bar, baseball bat, something with Michael's blood on it. You find that someone or you can take it from me there'll be one big, very public fuss.'

It was good to be in her own bed again, with Robert bringing the breakfast and sitting by her as she tucked into tea and buttered toast. It was all in the past, all that misery and pain, Hilda and Reg – Hilda running at him, trying to hit him in the face with her clenched fists while the receptionist held her back . . . Hilda weeping helplessly in the train on the way back, unable to stop, with Hetty holding her and Geoff keeping the other passengers at a distance. No good dwelling on that, on anything like that.

Hetty said, 'Schizophrenia. I couldn't manage, Robert. I couldn't manage at all.'

'If it was me?'

'You're too old. Couldn't happen.'

'If it was Geoffrey?'

'He's not our son.'

'Who else would look after him?'

Safe as Houses

Five-thirty a.m. and stacks of daily newspapers were waiting for collection outside the Parcels Office of the railway station. The big newsagents had collected already but now a rickety old van, driven too fast, arrived, braked and backed up to the collection point to the sound of pop music on local radio from the cab. Merv, the driver's mate, seventeen years old and with the acne to prove it, jumped out of the cab and opened the back of the van for loading while Trev, the driver, put his feet up on the dashboard, reached out for a dog-eared paperback and began to read. Trev did driving; he did not do lifting and heaving.

Merv hefted bundles of newspapers from the stack and hurled them into the van. Suddenly he saw something strange, stopped what he was doing, and peered to examine it more closely. In the middle of the stack of bundles was a baby, about six months old, neatly dressed and wearing a bonnet and a luggage label with an address. It smiled at him.

Inside the cab, Trev became aware of someone knocking at the door. He put down the paperback, lowered the window, and looked out. Merv was standing outside, the baby's face pressed against his own cheek and the baby's arm in his hand. Merv was moving the tiny arm up and down so that the baby, which seemed to enjoy the process, was waving at Trev.

Trev was a family man. He dialled 999 from the phone in the Parcels Office and an ambulance arrived to take the baby from Merv, who relinquished it with regret; he was already beginning to feel like a teenage father. There were more vans by this time and the collection of newspapers had been delayed by the general interest, the ooohing and ahhhhing, the wiggling of fingers and who's-the-pretty-one-ing of the hard-boiled veterans of the early-morning run. A paramedic took the baby into her temporary care; it seemed unfazed by the change in substitute parents. The ambulance was driven away, its blue light flashing.

Chrissie Hedges, sixteen, had watched the whole incident from the station car park. When she saw the baby being handed into the paramedic's care, she turned away and began to walk towards the main road; the ambulance passed her. Chrissie was the baby's mother.

Hetty was almost ready to go shopping. Her basket was on the table with a large canvas shopping bag in it and next to it her list, with a pen standing ready in case she needed to add anything to it at the last minute. But she delayed. Something was troubling Robert. He would not look at her and kept clearing his throat. She knew the signs.

Robert said, 'They were talking in the bar of the Goat and Compasses. Some programme on the telly.'

They were out of salt. Just as well she had remembered. She added it to the list. 'You've been using it for those slugs of yours.'

'They're not my slugs; they're free-range. Twenty pounds an hour.'

'Don't pay. It's too much for slugs.'

'Private detectives. It were a documentary on telly. Twenty pounds, the going rate.'

'That's London rates.' She picked up her list. 'It's no

good, Robert: we charge what our public can afford. When we're established we'll put our prices up.'

He cleared his throat again. Worrying! Whatever it was, it was not out yet. But she could delay no further or she would miss the bus. She put on her coat in the hall, where Geoff was waiting. 'What's the matter with him?'

'I think he's got something to say to you, Mrs Wainthropp.'

Better out than in, bus or no bus. She returned to the kitchen. Robert said, 'I've been meaning to tell you; I've taken a job.' She stared at him. Secrets? What job? 'Part-time. Three days a week, collecting trolleys. The detective business doesn't pay; it's been eating into my redundancy money. Something had to be done.'

Too many thoughts rushing together. Shame. Anger. Concern. A helpless surge of love. Now that he had told her straight out, he could look at her, but she discovered that she could not look at him. 'You'll give it up the moment we can afford it,' she said. 'I'm not having a husband of mine going out to work. Your job's here.'

The phone rang.

Geoff took the call. It was a Mrs Baynes from Bolton, who would speak to no one but Mrs Wainthropp herself. 'Must be a client,' said Geoff as he handed the receiver to Hetty.

'Notepad.'

'By the phone. With a pen. As always.'

Mrs Baynes was a foster-mother, fostering at present a teenager, Chrissie Hedges. Chrissie had been in care since she was two and a half. There had been five foster placements, six different Children's Homes, four suicide attempts. Now she had left her young baby hidden in a stack of newspapers at the railway station and legged it to God knows where.

'Wants us to find her?' asked Geoff.

'Doesn't say. Wants to meet me first. Makes you think, Geoffrey – four suicide attempts!'

'Real ones?'

'You can tell the difference, can you?'

'Sometimes it's just what they call "cutting". Watching the blood spurt out, so they know they're there. Proof of existence. It's the girls mostly. Boys have other ways.'

'You know a lot about it.'

'Kids from a Children's Home used to come to our school. It's depression, you see, and low self-esteem. Lack of feeling. They'd been left in care so long.'

'No so much a death-wish, more a life-wish?'

'Wish for a different life, yeah.' She had opened the front door. She was leaving. 'Am I not coming with you?'

'Not this one, Geoffrey. Not today.'

'You need me. It's our first job for . . . for a long time.'

'And maybe we won't get it. But it's beyond Bolton. Easy enough for me with me bus-pass, but the way things are at the moment, we can't afford your fare.'

'I'll hold the fort, then?'

'You hold the fort.'

Robert said, 'I do that. I hold the fort.'

'Not if you've got a part-time job three days a week. Still, if you're working for a supermarket you might as well do the shopping. The list's on the table.'

Chrissie was in the forecourt of a Greasy Spoon, leaning against the wall by the entrance. She had been given two lifts by lorry-drivers, neither for long because she had quit when the drivers began to be over-attentive. A neat bespectacled middle-aged man came out of the café. He looked like someone who would have few ideas and those he had would be easy to control. She smiled at him as he passed, just a small friendly smile, nothing too heavy. He stopped and turned back.

Chrissie was looking at him. No smile this time, just a direct look asking no favours. He nodded, and they walked together towards his G registration Volvo.

His name was Alec. He was a rep, travelling in phosphates – not a commercial traveller. The difference was important; a rep did travel, but was received with more respect. They booked into a motel. He signed the register, she remained with the suitcase and did not see what names he gave.

The female receptionist was a right old battle-axe, HMS *Dreadnought* with all flags at half-mast. She stared suspiciously at Chrissie, who lifted her chin and stared right back.

They were given a key and went together to the room in which they would be sleeping. Alec began to unpack the suitcase. It contained some kind of fancy dress. He reached in and felt the different textures of the materials between his fingers. There was a low-cut frilly blouse, black lace underwear and a black leather mini-skirt, a peroxide wig and long black high-heeled boots. 'What do the initials "S" and "M" mean to you?' he said.

'Sausage and mash. Why? Is there room service?'

Mrs Baynes, the client, opened the door.

'Good morning! Hetty Wainthropp, Private Investigator.'

Mrs Baynes stared at Hetty. 'You're not!'

'Indeed I am.'

Over the road the net curtains of a front room twitched. Mrs Baynes gestured to Hetty to come in. 'Quick! Inside! One evil eye from that window over there and you'll wither on the spot.'

Hetty looked across the road. 'We've got one of those where I live.'

They went into the house. Mrs Baynes said, 'A private detective? I don't believe it.'

'Perhaps I should have brought a letter of recommendation from the Chief Constable of Merseyside.'

They went on into the living room. It was clear that this was a home with children in it, since all the furniture was inexpensive and much used, but there was a piano and on it a framed photograph of two young women in concert party costume – matching blouses and skirts with huge buttons, frills round the neck and pointy hats with pom-poms. Mrs Baynes said, 'Fetch me the Magna Carta signed by Barry Manilow, and you still couldn't detect a gas leak with a blow-torch.'

'Then why phone me? Wasting my time and money!' Hetty wasn't having it: the woman would have to pay bus-fares at least.

'You were the cheapest.'

'We're doing a special rate at the moment.'

'Of course you are. You'd have to.' Mrs Baynes sat at the piano and began strumming the intro to a song. Hetty thought, I'm with a madwoman here. Then Mrs Baynes began to sing:

> *'Why does a cow have four legs?*
> *Why, oh why, oh why?'*

And the penny dropped. 'If you're a detective,' Mrs Baynes said, 'tell me who I am.'

She couldn't be. 'Alice Endersby?' She was. Alice Baynes now. 'You never could get the words right. Play.' And Mrs Baynes began to play again as Hetty sang:

> *'Why does a cow have four legs?*
> *I must find out somehow.'*

and Alice joined in:

> *'You don't know, and I don't know,*
> *And neither does the cow.'*

What a turn-up! Hetty picked up the framed photograph. It had been nearly forty years ago, one season semi-professional at the Floral Hall, Fleetwood, before commonsense took over. 'Hetty Ponsonby aka Chuckles Chinchilla. All that wriggling about in fur and fishnet!'

'And that squeaky voice you put on when you wrinkled your nose to giggle.'

'I had the devil in me in them days.'

'Still have, by the look of it. I saw your picture in the *Record*.'

'They used the wrong profile.'

'Supergran Sleuth! Something to do with an old woman dead on the stairs. I cut it out and kept it. Then, when I needed a bloodhound myself I remembered Chuckles Chinchilla.' There was the noise of a baby crying from the kitchen. 'Fred!' Alice left the room at a run and Hetty followed.

The baby was in a carry-cot. Alice picked him up and rocked him. Hetty said, 'Must be quite a challenge being a foster-mother. When did you start?'

'When we knew we couldn't have any of our own. After Jim died, I just kept on.' The baby stopped crying. 'Would you like to change him while I do his bottle?' She popped the baby into Hetty's arms without waiting for an answer and handed her a clean nappy from the clothes-horse. 'It's like riding a bicycle. You never forget.'

She heated water to warm the bottle while Hetty began undressing the baby. It had been a long time since Hetty had changed a nappy so she went about it cautiously, but a hidden watcher might have noticed a lift in her expression to pleasure and even gooeyness.

Mrs Baynes rattled on. 'Now the Social Services seem to take a delight in sending me the difficult ones like Chrissie. Total cost of damage by age thirteen – sixteen thousand eight hundred and sixty-four pounds.'

'The precise way they tot it up! The kids must get competitive.'

'She reckons the best year of her life was the one she spent in a Secure Unit when she was nine. Knew who she was and what she was, and didn't have to think about it. The rest of her life has been spent either on the run or being returned. When she came to me she was five months pregnant. We knitted and shopped and planned. At first I thought the baby would be the making of her. She was too heavy to run before she had him and too tired after.'

'But now she knows perfectly well you're besotted with him. As far as she's concerned, you've got two foster-children so she can come and go as she likes.'

'Right. You're not such a bad detective after all.' Hetty thanked Alice for this unsolicited testimonial. 'But be careful with young Fred. He saves up his wee-wee till you start changing him, so watch his line of fire.'

Alec was lying on the bed, wearing no more than thin black socks and white jockey shorts. The suitcase had contained handcuffs as well as the fancy dress. He was shackled by his wrists and ankles to the four corners of the bed.

Chrissie was wearing the peroxide wig, high-heeled boots, frilly blouse and mini-skirt. She stood at the foot of the bed, holding a whip and went through a routine of posing, pouting and running the thong of the whip through her fingers.

'It's nothing untoward really, you know. It just adds to the excitement.'

It did nothing for Chrissie, but if that's what he wanted . . . 'I think, if you're quite ready, perhaps you might let me have it now,' he said.

'I thought I was supposed to deny you. Treat you with brutality and contempt.'

'Yes, well, up to a point, but just remember who's paying. Now! Don't wait! Go!'

Chrissie flicked the whip in the air above her head. It made a satisfactory crack. 'Wagons roll! Rawhide!'

'Yes – that's the spirit. I love you. Sting me! Hurt me! Yes . . . Now . . . Yes!'

Chrissie threw the whip on top of him, and, all in one smooth action, took his trousers and jacket from the back of the chair where he had left them, removed his wallet and credit cards, then grabbed her own clothes and threw them into the suitcase, closed it, and took it with her out of the door of the motel room.

Alec watched. He could hardly do anything else.

'You want me to find her?'

'That's not the problem.'

Alice took Hetty into the living room and switched on the television and video-recorder. There was already a video-cassette in the machine. Alice played it – a clip of film from a local news programme showing firemen fighting a blaze with people watching. Among the gawpers was a young girl. '*That* is the problem.'

'That's your Chrissie?'

'I wanted the Paul Newman film, but I set the damn thing wrong as usual and got the local news. It's showing the fire at Preston last week. What's Chrissie doing there?'

'Watching?'

'Why?'

'People do.'

'The year she spent in the Secure Unit was for setting fire to a school.' Alice turned off the television. 'There've been two house-fires in the North-West recently, both started deliberately. Nobody got hurt; they were all away on holiday. And both times Chrissie was doing one of her runners. It's been touch and go, the powers that be allowing her to keep Fred. Luckily they only find out half of what goes on.'

'What do you want me to do?'

'Prove she didn't do it.'

'You can't prove a negative.'

'You can if you find the person who did do it.'

'And if that was Chrissie?' No answer. 'Alice?'

'I can't shop her. I'm the only person she trusts. If I shop her, then she's nobody.'

'If I find out she's setting fire to houses, I'll shop her. Next time there might be somebody home.'

They had been partners; they had shared a dressing-room. They had been friends, who had drifted apart and found each other again. Now they were suddenly on opposite sides. Alice said, 'That's your decision.'

'You're taking a risk.'

'I have to believe in her. For Fred's sake.'

'I can try to find out where she goes and what she gets up to when she runs away.'

'It's a start. Her last Children's Home is ten minutes away. She still has a few friends there. I'll give you the address.'

The receptionist at the motel watched from her desk. Chrissie was out on the main road, now wearing a peroxide wig, leather mini-skirt and high-heeled boots, and carrying the suitcase brought by her paramour, whose Volvo was still on the forecourt.

The girl was trying to hitch a lift. Cars approached, slowed, then accelerated away. She'd have a job, dressed like that. Faintly from one of the rooms there came the sound of a man's voice, shouting for help.

Let him shout a while; it would exercise the vocal cords.

She reached for the pass key which was kept on a hook below the desk, and made her leisurely way towards the shouting. She reached the room and looked through the window. The man was stretched out on the bed, wearing only his undies and a pair of black silk socks, shackled to the four corners and struggling to get free. There was a whip lying across his stomach. She opened the door and entered the room.

The man said, 'I assure you there's a perfectly simple explanation.'

The receptionist picked up the whip.

A small saloon car approached Chrissie, who was still standing in the road. The driver was a mouse of a man in his early sixties. He drew level, stopped, leaned across and opened the window. 'Where you going?'

'Anywhere.' Chrissie opened the passenger door and got in, uninvited. The car drove on.

The driver said, 'I hope you don't mind, but I couldn't help noticing – your hair's not your own, is it?'

'Just something I picked up.'

'My name's Stanley, by the way.'

Hetty found Chrissie's friend, Damien, in the Independence Training Unit of the Children's Home. Five sixteen-year-olds, three females, two males, were learning how to shop and cook for themselves. Hetty had been allowed to detach Damien (dark curly hair and bedroom eyes) from the class on the promise that she would complete the lesson herself. 'Try to make him understand,' the Instructor said, 'that cooking isn't about throwing in a bit of this and a bit of that, and swigging at a bottle of cheap plonk like the man on the telly. And shopping is about a budget or it's nothing, and there are alternatives to mince.'

They watched the other teenagers clear up after the lesson. Damien said, 'Have you seen the baby? Isn't he smashing?'

'I'm told she won't let on who the father is.'

'No, she won't.' Damien's agreement was a little too quick.

'Because she's slept around so much that she doesn't know herself?'

'She knows. She just won't share.'

'And you want to share?'

Silence. Then a smile. He did. But knowing who Fred's father was would not help her find out whether or not Chrissie was starting the fires. Hetty said, 'She won't let anyone share him, but she keeps dumping him and running away. Why?'

He looked at her. She must be sixty, older than his gran. It wasn't likely she'd understand, but she had listened to him so far, which was more than his gran had ever done. People her age *should* understand, if the world was ever going to be a better place. He'd give it a whirl. 'When they first put you into Care, you own nothing so you've no respect for anything, not even yourself, right?'

'Go on.'

'Then when you're free, after years in a place like this, it's a bit of a shock. You get into everything – drink, drugs, shoplifting, quick fixes. They take us into Care because we've been deprived of love and money, then wonder why we end up on the game.'

The other kids and the Instructor had gone. Hetty said, 'I promised to finish the lesson, so let's get cooking.' They rolled cubes of stewing steak in seasoned flour while the oven heated up, chopped carrots, potatoes and onions, crumbled a stock cube into boiling water. Damien seemed to know what he was doing. Hetty said, 'Is Chrissie on the game.'

'Not really. She runs away for the same reason she's always run away. Looking for her mother. I'll brown the meat.'

'Herbs?'

'Too expensive. There's herbs in the stock cube.'

'Does she know who her mother is?'

'No, she gets notions. Someone out of the past who's been kind to her – no real reason, but Chrissie'll track her down, hang about till she's rejected, then give up and start over with someone else.'

'Does her foster-mother know this?'

'No, she'd be cut up if she did; she's more than the usual foster-mother. Fred's special for her. Chrissie doesn't talk about why she's going or where she's been. Just runs off and comes back. Now we turn the bits of meat over.'

'But you know?'

'Yes.'

He did want to share. He was much too young but might make a good father. Still, hers not to interfere. 'What would Chrissie do if she found her mother?'

'Ask questions and hope to believe the answers. Stock in the pan, please, with the vegetables.'

'And you'll swear on little Fred's dimples that you've no idea where she is now?'

'Could be anywhere. Casserole cover on and into the oven. Total cost one pound-fifteen. Not that you'd ever bother to do it just for yourself when you can always buy a bag of chips.'

'Well, I've certainly learned a lot today.'

Geoff, left to hold the fort, attacked the stair-carpet with dustpan and brush. Through the open door to the kitchen he could hear Local Radio.

'Newsflash for all would-be Sherlocks! Someone's setting the North-West alight: it's official. Police are now convinced that house-fires in Preston and Bolton were seemingly motiveless arson attacks, almost certainly by the same person.' Geoff's interest had been aroused. His face appeared between the banister rails, listening intently. 'The insurance companies concerned have combined to offer a reward of fifteen thousand pounds for information leading to an arrest.'

Fifteen thousand! It would lift the Wainthropp Detective Agency from its financial doldrums as a mere runaway teenager could never do, and Robert could give up the job at the supermarket. Geoff would need to borrow the scooter on a semi-permanent loan until the job was done.

He had allowed Mr and Mrs Wainthropp to believe that the scooter belonged to a mate of his. In fact, it belonged to Miss Apthwaite, once his Geography teacher, now retired, who seldom used it these days, except for occasional trips to churches in the Cotswolds to do brass-rubbing, which was why it was often available. He left the fort to hold itself and took the bus to town.

Miss Apthwaite said, 'Very well, Geoffrey. A week. And a full tank and clean plugs, please, when you bring it back. Two helmets, I suppose, as usual?'

He would do this job on his own while Hetty looked for the teenager. 'One will do this time, thank you.'

Miss Apthwaite gave him the helmet. Then she was struck by a sudden thought. 'Put it on. Let's have a look at you.'

'What – now?'

'Well, I'm not making an appointment to view.' He put it on. She walked round him, scrutinising him. Geoff began to feel uncomfortable. 'Yes. That should do nicely. Come with me.' They left the shed where the scooter was kept and went into the garden. He needed the scooter and would have to oblige her, but what did this bode? They came to a deep hole, recently dug. Miss Apthwaite had never struck him as the kind of woman to become a serial-killer, but one could not know; retirement sometimes took people in funny ways. 'If you'd be kind enough to stand in this hole with just your head protruding . . .' she was not a young woman: he could fight her off '. . . while I snap at you with my faithful Instamatic.'

She produced a small camera from the pocket of her smock. Slowly, with deep suspicion, Geoff climbed into the hole. 'I was going to get in there myself,' Miss Apthwaite said, 'and find someone else to take the picture. But you in that helmet wearing your famous "Please help me 'cos I'm only small" expression is a much better idea for the *Record*'s Funny Photo Competition. This is to be my year for winning, Geoffrey. I'm relying on you.'

Hetty called in at the police station on her way home and asked to see DCI Adams. After longer than she expected he came out to her and stood, shaking his head slowly from side to side.

'You haven't asked me why I'm here yet. I could have the name of a mass-murderer in my pocket.'

'If you'd shrunk the miscreant and given him house-room in your handbag, I'd still find it hard to summon up surprise.'

'These fires. This arson.'

'You want the times they were reported and by whom, names of next-door neighbours, addresses of nearest relatives, any other information the police are prepared to give.'

'How did you know?'

DCI Adams took Hetty's arm and steered her slowly towards the way out. 'Let's just say that I may bring a charge of wasting police time against Radio North-West for all the DIY detectives they've sent here, asking questions that could easily have been answered by ten minutes with last week's local papers at the Reference Library.'

'It's closed.'

'It was open when some idiot DJ told the listening public about the fifteen-thousand-pounds reward and it dashed round here in a body. So what kept you?'

'I've come straight from a client. Nobody told me about any rewards.'

The DCI stopped abruptly. They were only two paces from the exit. 'Straight from a client?' Hetty nodded. 'And you want to know about the fires?' She nodded again. 'With no hope of a reward?'

'I don't know what you're on about.'

The DCI turned on the spot, still holding Hetty's arm, and led her back towards his office, speaking gently, almost tenderly. 'Then what is the connection between your client, Mrs Wainthropp, and these fires?'

'None, I hope. But if my investigation is to be blocked by petty officialdom, pique and the fact that you're manhandling me, we may never know.'

'And the name of this client?'

'Confidential.' They were nose to nose, but Hetty could not be faced down and he knew it. 'You know damn well I'm not the sort of woman to sit on fires. If what I find is a criminal offence, you'll be told and quickly.'

'What do you want?'

'If there's another fire I want to know at once. I want to be there. I need to be sure someone isn't hanging about watching.'

'And if they are?'

'Client confidentiality stops.'

They were at the door of his office. The DCI nodded gently. 'You may be assured of my co-operation.'

So he took her in and summoned a disapproving Detective Sergeant to provide her with the information she had requested. When she had gone, he said, 'You've got her phone number. The moment we know, she knows.'

'A member of the public!'

'She's an extraordinary woman. Not exactly Miss Marple, but—'

'Mind like a steel trap sort of thing?'

'More like a plate of pilchards. You think you've finished with it, but somehow it persists.'

Hetty reached home to find Robert with his feet in a bowl of warm water, a glass of Dubonnet at his side, and Geoff ironing shirts. She looked from one to the other. 'I do that.'

'It's only shirts.'

'I don't mean the ironing.'

Robert said, 'My need is greater.'

'Well, we've got the case, though I don't see it making us rich.'

'Have you been listening to local radio, by any chance?'

'On the bus?'

'These fires. There's a reward.'

'I know about the reward. We're going to need the scooter. Do you think your friend would let us have it for a few days?'

'Funny you should say that, Mrs Wainthropp. Just by chance I have actually borrowed it for the entire week.'

'While you were stuck here holding the fort?'

'The only problem is . . . there's just the one helmet.'

She was staring at him, hardly able to believe what she had heard. He was deeply ashamed. 'What are you trying to tell me, Geoffrey?'

'You always said I should use my initiative.'

'Hell's bells and little fishes!' She had finally exploded. 'I've only to turn my back for ten minutes, and Robert's at the Dubonnet and you've started taking cases on your own.'

There was a loud snore from behind her. If she'd had a long day, so had the part-time collector of trolleys. Robert had fallen asleep, his head on one side, the volume of his snores now diminished to hardly more than heavy breathing. Well, the new job would probably do him the world of good, getting out and making new friends. She wondered whether part-time staff at the supermarket were allowed discounts.

Chrissie was trying to sleep in a bus shelter, hugging herself for warmth. Her clothes were soaked. She had got rid of the suitcase and its contents to Stanley, who had paid her for them, not very much but probably as much as he could afford; he had not seemed rich. She would see Mum tomorrow, maybe take her something, then go home, say 'Hello,' to Fred and endure whatever reproach Alice might throw at her.

A fire engine passed her, going like the clappers, siren sounding and blue light flashing. Then a police car. It was all go tonight.

In the Wainthropp home the telephone rang, and Robert answered. It was the police. There was confusion as Hetty reached over him in the bed to grab the phone. 'Hello? Hetty Wainthropp here. Just a minute. Robert, put your teeth in, and get me a notepad and pen.'

The fire was in a street of detached houses in Burnley. Once again the arsonist had put nobody at risk: the house was set well apart from its neighbours and the owners were away. The firemen were there, hoses already sending out great jets of water, and a film crew, assorted photographers and a couple of reporters, and would-be detectives all taking notes among the small crowd of neighbours and gawpers who would be there anyway.

Mrs Parry-Jones from next door, in housecoat, fluffy slippers and a chiffon headscarf, stood in a pool of hastily rigged lighting being interviwed by the media. 'Stilettos, they were. Well, I don't sleep, you see, and when I do it's only to rest my eyes. So when I heard this tippy-tap, tippy-tap, going up the path next door and then a little rattle at the letter-box, I thought, "Nobody does canvassing for the local elections at this time of night. I'd better have a look see." Well, you can only see the front door of Number Twenty-Seven from the spare room, and I could hear them stilettos again, tippy-tap back down the path and into the street, so I scurried to the spare room, looked out of the window and *whoosh!* Up went the front door in a sheet of flame. If I hadn't dialled 999 at the speed of light, there's no telling what lives we'd have lost.'

'None. They're away on holiday just like the others.' Hetty had heard enough. She motioned Geoff to come with her and moved away from the circle of light. The beam of her torch searched the pavement.

'What you looking for?'

'Not broken stiletto heels, I can tell you that much. Who in their right mind would wear high heels to go out starting fires?'

'What, then?'

Hetty spoke with heavy patience. 'I'm looking to see where I'm going because I think I may have trodden in something. They walk their dogs on this estate.'

'I didn't see anyone like Chrissie Hedges there, did you?'

'No. She wasn't there, thank goodness.'

Chrissie was still huddled in the bus shelter, still soaked through and trying to sleep. The fire engines and police cars were long gone; there was no traffic to speak of and no all-night buses. A shadow fell over her face. She opened her eyes.

Stanley was standing over her. He was wearing an ankle-length waterproof raincoat and looking down at her, not unkindly but as at a friend.

'Hungry?'

She nodded.

'I can give you food.'

Back at the Wainthropps' house Geoff was making instant coffee for two, while Hetty examined the sole of her shoe. She had done the people of the estate an injustice. It was not dogs, but a piece of plastic.

She pulled the plastic from her shoe and examined it. It was all shrivelled up, but there was something written on it. 'Interesting! I can feel the little grey cells beginning to stir.'

'In what direction, Mrs Wainthropp?'

'How were the other two fires started – and probably this one?'

'Rags soaked in petrol.'

'And how would you carry rags soaked in petrol to the scene of the crime?'

'Plastic carrier-bag.'

'Right. And plastic doesn't burn at once. It shrivels up first and bits of it could blow away and stick to someone's shoe.' She placed the bit of plastic carefully on the table.

'That's forensic evidence, Mrs Wainthropp. If we've

found anything, the police should have it.'

'And so they shall. But I've got my own job to do, and there's also the little matter of the reward.' Geoff closed his eyes. It was Malcolm Stone's camera all over again; Hetty seemed to have no notion of the sacredness of evidence found at the scene of the crime. 'See if you can make out the writing. You'd better use Robert's spectacles as a magnifying glass.'

He brought Robert's specs from the dresser and held one lens at a little distance from the shrivelled piece of plastic. He could make out the words:

FAMILY

BURN

He was horrified. 'We're dealing with a maniac here.'

'Family butcher – Burnley, I expect. It's just a manner of speaking. I don't think they ever do butcher families these days, even in Burnley.'

Morning. Different people in different places.

Chrissie was at Stanley's house. There was the sound and smell of sizzling sausages. She stood in the hall, wrapped in an old dressing-gown while her own clothes were drying, sniffing in the aroma like a Bisto Kid. The long raincoat Stanley had been wearing the night before was hanging up with other clothes. She investigated the pockets and found a screwdriver and two brass numbers of the size one finds on doors, a 2 and a 7. She looked at them, could not make anything of them, and put them back.

Geoff had taken the scooter to Preston to interview Mr Nygate, neighbour to the people whose house had been burned the week before.

'You one of them amateur detectives?'

'Just a few questions.'

'It's fifty pound for an interview, fifteen if you take photos from inside the house and ten for an Eccles cake and a mug of tea in the back garden. No credit cards.'

'Can you tell me where they went on holiday?'

'Five.'

'It's only a fire, Mr Nygate, not a mass murder. If you've told the local press I can find out for the price of a paper.'

'One, then. One pound in my hand.'

'Fifty p.'

'Done. Tenerife.'

Hetty was in Burnley, visiting butchers' shops. It would have to be an old-fashioned independent shop, not a chain. Chains never advertised themselves as butchering families. She had looked in the Yellow Pages and bought a street map but it was still, as detection had always been, murder on the feet.

The sixth shop was in an alley away from the main shopping centre. She stared through the window at the plastic bags hanging up inside, then compared them with her scrap of plastic. Could be. She had a collection of plastic bags already in her handbag; they all seemed to be much the same. She entered the shop.

'Excuse me. I'm doing a survey on the shopping habits of the Ribble Valley meat-eater. I wonder if you could tell me roughly how many carrier-bags you give away in a week.'

'None. They're five p each.'

'How many do you sell, then?'

'Not many. Folk don't like paying for them.'

'Has anyone bought a bag recently without buying meat?' The butcher shook his head. 'Are your bags ever stolen?'

'Who'd steal a carrier-bag when you can get one free from the supermarket?'

'I'll ask the questions: you concentrate on the answers.

Can you remember how many bags you sold yesterday – as between men and women?'

'No.' He gave it some thought. 'There'd be more women. Always are.'

Hetty produced a photograph of Chrissie, supplied by Mrs Baynes, from her handbag. 'I'd like you to look at this photo. No, you don't get blood on it; I'll hold it for you. Have you seen a young woman like this come in recently?'

He shook his head. She took a 5p piece from her bag. 'Thank you for your co-operation. Now I'll have a carrier please.' Bemused he took the money and gave her a bag. She started to leave, then turned back. 'I hope you don't mind me saying this, but speaking as an expert in Market Research, if you really want to sell those pork chops, you'd do better with most of that fat cut off.'

Then she had gone. Stanley came from the back of the shop, carrying a carcass of beef.

'What she want?'

'Taking down a peg, in my opinion.'

Robert was in the car park of the supermarket, pushing a line of trolleys from the various dumping points to the main entrance. Through the revolving doors came a housewife and her fat friend, both pushing loaded trolleys. They passed him. He could hear what was being said.

'Met at Manchester Airport by a man from the insurance holding up a card with their names on. "I'm sorry to have to tell you you're underinsured," he says. "We can't pay out in full."'

Robert turned slowly, wishing to hear more.

'"But where are we to live?" says Muriel. "Our house is all burned down. We should be accommodated in a four-star hotel while you rebuild." "It's not in the policy," he says. And the upshot was they've ended up in a trailer site outside Padiham with no prejudice on either side.'

Had he heard what he had heard? Was it a clue? Was it important information to be followed up? They were obviously talking about one of the fires. The two women had passed him, gone out of earshot to a car in Section C with its boot open and a husband standing by to load the carriers, where the woman stopped but the friend went on.

Robert dithered. He should follow, get back into earshot, ask directly who they were talking about. But there were the trolleys. The woman was settling into the car, her husband getting rid of the trolley, leaving it dangerously in a parking bay instead of at the proper disposal point. Now he had returned and was starting the car. He would have to go up one way and down another before joining the lane which led to the exit, and could be cut off if Robert were quick and scrambled through a few shrubs and the Bottle Bank. He pushed the line of trolleys away from him and began to run.

The line of trolleys sped like an arrow up to and through the revolving doors and pinned a lady of substance in a floral hat to a display of Galia melons at a giveaway price. Robert did not see the collision or hear her cries. He stumbled through potentillas and over broken glass and reached the exit just before the woman's car. 'May I have a word? It is important.'

Hetty returned with seventeen plastic carrier-bags, sore feet and a dry throat, Geoff with aching thighs, just as dry a throat and the information that every one of the three couples whose houses had been burned, had been on holiday in Tenerife when the arson took place. A large pot of tea seemed to be the immediate answer to their most immediate problem; they found that Robert had already made one and was in the kitchen drinking it and eating one of the very large sandwiches he only made for comfort.

'You're back early.'

'Got the sack.'

'What for?'

'Bit of a how-de-do over some trolleys.'

Hetty sat heavily while Geoff poured tea into mugs. 'I've been all round Burnley – back streets – shopping centre. I don't know what good it's done.'

'None,' said Robert.

'You can't know that.'

'Yes, I can. Just take our supermarket. There's recycling bins – glass, newspapers, tin cans, plastic bags. And litter-bins all over town. If I wanted a carrier bag to burn down a house, I wouldn't use one of me own.'

'You're too logical sometimes. It'll make you enemies.'

'That's as may be, but I've found a piece of your jigsaw.'

The mugful of life-reviving liquid was already halfway to her lips but she put it down untasted. 'You what?'

'One of them couples whose house burned down last week – they're on a caravan site near Padiham.'

Geoff looked at the expression on Hetty's face and began to be afraid that he was not going to get anything to eat. But the danger passed. Hetty said, 'We'll finish our tea and have a quick bite and then go.'

It's surprising how much a growing lad can put away in a quick bite. Geoff sat, with Hetty beside him, on an upholstered bunk in a Deluxavita Mobile Home on the site near Padiham, his notepad open and ready for notes, feeling quite refreshed. Alf Kenny, a corpulent man in his fifties, was fixing drinks at the bar while his wife, Muriel, warmed her hands at the Calor-Gas heater. Muriel's hands were heavy with rings, her wrists with bracelets. They were a well-preserved, sun-tanned couple, glittering with gold. 'Time travel for us, is this,' she said.

Alf agreed. 'Takes us right back.'

'Back to our roots. Long before we bought the apartment in Tenerife we took holidays like this.'

Alf brought over the drinks, gin-and-tonic for his wife and himself, fruit juice for Hetty and Geoff. Gin-and-tonic at four in the afternoon! The way some people lived these days!

Alf said, 'Except our caravans moved, mostly from side to side if you did more than thirty miles an hour. There was one we called "The Ark". Solid wood and gas-mantles. Took eight hours to get from Accrington to Torquay.'

'Alf had the runs that trip. He had to aim for a china pot in the cupboard.'

'You don't seem too upset at having your house burned down.'

'It's just possessions, isn't it?'

'You've no idea who might have a grudge against you?'

'Not a clue. The Mitchells thought their fire might have something to do with a loony nephew, but he's doing time.'

'And the Saunders wondered if theirs was political in any way, with him being on the Council.'

There was something funny here. These people seemed to know the other two couples, yet they had only just returned from holiday. Even allowing for the Tenerife connection, that seemed unlikely when you consider how many people arrive in Tenerife for holidays every week. 'Are you saying you know the other couples – that there's some connection?'

'Of course we know them. We all live in the same apartment block.'

'Eureka!'

Geoff coughed. 'Excuse me, Mrs Wainthropp. Before the little grey cells settle in for the hundred-yard dash, just one question.' He addressed it to Muriel. 'Do the police know the connection between these three fires?'

'Oh yes, the police were very interested. I mean, three fires in different parts of Lancashire, but all of us in the same apartment block. It's hardly coincidence.'

Chrissie went to Cashmere Heaven and bought a scarf. Then she waited until evening, and took the bus to where her mum lived.

She walked down a road in a rundown housing estate and stopped under a street-lamp, looking at the semi-detached house opposite. The scarf was in a gift-wrapped parcel in a plastic carrier-bag. She looked up and down the road to make sure the coast was clear.

Inside the house, May Foley was listening to the radio in the living room in the dark. May lived alone: there was no point in turning on lights and wasting electricity when the fire gave all the light she needed. She was restless. She got up and went to the window, moved the curtain and looked out. There was a girl standing under the street-lamp opposite. Not for the first time.

The girl was crossing the road towards the house. May Foley let the curtain fall back into place and went into the hall.

Something was being fed through the letter-box. It fell on to the mat. It was a wrapped parcel, the paper slightly torn by the flap of the letter-box. May Foley picked up the parcel, her face impassive, and unwrapped it. Inside was the scarf with a card. Printed on the card were the words *I Love You, Mum.*

There were two large bolts on the inside of the door. May Foley slid them into position.

Then she turned towards the mirror of the hall-stand, put the scarf round her neck to admire it in the dark, then removed it and placed it in the drawer of the hall-stand, in which there were other cards, other scarves, bracelets and bottles of scent.

Chrissie walked back up the street. She dropped the plastic carrier in the front garden of one of the houses she passed.

Case Conference.

Hetty sat at the head of the kitchen table, head in hands, deeply depressed. Geoff and Robert were in their usual places opposite each other, both extremely apprehensive. They knew what had to be done, but dared not say so.

'It does seem quite clear, Mrs Wainthropp. Except for the piece of plastic, everything we've managed to find out, the police already know.'

'That piece of plastic won't run, Hetty. I told you.'

She lifted her head from her hands and stared at him balefully. 'All three in the same apartment block in Tenerife!'

'We can't afford the air-fare. It's not two days since even the bus to Bolton was a major stumbling block.'

'I have to say, Mrs Wainthropp, the Agency went into this to prove . . . was employed to prove . . .'

'A negative.'

'And we've proved it. If the answer's in Tenerife, Chrissie can't have had anything to do with it. It'd be dishonest, Mrs Wainthropp, to go on taking the client's money.'

Hetty brooded. Neither of them understood. Both were against her. Dishonest! How dare he! It was not dishonest to be reluctant to give up. But all the time, beneath the resentment, her commonsense was working away at what they had said, and her commonsense told her that they were right.

She stood up. 'Very well. I'll take that bit of plastic into the police station in the morning and then go on to Alice Baynes. I'll tell her Chrissie has to be in the clear, and collect our fee. Geoffrey will return the scooter. Case closed.' She marched out of the kitchen and could be heard going upstairs.

Robert said, 'Best to leave her be. She doesn't like anyone with her when she's upset.'

The piece of plastic lay on the desk between Hetty and DCI Adams.

'You found it at the scene of the crime and you took it away?'

'Trod on it. I didn't find it till we got home.'

'And you kept it for twenty-four hours. You did not keep it under sterile conditions, you—'

He was keeping his temper. She lost hers. 'What sterile conditions? It'd been in all the muck of the street.'

'Who else has touched it?'

'My assistant, Geoffrey. He wanted me to hand it over to you. It was me took the decision to keep it. I may have acted rashly.'

'And consequently you've forfeited all co-operation. I am asking you now – officially – for the name of your client.'

'It's still confidential. Anyway, I'm now satisfied that my client had nothing to do with these fires. You know perfectly well the connection's somewhere in Tenerife.'

'I know perfectly well the fires were not started in Tenerife. Are you refusing to assist me with my enquiries, Mrs Wainthropp?'

Hetty lifted her chin. She *was* refusing.

'Very well. Go now, please. You and your potty little business exist on my sufferance. Remember that.'

She got up and left the office.

Meanwhile Chrissie had returned home. 'Look, Fred!' said Mrs Baynes. 'Look what the fleet's sent home.' She looked Chrissie up and down. 'You've been away two nights.'

'Who's counting?'

'I am. You've been with someone.'

'If you like.'

'Did he use anything?' Chrissie walked away from her, leaned over the baby's cot and put her face close to his. 'Did he use a rubber?'

'What for? To rub out a mistake?' She kissed the baby and stood up, and Alice hit her across the face with the flat of her hand. There was a silence. Both women were profoundly shocked. Then Chrissie spoke quietly. 'They can do you for child abuse these days, Mother Hubbard.'

Alice left the room without speaking and went upstairs. She returned with a towel. Chrissie said, 'He'll want a feed.'

'I'll give him his bottle.'

'No need. I'm back now. I've got milk.'

'Your milk stays where it is until some tests have been done. There's a hot bath waiting for you upstairs.'

'More than your job's worth to let me feed him when you don't know what I might have caught?' Alice nodded. 'But we're not much of a job, are we, me and Fred, not for somebody with your talents?'

'You know you're going to lose him, don't you?'

'He's a child of the State, Mrs B. Ward of court. Never really mine in the first place.'

And she left the room, left the house. Fred, who was sensitive to atmosphere, and anyway preferred to be the centre of attention himself, began to cry.

At the motel, the hard-faced receptionist was looking at the front page or the *Record*. Splashed across three columns was the blurred photograph of a woman with peroxide hair, a leather mini-skirt and high-heeled boots. The headline was:

BABY, DON'T YOU LIGHT MY FIRE
Reader's Photo Gives Clue to Fire-Bug

The receptionist punched the 999 buttons of the telephone on her desk. 'Police, please.'

Hetty and Alice Baynes were looking at the same front page. Alice said, 'I wouldn't let her go around looking like a floozie who had missed her sell-by date. It's not a bit like Chrissie.'

Chrissie herself, who did not read local papers or anything very much, was buying a diamanté brooch for her mum, using one of the credit cards she had stolen from

Alec. The assistant looked at the card and looked at Chrissie, then looked to right and left. Two large Store Detectives approached from different directions, leaving nowhere to run.

Hetty said, 'Is it even a her, I wonder?'

Alice looked more closely at the photo. 'Y'right. Do you remember Percy Higginbotham?'

'With some reluctance.'

'We used to strike artistic poses at the back of the stage while he pretended to be Gladys Camiknickers or some such, doing that "Over the Garden Wall" patter he'd pinched off the radio. He stood just like that.'

'Those knees certainly don't belong to a woman. They've too many knobbly bits.'

The phone rang in the hall and Alice went to answer. Hetty continued to examine the photo in the *Record*, giving it the hawk-eyed scrutiny of a trained detective and singing *Why Does A Cow Have Four Legs* quietly to herself. Alice came back into the room.

'Chrissie's been arrested. Something to do with a credit card. And for the fires.'

Miss Apthwaite also had a copy of the *Record* but the photograph in which she was interested was not on the front page. 'Look at this!' she said. 'Have you ever seen anything more ridiculous?'

It was the winning photograph in the Funny Photo Competition. It was not of Geoffrey standing in a hole in Miss Apthwaite's garden with his head in a skid-lid protruding like a tulip from the freshly turned earth. It was the photograph of a grave in a cemetery and on it, instead of flowers, were two name-plates of the sort one finds on suburban houses – DUNROAMIN and BIDEAWHILE.

'Dunroamin on a grave! It's not at all funny and in extremely bad taste.'

So Geoff did not have a chance to see the front page

properly until he had made his way home.

Hetty returned to the police station where the DCI reluctantly agreed to see her. Alice had come with her, not to remonstrate with the authorities, but to visit Chrissie who was being held in a cell.

Hetty said to the DCI, 'You've made a mistake.'

'The girl who stole the credit card was seen wearing this wig and these clothes. She stood on the side of the road for a considerable time, trying to hitch a lift. We have a positive identification.'

'That's as may be. She wasn't at the fire.'

'This photograph says she was.'

'Look closely at it. Look at the knees.'

'It's blurred. Taken by an amateur at night. You wouldn't know those knees *were* knees except for their situation below the thighs and above the calves.'

'I knew a concert-party comedian used to stand the same way.'

'And you're suggesting he started the fires'?' She couldn't answer. 'Come along, Mrs Wainthropp, what did I once try to teach you about cost-effectiveness in police work?'

'You won't do what you can't afford unless you're forced.'

'Right. The first principle of detective work is, once you've settled on a suspect don't waste time and money looking for reasons why that suspect might not have committed the crime. All suspects are guilty until proved innocent, usually by someone else or some years after they've been sent to prison or, in the old days, hanged.'

Hetty said, 'I never know when you're serious.'

'I don't always know myself, to tell you the truth.'

Two floors lower down, Alice Baynes was with her foster-child under the watchful eye of a Woman Police Constable.

Chrissie said, 'They're trying to find a Secure Unit for me.'

'You'll know where you are, then.'

'Right.'

'Are you sure you don't want to see Fred?'

'Got to start trying to forget him, haven't I?'

'Not sure that's possible, is it?'

Chrissie shrugged. Mrs Baynes could not take her hand or hug her: she had been told she would not be allowed physical contact of any kind. She kept on looking at Chrissie. Contact had to be by eyes.

Chrissie said tenderly, 'You really are an old bat on a broomstick when you want to be.'

The Woman Police Constable sniffed. Whether it was in sympathy or disapproval could not be told.

Geoff had returned from Miss Apthwaite and, for want of anything better to do, was studying a guidebook to Tenerife brought from the Public Library. Robert was peeling potatoes moodily. A copy of the *Record*, with the front page upwards, was on the kitchen table.

Hetty had returned from the police station in a fury. 'She's not guilty and I intend to prove it. We'll need the scooter.'

'I've took it back.'

'Then get it again.'

'The trouble is, she's not pleased with me. I didn't look enough like a tulip when the chips were down.' He riffled through the paper to find the Funny Photo Competition. 'See? That's the photo that won.' Robert put down a half-peeled potato and came to look. 'Should have been me with me head poking out of a flowerbed. Miss Apthwaite's very disappointed.'

Hetty hardly glanced at the picture. She was not one to be diverted by Funny Photos. The *Record*'s faithful readers had done enough damage with their photographs already.

Robert said, 'Ingenious! Dunroamin – that's the name of a house.'

Suddenly the air of the kitchen became charged with electric particles. Hetty said slowly, 'That's the name of a house which was burned down last week.' She looked again at the Funny Photo. 'And Bideawhile. That was the other.'

They found out from their old acquaintance, the Picture Editor of the *Record*, the location of the cemetery. Hetty went with Geoff to make the acquaintance of Miss Apthwaite and borrow the scooter. They stood side by side in the cemetery and looked at the grave. Two brass letters, 2 and 7 had been added to the two name-plates.

'Twenty-seven, Arbutilon Avenue. The third house.'

Hetty was reading the memorial on the grave. '"Ethel, dearly beloved wife of Stanley". I don't think we'll bother the police yet with this one.'

Alice Baynes had brought Fred in his carry-cot to show to May Foley.

'I used to work in the kitchen of a Children's Home,' May said. 'Chrissie was such a funny little object; I quite took a fancy to her. I used to sneak her treats from the kitchen: I suppose she thought that meant more than it did. Then they cut back with the rate-capping and I lost the job and moved away. I don't know how she found me.'

The two women looked down at Fred. Alice said, 'I so want him to grow up to live a normal life.'

'What's normal these days?'

Hetty just needed the final confirmation before risking all and going public.

They had come by bus to Burnley. Geoff would not have been able to ride the scooter, dressed as he was in peroxide wig, leather mini-skirt and high-heeled boots; skirts are not practical on a scooter, and anyway it would have attracted attention. Procuring such an outfit had not been easy. The

Oxfam shop had been unable to provide it and there had been remarks made by the Sales Assistants of the department store where they had been forced to purchase it outright after an embarrassing attempt to hire.

Geoff was carrying the plastic carrier-bag with FAMILY BUTCHERS BURNLEY on it which Hetty had bought while pretending to be a market researcher. 'These rags may be triple-wrapped,' he said, 'but you can still smell the petrol. I don't like to think what'll happen if we pass a heavy smoker.'

'Nothing venture, nothing win.'

'And the tape-recorder's pushing me breasts out of true. There was a lady sat opposite in the bus kept looking at me very peculiar.'

They had reached the shop. Hetty made a few last-minute adjustments to Geoff's wig and neck-line. 'Now you want half a pound of skirt to be minced while you wait. That will give you time to chat him up while he's mincing. And if he tries anything, I'll be right behind you.'

'Let us give thanks for small mercies.'

'One last word. If you see you're penetrating his defences, don't hesitate to use your initiative. Now off you go.'

He gave her a last desperate look and began to cross the street. Butchers had knives. They kept them handy and kept them sharp. He entered the shop.

Stanley was alone in there, cutting up meat on the wooden counter. As Geoff shut the door behind him, he turned the sign on it from OPEN to CLOSED.

There was a long silence. Stanley was staring at him, still holding the knife, as Geoff approached. 'Chrissie?'

'You know it's not.' Slowly Geoff lifted his plastic carrier-bag to show it. Stanley watched him as if hypnotised. 'What have I got here, Stanley?'

He emptied the packet of triple-wrapped petrol-soaked rags from the plastic bag on to the wooden counter. Then he removed the wrapping from the packet and the rags fell out. Stanley watched. They would have to scrub the counter very thoroughly or the petrol would taint the meat.

'Got a match? Cigarette lighter? Bit of lighted paper? Say something to me, Stanley, even if it's just "Goodbye".' He took a box of matches from the tiny pocket of the mini-skirt and extracted a match. Stanley was sweating now and beginning to breathe heavily. Geoff held the match ready to strike on the side of the box.

'No!'

'No?' He struck the match against the side of the box. There was a loud cry of terror from Stanley. The match did not light.

'Shall I do another?'

Stanley covered his face with his arms, his back against the tiled wall of the shop, and collapsed down that wall slowly. He was making a curious noise, half-gasping, half-weeping. Was he having some sort of attack? Had Geoff gone too far?

It was certainly time to be reassuring. 'Don't get into a tiz-woz, Stanley.' This was Geoff in reassuring mode. 'You're quite safe. They wouldn't strike; I wet them. Is it your heart? Do you want pills?'

Hetty had come into the shop. Geoff remembered that he had not asked for mince, and hoped she would not be cross at this departure from plan. Hetty said, 'Was it your wife, Stanley? Was that the reason?' Stanley had gone quiet. Either the attack had passed or it had got worse. 'Was it because of Ethel you did the fires?'

He looked up at them. 'She had emphysema. They said the air was dry in Tenerife. We spent our savings to buy a place out there, but we were cheated. There's others live in our apartment now. And Ethel died.'

'It wasn't ever their apartment,' the DCI said to Hetty. 'The firm that was building the block went bankrupt and a new lot took over with no obligation to the people who had put money down. He'd lost his savings and he had to take what job he could find. Lucky to get any these days.'

'And Chrissie?'

'There's no justice: she won't be charged. Even the stolen credit cards, the man doesn't want publicity.'

'All's well that end's well?'

'If you like. Seems I owe you an apology.'

'You do.'

'Well, I'm offering it.'

'Well, I'm accepting it.'

The presentation of the cheque was held in the Functions Room of the classiest hotel in town.

The cheque itself was rather large in size, too big to be paid into a bank, more of a cheque to be photographed for the newspapers, but it was for £15,000 – which ought to put the Wainthropp Detective Agency back into the black for years to come. Hetty was stood up on this platform with a piano (why a piano?) and the Public Relations Officer representing the insurance companies handed the cheque over, while everybody clapped and the flash-bulbs popped. Then Hetty made a great, 'Come to me,' gesture with open arms, and her two men, Robert and Geoff, came to stand on either side of her, but lower so that she could place those arms on their shoulders, and there was more clapping and cheering and more photographs and champagne corks popping and smoked salmon for all, especially the press.

DCI Adams was there, and Alice, May Foley, Chrissie and Damien with little Fred (who had his forehead wetted for no good reason that Hetty could see), Miss Apthwaite, even Alf and Muriel, the Picture Editor, Malcolm and Penipha Stone and his mum and dad, Ambo the graffiti art critic, various people with whom Geoff had been at school and many from the village. All sorts were there, more people than Hetty could honestly say they knew.

Then there was a whispering and a giggling, and Alice led Hetty away to a side room, where two costumes had been laid out, male evening dress with top hats, and Alice explained to Hetty Wainthropp aka Chuckles Chinchilla of the Floral Hall, Fleetwood, that the public could not and should not be disappointed.

And *that* was what the piano was for.

Alice sat at the piano and Hetty stood on the platform and together they sang:

'I'm Burlington Bertie.
I rise at ten-thirty,
And saunter along like a toff.
I walk down the Strand
With my gloves on my hand
Then I walk down again with them off.
I'm all airs and graces
Correct easy paces
Without food so long
I forgot where my face is.
I'm Bert . . . Bert . . .
I haven't a shirt,
But my people are well off, you know!
Nearly ev'ryone knows me
From Smith to Lord Roseb'ry.
I'm Burlington Bertie from Bow.'

She was singing. She was tap-dancing. She should never have left the stage.